Praises for Pa...
84 Ribbons

Author Paddy Eger realistically portrays the daily life of a professional ballet dancer in this wonderful coming of age novel. The setting of 1950's America adds to the appeal of the story.

Cheryl Schubert (Librarian)

This was a very good coming of age story that follows Martha Selbryth as she attempts to follow her dream of becoming a professional ballerina.

Courtney Brooks (Net Galley Reviewer)

It's a realistic look into the struggle of making it dancing professionally, including the pain, blood, sweat, and tears required, as well as the devotion to perfection. Marta doesn't have an easy ride at the Intermountain Ballet Company, but she's determined to prove herself and succeed. ...it's more than just a ballet book.

Leeanna Chetsko (Net Galley Reviewer)

I loved this short book's quiet, deceptively simple voice; its strong sense of time and place (Billings, Montana in 1957); and the timelessness of its topics and themes, which include moving away from home, making friends and enemies, and dealing with first love, loneliness, temptations, and career decisions. It is squeaky clean in terms of language and content yet also candid about things like eating disorders.

Hope Baugh (Librarian)

As a former bunhead who grew up in Washington, I thought this book was both credible and enjoyable.

Amy Anderson (Librarian)

Praises for Paddy Eger's 84 Ribbons

This was a great look into the world of ballet. This would be entertaining for readers of all ages from teen to adult.

Jessica Rockhey (Librarian)

...Overall, this book was a pleasant surprise. It is the best ballet book I have read in a long, long time and I'm excited to see that Paddy Eger has a follow up planned as I'm keen to see what happens next.

Trish Hartigan (Net Galley Reviewer)

84 Ribbons is a real story for young adult ballet fans. It's not one of those melodramas all about some hot boy. ...This was one of the better YA theatre/sport oriented books I've read. ...If you liked the Drina books by Jean Estoril or Girl in Motion by Miriam Wenger-Landis; then I'd also recommend this book to you.

Sonya Heaney (Net Galley Reviewer)

I could see the whole thing unfold in front of me like a movie. ...I will continue to think about this story for a good while, it's just one of those books. ...Thank you thank you thank you for the opportunity to read this beautiful story!

Holly Harkins (Net Galley Reviewer)

I really enjoyed this book. It reminded me of Laurie Halse Anderson's "Wintergirls" in a great way. ...I loved how ballet provided the framework, but how the characters really took over. ...We'll be ordering a copy for multiple collections.

Stephanie Nicora (Net Galley Reviewer)

When the Music Stops

Dance On

Paddy Eger

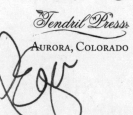

Tendril Press
AURORA, COLORADO

Dance in whatever you wish to explore

When the Music Stops—Dance On

Published by Tendril Press™
www.tendrilpress.com
Denver, CO
303.696.9227

ISBN 978-0-9858933-7-8

Library of Congress Control Number: 2015932943

First Publishing: September 15, 2015
Printed in the United States of America

Author Photo by: Yuen Lui
www.YuenLuiStudio.com
Lynnwood, WA
425.771.3423

Cover Photo by shutterstock.com

Art Direction, Book Design and Cover Design
© 2013. All Rights Reserved by
A. J. Business Design & Publishing Center Inc.
www.AJImagesinc.com — 303•696•9227
Info@AJImagesInc.com

To all who love ballet.
May it fill your heart and soul with joy

Dance is the hidden language of the soul.

— Martha Graham

*M*arta straightened her shoulders, gathered her belongings, and descended the metal stairs onto the train station platform. She glanced at the crescent moon that hung in the darkness above the depot roof and briefly closed her eyes. Her injured ankle throbbed as she hobbled through the crush of tired-looking travelers and entered the waiting room. Only two people waited inside the depot. Neither was her mother.

A uniformed man stood on a platform high above the large room beside an illuminated clock which read 12:21. He adjusted the removable lettering to read the new day's date: May 28, 1958. She'd left Billings, Montana, less than twenty-four hours ago, but the absence of her friends already stung.

The porter took his time pushing the overloaded cart into the waiting room. Once he'd unloaded the cart inside a roped off area, passengers crowded forward to redeem their bags and hurry out the exit. No mom, no rush. Marta waited until the area cleared, then collected her two bags and checked the clock again: 12:35. She bit her lip as she scanned the waiting area. Where was her mom?

A tall, thin man entered from the street and looked around. Whoever he planned to meet didn't appear to be there. He hurried to the ticket counter.

"Marta Selbryth to the ticket counter," boomed the PA system.

As she approached the counter, the man smiled. "Hi, Marta. I'm Elle's friend, Robert Marsden." He handed her a folded paper. "Your mother sent this note. She had an emergency with the costume delivery. I'm here to drive you home."

Marta gave him a quick once-over as she opened the note. He didn't look like she'd pictured him. He was taller than her dad had been, and younger. He looked pleasant.

> *Honey,*
>   *I am so sorry I'm not there to meet you. Robert volunteered to drive you home. The delivery truck carrying our costumes broke down in northern California three days ago. With the recital in two days, I need to take delivery whenever it arrives tonight. I'll see you soon.*
>   *Welcome home!*
>   *Mom*

Marta's excitement to be home withered. Her spoiled child pout crept onto her face, so she swallowed down her disappointment and replaced it with a stage smile. "Shall we go?"

"Do you want to stop and call her? I saw a pay phone by the exit."

"No. It's okay."

Robert gathered up her luggage, turned, and moved toward the exit. Her uneven gait beside his long strides made her feel five years old. Great. No mom and now a near-stranger who moves as fast as a marathon walker. Welcome home, self.

The white face of the Union Station clock lit up the otherwise dark Tacoma skyline. They traveled north, passing Stadium High School with its castle-like appearance. It reminded her of twelve months ago when she'd been in Tacoma. She'd had dinner at the Towers with her neighbor Leo before they attended her senior prom. That felt like years ago.

"Few red lights to stop us," Robert said. "One benefit of driving late."

"Same thing happens in Billings," Marta said, "but there are fewer signals and a lot less people driving around even on busy days."

"I doubt you'll see many changes in Bremerton over the past nine months beyond an exchange of Navy vessels in the shipyard. You're back in time for the beginning of the Saturday markets."

"That's good," she said. "Has my mom planted her garden yet?"

"Only set onions and lettuce. I think she's waiting until things dry out before she puts the rest in the ground. She joked about not wanting her seeds to float away."

As they approached the Narrows Bridge, Marta leaned forward to view the bright lights illuminating the sweeping spans. "I love this bridge."

"Your mom told me you called this the fairy bridge."

"I did. I thought a magical land waited beyond the darkness."

"Maybe it does," Robert said. "It's taking you home."

"It's good to be back." Marta felt rather than saw the shelter of evergreens guarding the roadside. She rolled down the window and inhaled the aroma of Douglas fir and pines. The salt-laden air felt thicker here than the dust-filled air of Billings.

She leaned back and closed her eyes. Soon she felt the car stop. When she opened her eyes they sat in front of her family home. She jerked herself upright. How on earth had she slept through the hour-long drive?

"Sorry I fell asleep. Thanks for driving me home."

"No problem. I know it's been a difficult couple of weeks for you. One day after you're settled in we'll have time to get acquainted."

Right, thought Marta. That's not on the top of my welcome home list. She shook her head, trying to release her grumpy mood much as she would have done at ballet rehearsals last fall.

Robert unloaded her luggage, opened the gate, and walked along the side of the house to unlock the back door. Marta stopped at the base of the steps to look around. The porch light illuminated her mom's wisteria as it climbed along the grape arbor, entangling with the grape vines. The light also reflected off the window panes of her playhouse. Lots of memories lived inside the tiny doorway. But that could wait as well.

Once inside the kitchen, the familiar aroma of cinnamon and coffee surrounded her. She dropped her purse on the kitchen counter and looked around. The light over the sink cast shadows on the dirty dishes left there. Not like her mom to leave the kitchen without tidying it up. Must have been in a huge hurry.

Robert turned on the overhead light. "I know your mom's sad she's not here. Can I fix you a snack or pour you something cold to drink?"

"I'm fine. Thanks again for picking me up."

Robert nodded. "I'll set your bags in your old room."

Marta watched him move toward the hallway. He acted comfortable in the house. Guess that's to be expected. Last spring she'd spoken with him when he took care of her mom during her bout with the flu. Plus, every time Marta called home, her mom and Robert were heading out to dinner or to visit with friends.

The kitchen felt smaller than she remembered, but the familiar surroundings opened a flood of memories. Same red Formica and chrome table in the kitchen nook where she did her homework last year. Same Bakelite phone on the wall where she'd talked with high school friends. Same lacy curtains edging the corner windows. Nothing new except Robert, hovering.

He returned to the kitchen and pointed to the basket on the counter. "Spare house key is in the basket. I'll leave you to settle in." As he stepped onto the back porch, he turned back and smiled. "Welcome home. Have a good rest."

"Thanks, I will."

After he exited the back gate, she locked the door and walked into the living room. A bouquet of red roses spilled from a tall vase, filling the muggy room with their heavy, velvety scent. She plucked the delivery card out of the arrangement.

> Marta,
>   You'll always be my favorite ballerina. I miss you already. Call me so I know you arrived safely.
>   Love,
>   Steve

A tear slid down her cheek and slipped between her lips. Her chest tightened as she thought about him and Lynne. She shook her head, not willing to let herself dwell on Bartley.

A postcard and a letter lay next to the flowers. Marta chuckled to herself as she read the postcard.

> *Miss me yet? I wanted you to know I started missing you the minute you handed me that box of costumes for the little girls. Be home when I call on Sundays, OK? Probably in the afternoon, unless I have a date.*
>
> *Lynne*

Lynne. Such a funny best friend. She'd mailed a postcard showing downtown Billings, the place Marta had just left. Not hearing about her dating fiascoes or seeing her every day would be a serious adjustment.

Marta picked up the letter with Steve's home address as the return. She turned it over in her hands and hesitated. Could she handle reading what Steve wrote before she went to bed? No. She returned the letter to the table and headed back to the kitchen.

With the overhead light turned off, darkness enclosed her in the small space. Was coming home an ill-conceived decision? Should she have stayed and auditioned at the end of summer as a new corps dancer? Three more months might have been all her ankle needed to be able stand up to the rigors of the Intermountain Ballet Company again. But it had already been nearly five months since she broke it. It had gotten stronger, but not strong enough for professional ballet. And even if it did fully heal, she wasn't sure the director, Madame Cosper, would give her another chance. Marta wasn't sure she could face another failure.

It was sad that shattering a tiny bone in her ankle ended her career in a few seconds. She still shuddered when she thought about how she slid across the icy porch and broke through the railing. Nothing happy about that New Year's Eve in the mountains.

When Marta stepped into her old bedroom, she gasped. That was fast! Her mom had reorganized. A work table and a kitchen chair filled the space where her second twin bed once stood. A double-headed work light replaced her frilly table lamp. Neatly stacked fabrics sorted by color filled an open bookcase. So much for my bedroom.

Her small window facing the backyard framed a black square of night. Hopefully the daylight view of the garden would brighten everything, including her mood. The room would never be as bright or spacious as her room in Billings; there was no space here for a rocking chair and no view of the neighborhood street. She'd need time to readjust how she'd handle her quiet times.

Marta changed into an old seersucker nightgown she pulled from the dresser and stepped into the bathroom to prepare for bed. When she climbed between the sheets, their coolness relaxed her tired body. She curled up to massage her throbbing ankle and waited for sleep to erase all thoughts of her recent disappointments. Could she have stayed in Billings and lived there without dancing? Not likely.

The next morning when she woke, she felt the silence in the house. Her mom must be gone already. She stretched and padded to the kitchen. No mom. A note rested against the sugar bowl on the kitchen table.

> Honey,
>> Sorry about last night. Got in about 4. Know you need your rest. Dress rehearsal until 8 tonight. See you after. I'm so glad you're home.
>> XOX,
>> Mom

After a long bath followed by a cup of mint tea, Marta unpacked. She hung her clothes, then moved her mom's sewing notions from one drawer to make room for her personal items.

The last item out of her suitcase was her cigar box filled with *pointe* shoe ribbons. She let her fingers slide through their satiny smoothness. She'd collected 84 ribbons, but the goal of attaining soloist status by that time had proven unrealistic. A featured role required at least another year of dancing, performing and competing, gathering another hundred worn out *pointe* shoe ribbons. And even more if Madame didn't like you.

Marta allowed her disappointment to wash over her like a chilling ocean wave. So many performances waited to be danced, now by someone else. She closed the box, stood, and looked around the room. The top of the curio her dad made would be perfect. She stretched and shoved the box back from view.

What next? Open the letter from Steve. Marta retrieved the letter from the dining room table and slid the letter opener along the top edge of the envelope. She expelled a long breath as she lifted out a single sheet of ordinary notebook paper.

Dear Marta,

　　The moment you walked away from the ballet company building, I started missing you. I knew you'd leave me and Billings. I understand it's what you need to do. Just know you haven't seen the last of me, Miss Fluff!

　　　　Love ya!

　　　　Steve

A smile, a laugh, tears, and a sharp pain mingled inside her. Thank heavens she'd shared her true feelings before leaving Steve. Otherwise he'd have sent an entirely different letter—if he'd sent one at all.

Marta scanned the room, looking for something to distract her. Nothing. A tour of the backyard would refocus her. The overcast morning matched her muted mood. On close investigation, the grape arbor bore only leaves. Soon hundreds of clusters of tiny green nubs smaller than peppercorns would push out. It would be months before they'd turn pink, then rose, then grow larger and become Concord purple and be ready to pick and eat. Her mom tried to keep them trimmed, but they needed her dad's long reach with the clippers. He'd trained the decades old branches to shade the back and one side of the garage on hot days. How he'd loved his grapes. Funny thing though, when he ate grapes, he always spit out the skins.

She cut a bouquet of late May blossoms and ivy for the kitchen table, then returned inside to put them in water. What did she want to do next: sew, sleep, bake, listen to music? What she wanted to do she couldn't. Nothing alleviated her restlessness, so she surrendered and sank down into her dad's overstuffed rocker.

ぷ

As dusk changed to dark, she put a chicken and new potatoes in the oven to bake, assembled a green salad, and set the kitchen nook table for two. At nine she turned down the oven and returned to the living room to rock.

When the phone rang she expected to hear her mom's voice on the other end.

"Marta! Are you OK? I've been frantic waiting for your call."

"Steve? Hi. I'm fine. I'm sorry I didn't call earlier. I got busy and… I'm sorry."

"Thank heaven you got home safely."

Marta shared her uneventful train trip, then asked about his college project.

"It's going well," he said. "But don't change the subject. You know how much I miss you, don't you?"

"Yes, because I miss you too." She twisted the phone cord with her fingers as she smiled, picturing his anxious face staring at her.

"That's good to know. Did you get my letter?"

"Yes, and the flowers. I loved both. I'm sorry I didn't call."

"You know, I think of you every hour of the day and night and wish you were here with me."

"I love you and miss you too. I'll be better about calling you from now on."

"How about I call you Sunday evenings like I did from San Francisco? That's when I know I'll have free time. My weekdays are so crazy, if you call I might miss it, Miss Fluff."

After they caught up on his week's activities, Marta stayed seated in the dark kitchen, feeling warmth like a smile glide through her body. "Miss Fluff" had been their joke ever since Steve called ballet "fluff news." After his first night attending the ballet, he quickly changed his tune, but the fluff nickname continued, cementing their connectedness that blossomed into love.

৵

Marta's mom returned at ten, with Robert following close behind.

Marta raced into her mother's outstretched arms and enjoyed the snugness of being held tight.

"Marta, honey. I'm so glad you're home. I looked in on you when I returned, but I didn't want to wake you." She held her at arm's length. "You look like you've lost weight. How do you feel?"

"I'm fine, considering."

She fingered Marta's short, curly hair. "When did you cut your hair?"

"While I was still wearing the cast. One less thing to worry about."

"Want to talk about your re-audition?"

Marta shrugged and wiped her eyes. "I danced as well as possible, considering. I didn't tell them about the new injury. I decided mentioning it sounded like an excuse, and I wanted to act professional. I expected they'd give me the summer to regain my strength, but they said 'sorry' and I was expected to say 'thank you' and walk away."

Marta watched Robert back into the kitchen as the conversation with her mom continued.

Her mom pulled her close and kissed her forehead. "You'll see. You'll prove them wrong. You'll get stronger and dance again, right?"

Marta nodded and stepped free of her mother's arms and returned to the kitchen to reheat dinner. She reset the table for three, noticing that not only did Robert hang around, he automatically sat in her old place at the table.

As they ate, the conversation settled on Marta. "So, honey," her mom said, "how was the trip? Better than last year when you were traveling on the bus to Billings?"

"Tons better. I enjoyed watching the world roll by my window. Mrs. B. made me a box dinner and snacks. Even though I told Lynne and Steve not to come to the depot, they showed up with a funny sign." Tears puddled in her eyes. She stifled a sob.

Mom leaned forward and squeezed Marta's hands. "I'm sure this is hard for you, but I'm glad you're home. You've got all summer to regain your strength and recover."

There it was again. Did her mother think she'd be prepared to dance by the end of summer? Didn't she realize dancing in *pointe* shoes might never be possible again? Did her mom expect her to pack up and move on by fall? Marta stared at her mother until she realized Robert was speaking to her.

"I'm certain you'll overcome that setback," Robert said. "Elle's been busy restoring your room when she's not at the dance studio all day and night."

Marta blinked as she struggled to focus on their conversation. She couldn't shake the strong evidence of changes in her mom, mostly because of Robert's presence in her family home. She sat taller and folded her hands to appear to be listening.

"Well, yes," her mom said. "But you know how I get my sewing all over the place. Two clients needed Masonic gowns in a hurry last week. After the recital's over I'll get in and clean out more things."

Marta pushed around her potatoes and swallowed a bite of chicken. "It's okay, Mom. I've got plenty of room. I've already unpacked, so don't worry about making changes."

After dinner her mom and Robert continued sitting in the kitchen nook. Her mom shuffled the deck of cards left on the window ledge. "I hope you don't mind. Robert and I usually play a few hands of gin rummy after dinner to unwind. I'm on a winning streak. You could join us if you'd like."

"No, but thanks," she said. "Just forget I'm here." As they started their game, she returned to the living room to sit in her dad's chair in the darkness, feeling her pout resurfacing. It would have been nice to sit and talk with her mom on their first night together. Marta closed her eyes and rocked.

When Marta heard Robert say good night near midnight, she stepped into the kitchen for a glass of water. She startled at the outline of her mom and Robert standing on the back porch wrapped in an embrace, their bodies melded into a single shape. She listened to her mom's laughter, followed by a long period of quiet. It appeared Robert wasn't going away any time soon.

Marta watched the silhouette break apart. "Okay," her mom said. "Call me tomorrow. Thanks for meeting Marta yesterday. Me too. Night."

Marta stepped back into the living room as her mother returned inside, yawning.

"I'm so tired after the costume delivery foul up. I wish I could sleep a week. But, there's too much to be done for Miss Holland. After tomorrow's recital I'll relax. Are you coming to watch?"

Marta shrugged. "If you need help."

"I really don't. Miss Holland has a great team of parents. But I thought you might like to watch the students you knew and danced with last year. You decide. Right now I'm off to bed. I'm so glad you're here, honey. We'll have a long talk after I get through the recital."

Her mom pulled Marta into a tight hug like the ones Marta remembered during her recovery last January. Suddenly her sobs exploded.

"Honey? What's wrong?"

"Nothing." Marta pulled away and wiped her face. "I'm, I'm so glad to see you. I...You should go to bed. You'll need every ounce of energy you can scrape up for tomorrow."

Her mom reached out and grasped Marta's hands. "Are you sure? I can stay up if you want to talk."

"No. I'm fine. Sweet dreams."

Within minutes, the kitchen clock marking off every second remained the only sound in the house. Tick, tick, tick, tick. Marta sat in the kitchen nook in her old spot. The last city bus of the evening stopped at the corner, then disappeared along the arterial. She turned on the overhead nook light and reached for the cards on the window ledge. Maybe a game of solitaire would invite sleep.

Tick, tick, tick, tick. Marta played solitaire until the first signs of dawn appeared behind the neighbor's house across the street. She put the cards back on the ledge and went to bed.

When Marta brought in the mail the next afternoon, she found two letters addressed to her: one from Steve, one from the Intermountain Ballet Company. She tossed the one from the ballet company on the dining table. The news it held could wait almost forever. Steve's letter, however, promised to lift her spirits.

> Dear Marta,
>   Missing you. Wishing you were here to help me finish my project or at least here to share a few kisses along The Rims or our river walk.
>   Please write. I want to hear all about how you miss me and how you can't live without me. I promise to visit as soon as the term ends.
>
>   I love you now and forever,
>   Steve

She crushed the letter to her chest and closed her eyes, letting her thoughts wander back to their time together in Billings. Numbness spread through her as though she lay buried in wet sand. Maybe she should have stayed in Billings. No, coming home remained her only realistic choice. She placed the letter with the earlier one from Steve in her bedside table, closed her eyes, and waited for sleep to wash away her wakefulness.

Marta wandered through the unplanted vegetable garden and under the grape arbor. She stopped at the playhouse. When she bent to enter, she inhaled the musty smell of the peeling wallpaper. She stared down at her tiny wooden table and chairs, remembering her years making grass tea, coloring pictures, and reading the picture books she'd kept on the tiny shelf in the wall.

Her favorite remembrances always gravitated toward playing with ballet paper dolls and hosting a tea party for her cousin. They'd laughed and made up different dances along the sidewalk next to the playhouse. Sometimes their moms became their audience and sat on the back steps and clapped. That decade also marked the beginning of life without her dad. Losing him created an emptiness she'd yet to fill.

Marta closed the playhouse door and continued her tour of the yard. Purple primroses lined the sidewalk, separating the lawn from the cement. That's when she saw a small sign attached to the front gate. The back side was blank, so she opened the gate to read the writing on the front side:

BREMCO
Bremerton Real Estate & Management Company
HOUSE FOR SALE

*T*he ground beneath Marta's feet fell away, or was it her knees bending, refusing to keep her upright? She stared at the sign. Her mom had never given any indication she planned to sell their family home. And why now? Hadn't there been enough changes recently without pulling away this last bit of security she'd come home to embrace?

Marta paced, circling the yard, the house, and the yard again. When it grew dark she rocked in her dad's chair. What if the house sold this week? Would her mom's plans include a place for her? If not, how could she find a job and earn enough money to move out? What a mess.

Her mom returned home near midnight, alone. She collapsed onto the couch. "What a long day. I didn't expect you to be up this late."

"How did it go?"

"The recital went smoothly, but I'm exhausted. As usual, the little kids stole the show when they turned the wrong way and made up their own dances. The audience gave Rosalia Marcus a standing ovation for her ballet solo. Reminds me of your performances last year. Looks like Miss Holland has another professional dancer in the making."

"She must be new."

"Her family is Navy. They arrived last September. She's almost as talented as you. I think she wants to follow your lead."

"I wish her luck. It's harder than she'll ever imagine."

"You'd have enjoyed watching her, but I imagine you were too tired to come to the recital."

"No. Not tired." Marta pulled in her lips as she stood and crossed her arms. "Disappointed is more like it."

"What's wrong?"

Marta looked away as tears filled her eyes. "I don't know where to start." She jammed her balled up fists into her robe pockets to give herself time to regain a civil voice. "How could you put the house up for sale and not bother to mention it to me?"

"What are you talking about? I've thought about it, but only when Robert's and my relationship becomes more serious. What brought this up?"

"Really? Then how do you explain the sign on the front gate?"

Her mom shot up from the couch, turned on the front porch light, and hurried out the front door. She returned, shredding the sign into small bits.

"Damn that woman! That's Connie Norton's doing. She's a friend of Robert's. I mentioned I'd give her the first chance to post the house when the time came. She'll hear from me first thing in the morning."

Her mom threw the sign into the waste bin, then returned and pulled Marta into a hug. "I'd never sell the house without talking with you, honey. You should know that."

Marta collapsed against her mother. "It's...the sign.... It shocked me." Marta sighed, then straightened. "So, you and Robert haven't made any marriage plans?"

Her mom looked quizzically at Marta's face. "Would it upset you if we did?"

Marta had thought about that a lot during her pacing sessions. "No. It's time, I guess."

"He's a good man, honey, and I enjoy his company. He makes me laugh, plus he's interested in my well being."

"Sounds like a good match, Mom. Really. Seeing that sign shocked me. So much has changed in my life so quickly."

"I know. Be assured that Connie will not get first dibs on selling this house. I'm angry that I ever met that woman."

Marta didn't reply.

Her mom shook her head. "I'm sorry you've been stewing about this all day. Try to get rested, honey. As soon as I put the last of the recital materials away, we'll get back to our old selves and take the time to sit and talk. Okay?"

Marta nodded and playfully pushed her mother toward her bedroom. "Off to bed, now. You deserve a good, long sleep."

Her mom kissed her then walked, yawning, into her bedroom.

When the tightness in Marta's chest eased, she picked up yesterday's letter from the Intermountain Ballet Company and stared at the return addresses, dreading the contents. She entered her own bedroom, closed the door and opened the envelope.

```
To Miss Marta Selbryth,

This letter is sent to inform you that your
contract with the Intermountain Ballet Company
is hereby terminated effective May 30, 1958. No
reply is required.

                              Anna Cosper
                              Damien Black
```

Marta squeezed her eyes closed as pain zigzagged through all the cells in her body. Breathing became difficult. Such a harsh send-off.

Careers weren't supposed to end this way or this soon. She returned the letter to its envelope and buried her face in her pillow to muffle her sobs.

She crumpled the letter in her hand as she lay sprawled across the comforter, letting the tears flow until dry heaves and then sleep took over. When she awoke, the bedside lamp blinded her but also pushed back the darkness festering inside her. The deep ache changed to a hollowness, an ever-expanding hole she anticipated might engulf her at any moment.

Marta realized she'd not brought in today's mail, so she opened the front door, turned on the porch light, and checked their mailbox that hung on the side of the house. Three pieces of mail. Back inside she set the two bills aside and smiled. Steve had sent another letter. After she climbed beneath the covers, she plumped up her pillows, leaned back, and ran her finger beneath the flap of the envelope.

> *Dear Marta,*
>
> *Thought of you today as I drove to class. I miss our drive-ins together and your sweet kisses.*
>
> *Finished my ed-op project. Just the newspaper mock-up left to be done. 6 months and 11 days until I'm set free from school. Know that I never want to be set free from you. I miss you.*
>
> *Love,*
> *Steve*

Marta kissed the letter and cried. Would her reserve of tears ever end? She slid the letter into the drawer of her bedside table and lay back. So much time stretched ahead in her life. How could she start over? Where to begin?

After breakfast, Marta sat in the nook and listened as her mom spoke with Connie Norton, sharing her frustration over the For Sale sign. After she hung up, Marta gave her a thumbs up. "Great job, Mom. You didn't give her much of a chance to reply."

"Why should I? She knew she'd overstepped her limits the moment she placed that sign on the gate. She'll probably play dumb and try to wheedle Robert about it, but she's done as far as I'm concerned."

Marta closed the heavy wooden garage door as her mom left for the dance studio. She looked around the garage. She'd spent many hours practicing in this space in the past. Was she ready to begin again? If she could dance it needed to start here and the sooner the better. Why did she hesitate about this and about seeing Miss Holland? Lynne would tell her to get a grip and start; she had nothing to lose.

She swept up the dirt and grit from the car tires, sprinkled sand on the grease spots, and rubbed it in with the toe of her sandal. Then she swept that up as well. Each motion became a hesitation, a way to lengthen the time before she'd begin exercising once again. She only planned to do warm ups, so why dilly dally?

She carried her ballet slippers to the garage and sat on the wooden bench inside the door. The soft-soled ballet slippers felt snug, but she forced her feet into them and stepped up to the make-shift barre her dad had installed over a decade ago. Deep breath in and out. She squared her shoulders, pulled her derriere snug, and began.

Slow *demi-pliés*, bending her knees, not lifting her heels, followed by forward, side, and back stretches while shaping her free arm into a gentle curve. Cautious *relevés*, lifting her heels, feeling her arches cramp and then release, allowing her to stretch skyward for a moment. Repeat on the left side.

Snail's pace *ronds de jambes à terre*, circling her foot on the floor, alternately standing on and using her injured left foot, feeling her toes refusing to support her need for proper balance. She ignored the stabs of electric pain shooting up her legs. Picture Lynne in her old car, remember Bartley smiling and dancing, visualize the ballet company practice room. When it hurts too much, don't think; just keep moving.

Sweat formed on her upper lip, her back, and under her arms. Six months ago, she'd executed these same warm-ups in the ballet company in Billings. How quickly her flexibility had slipped away. By now, when she should hear the piano music moving through her, no music played in her head to overcome the silence around her.

She looked around. Playing her warm-up record would ease her jittery attempts as she worked through the tightness in her left foot. The record player she'd remembered in the garage was missing. So much for music. Today she struggled through a silent practice followed by icing her ankle while she waited for the possibility of a letter from Steve.

Marta retrieved the mail: the electric bill, the telephone bill, and A & P's weekly grocery flyer. No letter from Steve. A small disappointment circled through her until she realized the selfishness of expecting a letter every day. Maybe she'd write to him. He'd be pleasantly surprised.

Seated at the console radio her dad had remodeled into a desk, Marta opened her mom's box of blue, scalloped-edge stationary.

Dear Steve,

She tapped the pen on the desk and looked around the room as if inspiration hung on the walls. Maybe she'd be more inspired if she wrote in the kitchen. She moved to the nook and started over.

Hi, Steve,
Thanks for writing. I love getting your letters. I've started exercising. I continue to ice my foot after I...

Now what? The view outside, kitchen towels hanging by the stove, and the large apple-shaped cookie jar offered no inspiration either, so she stopped and wadded up the paper. Steve cared about her, but she doubted he'd want to read a listing of her complaints.

She restarted the letter several times, then gave up and discarded her pages in the trash burner bin. At this rate she'd need to buy her mom a replacement box of stationary before she'd write anything worth mailing. She'd buy a handful of crazy postcards, tell him she loved him, and once she did something of value, she'd write a letter.

With dinner assembled and simmering on the stove, Marta went to the garden to pick green onions for their dinner salad. When her mom drove up, she hurried to open the garage door for her. In return she received a wave as her mom turned off the engine and retrieved a bag of groceries from the back seat of the car.

"Hi, dear. It's nice to have a smiling door valet. What a crazy day! Today was more hectic than you can imagine, even without students."

"How's your pile of catalogs and samples? Sorted out for next year?"

"Hardly." Her mom laughed and shook her head. "I spent the day trying to find the top of my desk and getting bills paid. Tomorrow we'll tackle the catalogs. I'm amazed at the cost of costumes. Do you know that a plain back leotard costs three dollars with shipping? Plain black."

Marta laughed. "Be glad you aren't paying close to four hundred dollars for a short tutu like we do at the ballet company. We need, I mean, they needed to replace costumes, but the cost is so great they've had to make do with threadbare costumes for many corps dances. They looked okay from a distance."

"So, ballet companies have money worries as well. Sad isn't it?"

They sat at the dinner table long after finishing their meal, enjoying iced tea while continuing their conversations.

"So, you exercised today? How'd your ankle hold up?"

"It's not totally flexible. That's going to take time."

"It will come." Her mom took a sip of tea. "So, the other day you started to say something that sounded like it might be important. Want to discuss it now?"

Marta shrugged. "Not really. My inability to dance keeps me restless. But since I've restarted warm-ups, my mood's improved. I'm disappointed and…"

Her mom covered her hands and patted them. "I understand how you feel. I have days like that. How about I give you a job. I could use your help at the studio. You could visit with Miss Holland. She…."

Marta shook her head as she popped up to her feet. "No, mom. I can't. Not yet."

A heavy silence swirled in the space between them. Finally her mom stood, patted Marta's shoulder, and carried their dishes to the sink. Marta picked up the drying towel and stood beside her. They worked together in silence.

სი

Week two. Marta sat at the kitchen table watching her mother back the car out of the garage. She left for the dance studio like clockwork at ten Monday through Saturday. Miss Holland's summer classes didn't kick in for another week, but acting as Miss Holland's right hand and fielding every situation outside the studio classrooms meant closing out the studio's finances mid-year as well as organizing and enrolling students for summer sessions.

What started as a part time job to pay for Marta's dance lessons had turned full time years ago. After avoiding any discussion of meeting with Miss Holland, Marta knew she owed her mother an apology or at least more support at home. Her mom seldom culled out time to sew for her private clients. Maybe she'd take on their sewing requests and earn a few dollars in the process.

Guilt over not visiting with Miss Holland poked at her like the pointed stick her neighbor Leo used to jab her with to gain her attention when they were little kids. If she didn't go to the studio soon, would she ever go? But how could she discuss her brief career and not the loss she felt or how sadness enveloped her every day? How could she talk about how she'd let Miss Holland down by failing to maintain her *corps de ballet* position?

Yesterday her mom had brought home a reel-to-reel tape deck and several of Miss Holland's recordings on loan for the summer. She'd gotten the message loud and clear from both her mom and Miss Holland: the time to visit needed to be scheduled soon.

After she placed the tape recorder on the garage workbench, she sat staring at the space. What held her back from using the space like she used to do? Before going to Montana, she'd hurry home and practice. Now everything, including this space, felt like a burden instead of a joy.

Once she moved to the barre, she began the tape. Even though she heard the music with her ears, she didn't hear it in her body or in her movement. It felt as if the music bounced off her or dissolved before it reached into her heart. She stared at the reel circling on the tape recorder, turned it off, then began her practice in silence. Maybe tomorrow the music would regain its magical spell. The dissonance she heard today didn't inspire her.

After finishing her daily ballet routine in the garage and a morning bath, Marta steeped her second cup of tea, snugged her robe belt, and turned on the television. Soap operas, game shows, and news broadcasts to mid afternoon. Children's programs at three-thirty, followed by the six o'clock news and evening dramas. The noise pushed aside the shroud of quiet that enveloped her. The near-daily letters and copies of articles Steve had written kept the post office in business. She enjoyed his newsy comments but still couldn't think of what to write in return. Should she lie and say everything was peachy? No. She wrote a love note, drew hearts all over the inside, and wrote:

> *I miss you and love you. I dream of you every night.*
> *I wish your arms were wrapped around me, holding me tight.*
> *XoXoXoXo*
> *Marta Fluff*

Then she found her mom's red lipstick, smeared it on her lips, and kissed the card. That should hold him. She owed him a reply for all his efforts to keep her smiling even though she continued to feel adrift.

The only daily jobs she'd taken on at home were making her bed, doing the laundry, and cooking dinner, except for the nights Robert took her mom out. The rest of each day she exercised, then sat and rocked. She watched the clock, waiting for her mother to return, hopefully alone but then not knowing what they'd talk about except Robert.

It wasn't that she didn't like him. She did. In fact he reminded her of her dad: tall and thin with brown hair, a quiet and gentle man of few words. But why did mom need to spend so much time with him? Did she desire to replace her husband?

Robert became the center of her latest phone conversation when Lynne, her fellow dancer and best friend in Billings, called as planned.

"Hey, Marta? What's going on? Are you ever planning to write or call?"

"I'm…it's hard to explain. Besides you said you'd call me, Lynne."

"True. So, I'm fine. The new ballet rehearsals are going well. I'm beginning lessons with our little angels. They miss you but love the fact that Mrs. B. lets us continue to use your old practice space in the basement."

Marta laughed and paced the kitchen as far as the coiled phone cord allowed. "Is Carol being a pest about you dancing near *her* laundry room?"

"No. She doesn't say much. I think I scare her. Enough about her. Tell me about you."

"Nothing to tell."

"Come on, Marta. Snap out of it. Shove that poor-little-me out of your voice."

Marta explained about the real estate sign, then about her mom's interest in Robert.

"Hey, it's ten years since your dad died," Lynne said. "Your mom deserves happiness and finding someone to share her life with is part of that. We all need it."

"I know. I'm acting grumpy because I'd like a little time with my mom. He's here most evenings and stays for dinner and gin rummy, then on weekends he helps with projects before they vanish."

"I thought you liked him."

"I do. It's just another change." Marta sighed. "My biggest problem is me. I fear I've lost my connection to the ballet music I've loved so deeply for so long. When I practice, none of it means anything. I feel hollow as a porcelain doll, like I've become a different person." Marta paused. "I'm scared, Lynne. I can't feel the music anymore."

"Don't worry so much, Marta. The music is still there. It's changed a bit. Think of me practicing beside you like we did at the company and in the boarding house basement. I'll gladly give you an imaginary little kick in the *derrière*."

Marta exhaled. "Okay. Thanks Lynne. I can always count on you to keep me smiling, even with all the changes in my life."

"Oh, Marta. Wait until I tell you the latest. Herbert didn't leave for back east as promised last spring. He's still in Billings, so Madame sees him after hours. She has no idea that I've observed their kissing sessions, and I plan to keep it that way until it serves a purpose."

"Be careful Lynne. Don't anger Madame."

Lynne laughed. "Who, quiet little me? Hey, I should take off. Got a date with a drummer tonight. Do you hear much from Steve?"

"He writes letters and calls me on Sundays when he has time. I miss seeing him."

"That guy's still ga-ga over you even at a distance. Have your feelings for Steve changed?"

"No. It's just—"

"Oh, oh. Larry the drummer's here. Gotta go. You've got scads of free time so write to me, promise?"

"I promise, I—"

"Hey, I'm tired of only opening bills, so get out and find a funny post-card to mail to me. It's the least you can do to save me. Love you, but I need to go. Write! Bye!"

Click.

Marta listened to the dial tone buzzing in her ear. Lynne was right. She needed to keep busy and be patient; the music would return.

After running a load of wash, Marta hung, dried and brought in the clothes from the backyard lines, folded them, and put them away. As she headed back into the kitchen, she caught her reflection in the large gilt mirror that hung behind the living room sofa. She hated the image looking back at her. That person had short, stringy hair and dull brown eyes with dark circles like a beat up prize fighter. She wore a scowl and no make-up. What did people see when they looked at her, if they even bothered to look? A loser with no job and no ambition? A person who didn't dress until late afternoon? A disappointment?

Shivers skittered down her spine. A diet pill would perk her up, give her energy to do *something*. When she rummaged through her handbag, she found two linty pills. She swallowed both, waiting for the familiar surge to begin. After these she'd quit.

Minutes later she jittered with energy. Tingly electric vibrations travelled from her core to her fingertips and her head, down her torso, and into her legs. She dressed, combed her hair, and headed for the kitchen to make bread.

By the time the local paper arrived, Marta had baked the bread, cleaned her bedroom, vacuumed the living room, shaken all the scatter rugs in the house, and swept the kitchen and hall. Now she sat in the nook and scanned yesterday's Help Wanted ads. Same ads everyday: secretaries, bookkeepers, carpenters, truck drivers, and gardeners. If she'd stayed in Billings she could have continued her part time jobs, but no Bremerton theatres advertised for ticket sellers, and none of the hotels needed night clerks.

When she called on a seamstress ad, the job had been taken. But a soft-spoken woman didn't slam that door. "I'll keep your name and number in case work shows up," she said.

Tonight's dinner, beef stroganoff, simmered in the oven and fresh bread lay sliced on a plate. Marta hummed the melodies of *Swan Lake*, swaying through the steps, realizing that the diet pills had created the spark she needed and kept the music playing inside her head. One day soon she'd need to stop taking the pills, but not quite yet.

She plopped down in the kitchen nook to play solitaire. Like usual, she lost before she ran out of cards. She watched the neighbor children across the road swinging on the lowest apple tree branch. Back and forth, back and forth. In past years their laughter lightened her soul; today their carefree laughter reminded her of how she empty she felt listening to Lynne talk about her busy life.

As she cleared away the cards and got up to stir the pot, the phone rang and startled her.

"Robert bought last-minute symphony tickets," her mom said. "I won't be home until late, so go ahead and eat without me."

"Okay. See you in the morning." Marta clenched her jaw as she replaced the receiver, turned off the oven, and set the pot on thick hot pads next to the refrigerator. Now what? She had to get out of the house. Do something, anything. A walk would help even though it caused her ankle to swell and throb. As she slipped on her shoes and grabbed a sweater, the phone rang. She ignored it and walked out the back door.

No destination sprang to mind. She missed The Rims of Billings, her chance to scan a vast plain and enjoy the mountains to the south and west. Here acres of evergreens surrounded her unless she traveled the three miles to stand near the downtown post office or drove to Kitsap Lake or Port Orchard to get a mountain view. Her mom had the car, so a neighborhood walk would have to do.

Callow Avenue, a main thoroughfare, began two blocks west of her home. Small businesses stretched out along the west side of the street; homes occupied the east side. Adults worked in their yards weeding, mowing, and watering, while the children rode bikes with playing cards flapping on their spokes, just like they did in Billings.

Marta took a side trip looping to Montgomery, past the dance studio where she'd taken lessons and where her mom worked. No visible changes over the last nine months. She should have gone to the recital and to see Miss Holland, but she didn't feel strong enough yet. This late, no one occupied the studio, so she walked back to Callow Drugs to purchase a pack of Chiclets gum, tooth powder, plus two packets of diet pills. She'd wean herself off the pills once she got back on track, probably next week.

As shadows grew long, parents called in their children and turned on lamps to make the day last a bit longer. A chill arrived. Back in Billings it would be too warm for a sweater, maybe too warm to be out walking. Was it the evening temperature or her isolation from her life in Billings that disturbed her? What was Mrs. B. doing? Who helped in the kitchen? Was her old room rented out?

What about Steve? Did he miss her as much as he told her in his letters? He began their relationship when he'd purposely interviewed her for a newspaper article. She had resisted his advances, but over time he'd become her tour guide and later her first and only love. She wished he walked beside her now as she turned toward home.

Mr. Dunbar, the elderly neighbor on Montgomery, sat on his white-washed porch swing. Pots of red geraniums marched up the edges of his front steps. She stopped, watching him rock back and forth. "Hello, Mr. Dunbar. How are you?"

"Oh, it's the little dancer isn't it? All grown up I see."

"Yes, I guess I am."

"Good." He removed his newspaper from the swing and motioned to Marta. "Sit with me."

She walked up the steps and slipped into the swing beside him.

"I thought you were dancing somewhere in Montana."

Marta swallowed hard. "I was until I broke my ankle. It was a fragile break, too severe to allow me to dance *en pointe*. So, here I am."

Mr. Dunbar shook his head. "I'm so sorry, but I'm glad to have your company." He shifted to face Marta. "Do you remember our berry contests when you were a little girl?"

"I do. My strawberries only ripened before your raspberries one time. You looked so surprised when I knocked at your door."

Mr. Dunbar laughed. "I was. My wife told me there'd be a time when you'd win. I always hoped she was right."

They talked about the neighborhood, then sat and rocked in the twilight. When he scooted forward and reached for his cane, Marta stood and steadied the swing.

"Thanks for joining me, young lady. I'll see you again real soon." He waved as he stepped inside his house and closed the door.

Marta trudged down the steps feeling a heaviness. Were the diet pills wearing off, or did her lack of direction tug at her? Something needed to change and soon.

Back home she stretched out on her bed thinking about the similarity of Mr. Dunbar and her mother. Both lived simple lives in simple homes. Both lost their spouses yet found ways to stay happy. Both believed in her. But did she believe in herself? She didn't know any more. Tomorrow she'd consider making a change, maybe.

$\mathcal{J}$he kitchen phone jangled, waking Marta. She stretched, listening to the rhythm of her mom's voice and decided to surprise her mom and get dressed instead of drifting back to sleep.

Her mom glanced up from her morning coffee, checked the clock, and looked back at Marta. A smile brightened her face, "Good morning! You're up earlier today. Feeling more like your old self this morning?"

"I guess," Marta said. "It's time to do *something*. I can't take another hour of Sean chasing Maggie and calling his wife Sue as if he's on a business trip when all along he's fathered Maggie's son and together they are stealing designs from his wife's clothing company. The soap is called *One Loving Life*, but it certainly sounds like more than one life getting messed up."

"You *have* been watching way too much daytime TV."

"Seems that way. I'm going to hunt for a job, any job. Got any ideas?"

"The local theatre group needs a seamstress and help with sets. Want me to call Hal, see if he's found anyone?"

"Sure." Marta paused. "No, let me call. Oh, who called you so early this morning?"

"Robert. He's going out of town for a few days and wanted to say good bye again."

Marta chuckled. Robert and Mom. Their relationship looked serious if he needed to say good bye again after seeing her last night.

The music of *Sleeping Beauty* pushed through Marta's head as she bathed and dressed in clean clothes for the first time this week. With her hair brushed back and gathered into a short ponytail, the music faded away before she captured it long enough to walk through the wedding scene choreography.

She added barrettes to her hair to keep it away from her face, then turned her head side to side. Why she'd hacked it off in the spring made less and less sense. Although she felt at odds with herself these days, she'd not dipped to the sadness she'd felt while wearing a cast earlier in the year.

♫

Marta called the community theatre and set up an appointment to meet the director, Hal Ryan, that afternoon. She took the bus to town and entered the old movie house they'd converted into a community theatre. She sat in the front of the auditorium waiting for Hal to arrive, letting her imagination create a ballet suitable for the small stage.

Hurried footsteps approached. "You must be Marta Selbryth," said a tall, middle-aged man as he approached the aisle where she sat.

Marta stood and offered him her hand. "I am."

"Thanks for meeting me here," he said as they shook hands. "Sorry for the informality. We're a low budget operation with only four or five performances a year. But you probably know that." He sat down next to her. So, Marta, let's talk about your theatre experience."

"I'm a ballet dancer, and I have no theatre experience."

"I see," he said. "Why am I talking with you if you have no art background or experience?"

Marta felt the sting of his comment but pressed on. "I sew," she said as she shook out two handmade costumes she'd brought with her. "I made these a few years ago. Sewing is a bit of a passion in our family."

He turned the samples over and checked the seams. "Very nice. And what about sets? Got any tucked in your bag?"

She laughed. "No, but I watched the ballet set team create backdrops. If someone shows me the basics, I'd like to learn."

He checked his watch and stood. "Give me a few days. We might need your sewing talents. If no qualified set person applies, I'll call you about that job as well." He headed backstage, leaving Marta alone in the auditorium.

"Thanks, Mr. Ryan. You're welcome, Marta." she said to the empty auditorium.

She sat in the dusky light and stared at the stage. Had he dismissed her? Was there any chance she'd get the jobs? She tucked the costumes back into her bag and exited the building.

The sunshine momentarily blinded her as she stood under the community theatre marquee and pawed through her purse for sunglasses. Oh well, she'd made an attempt. Next stop, the drug store across the street. She spent most of her last three dollars on diet pills, then took the bus home. Back to the afternoon soap operas, *One Loving Life*, *As The World Turns* and *General Hospital*.

The call came four days later. Marta took the call from Mr. Ryan while dressed in her robe seated in the kitchen playing solitaire.

"Miss Selbryth," he said. "If you're still available, I'd like to hire you to sew costumes for our summer children's theatre. Our six actors are students from the local junior highs. We're doing an original children's play called *Come Out and Play*, written by a friend of mine. The storyline calls for the animals to plan a surprise party. Our costume shop has a few items that need repairs, plus we want several animal costumes sewn. Does that interest you?"

Marta sat up. "Yes, it does. Thank you for remembering me. When do you want me to start?"

Mr. Ryan laughed. "We need the costumes yesterday. They must be flexible so the characters can dance as well as run around. Sound do-able?"

"Sure. I'll come by this afternoon and see what you have and what you need. Who's teaching them the animal dances?"

"The Holland Dance Studio. Do you know the place?"

"Very well. I took my training there. Miss Holland prepared me to become a professional dancer."

"Really? Would you want to teach our teenage actors a few steps?"

Marta twisted the phone cord around her finger. "I'd love to, but let me contact Miss Holland. She may already have someone in mind."

"Great. Let me know when you stop in this afternoon. The kids will be here as well. Thanks, Marta."

Marta felt a flutter of anticipation in her stomach when she dialed the dance studio.

"Holland Dance Studio. This is Elle."

"Hi, Mom. Is Miss Holland busy?"

Hi, honey. She's standing beside me. Just a minute."

"Marta?" Miss Holland said. "How are you? How's the ankle?"

"I'm fine and my ankle is coming along. I'm sorry I haven't stopped by the studio yet."

"Are you coming in today? I'd love to see you."

"No, not today." Marta explained about the community theatre.

"If you're up to teaching them, I'd be grateful. The girl I had in mind is away. Hal will be lucky to have you helping him. Just don't overdo it. I'll call Hal and let him know. Wait.... Your mom sends her best. Now that I've got you on the phone, when will you stop in so we can talk?"

Trapped. She knew Miss Holland was bound to ask. "I'll call you once I've figured out my hours with Mr. Ryan."

"Good. I'm anxious to see you and hear all about your experiences. Call me when you're ready."

Bathing in the small bath tub forced Marta's knees to touch her chin. She missed the showers back in her Billings boarding house, but being home mattered more than having a shower. Her mom had remained patient about her moping around, but now she had a job. Good fortune or at least a change offered her a distraction. She walked to the drug store on Callow and bought postcards, vowing to send them to Lynne and Steve later in the day. From there she caught a bus downtown to the community theatre.

The play's costume list hung on the bulletin board in the prop room. She'd investigated the raggedy costumes and decided she could repair, clean, and embellish a few, but four new costumes needed to be sewn. She closed her eyes and visualized a plan for sewing them: chenille with rag mop accents and feather-light wings. After all, they'd created the play for children; their imaginations created vivid costumes out of flour sacks or brown paper bags.

Now Marta sat in the center section of the dark auditorium waiting for Mr. Ryan and the teenagers to arrive. Just then a handful of young teens tromped down the aisle, chatting and laughing. Marta stood as Hal appeared on the stage. "Welcome, everyone! Please join us in the front rows, and let's talk about the play."

The shuffling bodies settled. Hal introduced the storyline of the play. "So you see, it's going to be fun, especially adding the dances Marta's offered to create for you. We're lucky to have a professional dancer. I'll let Marta explain her ideas to you."

Marta stood and felt their eyes follow her as she moved to sit on the edge of the stage. She straightened her spine and scrutinized the students. "We'll be using the music from *The Carnival of the Animals* to create dances for each animal. I'll teach you the basic steps, then create details to make each of your animals distinctive. But don't worry, these will be simple steps, enough to keep it fun and not embarrass you in front of your friends. You'll perform an opening group dance, a solo, and another group dance during the final party scene.

Hal announced their roles. "Neil, you're the tortoise; Pam, the butterfly; Terry and Valerie, the hens; Willis, the elephant; and George, the kangaroo. You're invited to ham up your dances as long as you don't get silly and forget your lines."

The teens laughed and poked each other but showed little enthusiasm for the play. Marta hoped they'd perk up and put energy into their roles as the production moved forward.

Hal continued. "We'll provide a schedule with the times you'll need to be here. Plan on Tuesday and Thursday mornings for practicing your lines and Wednesdays afternoons for learning your dances. Tell your parents each practice lasts ninety minutes and we need you here on time, every day. Questions?"

No hands raised so Hal handed out the scripts. "You're on your own learning your lines. Come ready to work, but also to have fun. Let's read through the script to familiarize all of us with the story."

Marta returned home with notes scribbled in the margins of her script and set to work creating simple steps for the teens. *The Carnival of the Animals* remained a personal favorite. Now she had the opportunity to use the music and steps she and Lynne taught the little girls in Billings, plus add her own touches. In all, she'd use seven selections from Saint-Saëns music. She'd create fifteen minutes of movements. That matched the time she'd traditionally be on stage when she danced professionally. Hopefully the teens were up for it.

Strangely, even though she guessed she was a scant five years older than the junior high actors, she felt a deep chasm separating them. Must be her year away on her own that created the gap. Regardless, she hoped they'd arrive for each rehearsal with more enthusiasm than they brought today, making her task considerably easier.

The teen play changed how she spent her day. She got up early and sat with her mom as she prepared for work. Then she spent time adjusting the dance steps and making or embellishing costumes before she hopped on the bus for the theater. Back at home she fixed dinner and once again readjusted the dances and costumes before her mom returned home. She forgot about taking diet pills, so perhaps her life had begun to change for the better and she'd focus on using her natural energy. Speaking with Miss Holland took a backseat to the teen play, but she needed to schedule her visit soon.

Wednesday afternoon dance rehearsals started with mixed results. Valerie, Terry, and Pam belonged to a dance team and learned their dances with ease. Marta added more detailed choreography to their two-minute solos.

The teen boys, Neil, Willis, and George, needed their simplified dances. Tortoise Neil's and Elephant Willis's slow-moving dances gave them time to think before they moved. Poor George shuffled like a lost cause. His feet became entangled throughout his brief yet fast-paced kangaroo solo.

"Marta, I don't know if I can do this," George said. "I mean I want to be in the play and all, but I don't want to be laughed at."

"George, you're doing fine. Lift your feet a little higher, like this." Marta demonstrated, then danced beside George to guide him. "Remember, this is a kids' play and it's supposed to be humorous."

Sure enough, when he lifted his feet he performed the steps perfectly and started adding humor to his role.

The end of June, Marta received another call from Hal Ryan. "I understand the dance lessons are going well. I appreciate your taking over that job."

"Thanks. It's fun working with the teens. It's a cute play. I'm certain the community will enjoy it."

"That's great to hear. Now more good news for you. Dennis, the set designer, hasn't found qualified help, so he'll call you before Monday to give you the opportunity to try your hand at building sets and helping paint them as well. It will be a bit of a time crunch with the sets needing to be completed as close to July tenth as possible."

"I'll do my best. I'm excited to help make sets. Watching the crew assemble them always fascinated me. Thanks, Mr. Ryan."

"Call me Hal. Prepare to get messy, Marta. Would you be interested in taking subscription calls and doing other odd jobs?"

"Yes, I'd love whatever work you have for me. I did reception jobs in Billings."

"How did you fit that in with your career?"

"I didn't. I worked at a hotel while I had a cast on my leg and couldn't dance."

"That must have been disappointing, but we're glad to have you working with us."

"Thanks, Hal." Marta hung up the phone and sat at the kitchen table feeling a mix of emotions. Hal, a near stranger, took the time to commiserate. Madame Cosper, artistic director of the ballet company, never shared any compassion for Marta's injury and recovery. Some day she hoped to understand why Madame didn't care or didn't like her.

Marta jumped up. No good came from dwelling on her past. Having jobs allowed her to send money to pay her doctor and hospital bills in Billings. If the set design job worked out, she'd start a nest egg toward getting a place of her own and a car.

"And that's the KING 5 News at Noon for Tuesday, July 7th, 1958." Marta clicked off the television. She retrieved the mail and flipped through it for her near-daily letter from Steve. No letter today; must be busy, or waiting until he received more than a postcard from her. Would he care to hear about her sewing or that she returned from set making each day wearing a rainbow of paint blots with splotches of dried wheat paste? Maybe. She really should write back to him.

Building sets proved to be backbreaking, but she'd learned a lot the past few days. Dennis, the carpenter who worked on set construction after hours, surprised her. Their first encounter reminded her of meeting Steve. Both began as a mishmash of misunderstandings.

That first afternoon, she'd arrived early and sat waiting on the apron of the stage. He was thirty minutes late. With her luck he'd be an old bald headed guy with a beer belly and unable to bend over.

As Marta prepared to leave, assuming he wasn't coming, a young, blonde man sauntered down the aisle carrying two tool boxes. "So, you're Marta and you want to become a set designer?"

"Not really," she said. Boy, her image of the carpenter missed the mark. "I need a job. Hal said you needed a set builder and someone to help paint."

Dennis grinned and shook his head. "Hal always caves for a lovely face."

Marta's smile faded. "Excuse me? I'm a hard worker, I can—"

"Forget I said that. It's just that I need more than a painter. My new carpentry business is taking off so I need someone to build sets, not just make them pretty."

"So, you took one look at me and thought I couldn't do this?"

"Yeah, that's right. You're what, five feet tall and weigh ninety pounds dripping wet? Many of our sets are eight feet tall and weigh more than you do. Do you even know how to swing a hammer?"

She pulled her mouth taut to hold back a retort that rushed to be spoken, but she knew her face gave away her frustration.

Dennis closed his eyes and shook his head. "Look. That sounded cruel but I need muscle more than art."

"Do you always judge people so quickly? How do you know I can't do it?"

Dennis lifted his hands in surrender. "Okay. Let's see what you've got." He opened his tool boxes. "Hand me the T-square, a claw hammer, and a dozen eight penny nails."

Marta rummaged through his tool boxes and handed him the square and the correct hammer. She held a similar hammer as she faced him. "You don't have any *eights* in your box. Is there another place I can check, or do you want to use *sixteens?* Or, would a lighter nail work?"

Dennis raised one eyebrow. His jaw dropped open as if he'd won a thousand dollar Bingo game. "Okay, Marta!" He walked to the wings and returned with a coffee can of nails. His sly smile and nod defrosted her anger.

Over the next three hours, they assembled frames, attached plywood, and moved on to building a platform. The steady beat of hammering released months of Marta's frustration one stroke at a time.

After they collected tools and prepared to leave for the evening, Marta sat on the apron resting with her feet dangling over the edge. A flutter of interest in Dennis ran through her as she watched his back muscles flex when he wrestled with the plywood tops. Too bad he acted like such a jerk. She'd like a few new friends, but expecting a busy guy like Dennis to become a friend was pushing her luck.

He sat down beside her and wiped his sweaty forehead. "I owe you an apology. How do you know so much about carpentry?"

"I only learned the basics when I helped my dad on projects."

"Is he a carpenter?"

Marta shook her head. "He worked as an electrician in the shipyard."

"What does he do now?"

"He died several years ago. I helped him on minor repairs."

"Good for you. When you need carpentry help, call me. I'll make time to help." He raised one eyebrow again like Sean on the soap opera. "Better yet, how 'bout we talk over dinner this weekend? My treat."

Marta fingered the necklace from Steve that hung on a chain inside her shirt. "Thanks, but I'm kind of in a relationship."

"Really?" Dennis drew a set of quotation marks in the air as he continued to speak. "How can you *kinda* be in a relationship?"

Marta closed her eyes and clamped her lips together. She hopped off the stage, snagged her purse from a seat in the front row, and took several deep breaths before she turned back to speak to Dennis. "We're done for tonight aren't we?"

Dennis nodded and cocked his head to one side. "See you tomorrow at five?"

"I'll be here," she said over her shoulder as she marched up the aisle toward the exit.

As she crossed to the bus stop, the necklace bounced against her sweaty skin. What was wrong with her? Flirting with Dennis, the first cute guy she met? She promised Steve she'd be in a committed relationship with him. He was buried in college projects as well as his job at the paper and still found time to write and call her. Dennis's pre-judgment of her skills made her furious, yet she continued flirting with him. This wasn't like her at all.

For the next two days, she worked diligently but didn't invite conversation with Dennis. He gave her directions, but his friendliness had cooled. "Now that we've primed the flats, I'll have the art students sketch the forest on the canvas backdrops. Follow the colors as indicated on each section. Paint them at night before you leave so they'll dry by the next morning's rehearsal. Set the maché cave sections aside; the kids will need to pretend for now. Any questions?"

Marta shook her head. "Nope."

"Okay then. I'm done until the next play. Contact Hal if you need any help." He packed up his tools and walked toward the wings. "Thanks for your help."

"Wait!" Marta swallowed hard. "I want to apologize for being huffy the other day."

Dennis turned to face her. His eyebrow lifted again. "Is that what you call it, huffy?"

"Okay. Rude might be a better word. Your offer for dinner caught me off guard."

"Are you always 'on guard,' Marta?"

Was she? She shrugged. "I guess."

"No need to explain. I got the message loud and clear. You're 'sorta' in a relationship." He shrugged. "I suggested dinner, not a wedding proposal."

"I know. I overreacted. How about I treat you to a meal? We're having a picnic at my mom's next Sunday at two o'clock. I'd like you to come."

"You're asking me on a date? That surprises me since you're dating Mr. Sorta."

Marta started to protest but stopped when she saw him point both index fingers toward her and wink.

"Gotcha, Marta." He bowed. "I'd love to come."

Before she could say anything else, he'd left the auditorium. What had she done?

The picnic proved to be more of an adventure than she'd anticipated. The guests were a mix of her mom and Robert's friends, plus his twenty-one year old daughter, Alice. Was it her button nose, her curly blonde hair, her curves, or her perky personality that attracted Dennis's attention? He couldn't take his eyes off her.

Marta watched the way he laughed at her jokes and nodded with interest at whatever she said. When she dropped her fork, Dennis handed her a new one. Marta might as well have been a bush or a tree in the backyard for all the attention he paid to her. Did his attention matter? Sure felt like it did. But why should it when she professed her commitment to Steve?

She struggled through a wave of embarrassment over the gnawing in her heart. Somehow she didn't want to share Dennis; as if she had any control over what he did or who he cared about.

Thoughts of Dennis, how they met, and her interest in him continued on as the work neared completion. Marta's paint-by-number sky, bushes, and trees made her arms and back ache, but getting paid made up for the discomfort. Only an hour or so left now and she'd be out of work, just when she'd gotten the hang of it.

"Nice job, Marta," a voice called from the back of the dark theatre.

She turned, careful to hold her paint-filled brush upright. As Hal approached the stage, her anticipation dropped. She'd hoped to see Dennis.

Hal hopped onto the stage and investigated each set and fingered the rack of costumes. "I like the terry cloth costumes idea and the way you stuffed the elephant with batting. The kids are thrilled."

"Thanks. They'll be able to move easily in them."

"I understand the dancing is coming along as well. You've influenced Pam. Says she wants to take lessons and become a ballerina."

"Good for her," Marta said, but inside she shuddered. If Pam knew what she was setting up for herself, how she'd need to sacrifice her free time and her active social life, she'd never want to become a dancer.

"Dennis also tells me you're a natural on sets. Sure you've never done them before?"

Marta laughed. "He made my job easy. It's exciting to see canvas, wood, and wheat paste become usable parts of the play's illusions."

"I hope you'll be available for future productions. You're just the spark of energy and creativity we've needed. The theatre board is anxious to meet you during the walk through on July 21. Looks like the teen play's a sellout, and our regular season subscriptions are starting to come in."

Marta felt her insides swell with pride from Hal's compliment. "Great," she said. "The kids are excited. Willis told me he wants to become an actor and perform on Broadway. But I told him that, like ballet dancers, only one in a thousand actors get auditions and only a few spots open up every year."

"Do you want to go back to dancing for a ballet company?"

She hesitated. What *did* she want? "Maybe, but not the one in Billings. I'll need to wait and decide after I'm fully recovered."

When Hal left for the evening, Marta remained behind enjoying the quiet of the theatre. Tonight she'd completed her jobs for the community theatre. The wages she'd earned from the set work, painting, and helping in the office would end as soon as the play ended. She'd need to find a new way to earn money until another play came along.

Since no one was around, Marta kicked off her sandals to make use of the stage. She stretched briefly, then recreated her final re-audition piece, *Rhapsody in Blue*. She imagined the long clarinet slide as she leaned back to add extension to the *grande developpe* followed by the swaying sidesteps, *balances,* and elongated sweeps of her arms moving toward the floor. Both ankles throbbed, but she continued dancing until the long string of *releves,* when she stopped and leaned forward with her hands on her knees.

Clap, clap, clap.

She looked up, startled to have an audience.

"You look amazing when you dance, Marta." Dennis stood in the center aisle holding a white paper bag. He raised it toward Marta. "Thought I'd bring dinner so we might celebrate your job well done."

"Thanks for the compliment. I thought I was alone so I took advantage of the free stage. But, I am also hungry, so thanks for the food as well."

Dennis spread out containers of Chinese food on a tarp on the stage and handed Marta wooden take-out utensils and a napkin. "It's self-serve tonight, even for dancers."

"I love it. So, what brings you back, and with food no less?"

"You. Hal called. Said you'd finished. Thought I'd check up on you and see how things were progressing. Didn't know I'd get a free dance performance as well."

Marta dipped her face as she felt a rush of heat spread through her body. "Painting is like dancing. It relaxes me, and I sometimes forget I'm hungry. It also gives me the chance to let my mind wander."

Dennis watched her face for a long moment and asked, "Where does your mind go, Marta?"

"I don't know. Nowhere and everywhere."

"Are you thinking of painting, dancing, or Mr. Sorta? Or me?"

How could she explain herself? She nibbled at bites of her dinner while she thought about where the conversation was heading. She had no intention of sharing her feelings with Dennis or saying anything more about Steve. Marta shrugged. "It's hard to explain. Images float through my mind like clouds moving across the sky. They reshape themselves every few seconds. Does that make any sense?"

Dennis shrugged. "Yes, But they're your images, so they only need to make sense to you."

Marta fidgeted and twirled a spiral of her hair around her finger. "Thanks for saying that. They are mine." His comment created a deeper respect for him than she thought possible after their first encounter.

When they finished eating, Dennis drove Marta home and invited her to join him for opening night on July 24. She accepted.

As they turned onto her road, she frowned when she noticed the line of cars parked along the fence. Damn. She'd pictured a hot bath and time to sit and rock before she went to bed. Why hadn't her mom told her she hosted Canasta tonight?

Marta stopped in the kitchen for a drink of water, then took a deep breath and placed her performance smile in place. Enter stage right. "Hi, Mom, Robert, everyone. Nice to see you again."

"Honey, you know everyone," her mom said. "Last minute change in plans since Marjorie is sick. Want to join us? We need another player."

"Thanks, but no. It's been a long day, so I'm sneaking through and heading for bed. Night, everyone."

A pleasant surprise rested on Marta's bedside table. It was a letter from Lynne.

Dear Marta,

Bad news. I can't make it to Bremerton this summer.

Got a great chance to teach at a dance camp in ole' Colorado until company classes resume. Need the big bucks (ha) so I can afford a not-quite-so-old car.

Saved an article about our final performances. Look for my name; it's not there. Next year, maybe I'll get a solo.

Will call with my phone number if they have any out in the wilderness. Might meet a mountain man! Better than meeting a mountain lion.

Lynne

No matter what Lynne wrote, she always made Marta chuckle. Who else would send a long article about a ballet when she wasn't even mentioned? The fact that Lynne wrote comments in the margins about what Madame said when she shared the article with the *corps* underscored just what a crazy friend she remained across the miles and mountains that separated them. She'd miss getting a humor boost from seeing her.

It wasn't until Marta drifted off to sleep that she revisited dancing on the stage and hearing the music play in her head. She rotated her ankle, felt a tightness but no sharp pain. Perhaps her life, like her ankle, was beginning to mend.

*S*weat ran down Marta's arms and legs as she hurried to the dance studio. Was it her pace, the unexpected July heat, or her nervousness? Most likely a combination of all three. With her tasks for the play winding down, she'd finally scheduled time to meet with Miss Holland.

She straightened her body as she crossed the last street and entered the dance studio. Her mom's reception desk looked bare. No sign of her or the usual clutter of catalogs, memos, and ledgers.

Ballet music streamed from the large practice room. Miss Holland's voice instructed her students, her hands clapping the beat. "Spot your turns...*Clap, clap, clap, clap*. Better...Nice finish."

Marta sat in the waiting area and looked around. At first she thought nothing had changed. Then she noticed her costumed photo hanging on the wall beside photos of Maria Tallchief and Alicia Markova. A warm feeling spread through her; for a brief while she'd been a professional dancer as they'd been. By hanging that photo, Miss Holland and her mom honored her accomplishment. She smiled and closed her eyes remembering her hours inside that room, working on *barre* exercises, center floor work, and ending her class time with turns and leaps. The familiarity of the music and routine relaxed her.

When the door opened, the smell of sweat filled the air. Teenage girls exited, pushing back their bangs and rushing for towels to dry their faces. They stepped around her, not noticing that they knew her, grabbed their bags, and headed out. One girl, a stranger to Marta, stopped and stared. She looked from Marta's face to the photo hanging on the wall and back to Marta's face again.

"Are you her? I mean, are you Marta?"

"I am. What's your name?"

The girl blushed and looked to the photo again. "I'm Rosalia. You dance for a ballet company, don't you?"

"I did until I got injured."

"But, uh…why are you here? I mean, when did you come back?"

"In May."

"And now she's here, Rosalia," said Miss Holland as she exited the practice room.

Marta stood and hurried to hug her long time instructor and mentor.

Rosalia stared until Miss Holland spoke. "Marta will be back to talk with your class one of these days. You can ask all your questions then."

"Can I have your autograph, please? I can't imagine how the others missed seeing you sitting here!"

Marta smiled and signed a recital program she found in her mom's desk. Rosalia hugged Marta, packed up her ballet bag, and waved as she left the building.

"Looks like you have an admirer, Marta. Welcome back. Let's sit in my office and chat."

The crowded office space sat tucked in a corner of the large studio. It held Miss Holland's desk, two chairs, and overcrowded shelves that reached to the ceiling. Pink *Capezio pointe* shoe boxes and stacks of costume catalogs and dog-eared magazines shared space with a dying plant, a box marked "old receipts," and several bags of colorful trims.

Despite her mom's efforts, Miss Holland's chaos hadn't changed over the intervening months.

Neither had Miss Holland. She was tall, blonde, beautiful, and thin with her long hair pulled into a sleek ponytail. Her damp leotard accentuated her muscular body. She didn't look to be as old as her mom, but she was. Maybe the sparkle in her blue eyes made her look younger. She cleared off the extra chair and sat behind the desk facing Marta.

"Well," she said. "How are you?"

"I'm fine. Sorry about missing the recital."

"Don't even think about it," Miss Holland said. "You've had lots to work through. Want to talk about it?"

Marta nodded. "It's hard to know where to start. So much happened over the nine months I was away."

"Start with the best parts. Tell me how it felt to be a professional dancer."

"Magic. Total magic. We practiced three hours every morning, doing many of the same *barre* and floor exercises I did here, plus we reviewed choreography."

"I knew I needed to push you ladies to practice longer hours."

"You were right to push us even though we complained. In fact the afternoons were more challenging. We learned new choreography and broke into groups to practice bits and pieces. Knowing ballerinas around the world followed the same routine and listened to the same music decade after decade, I felt like I'd joined a fellowship of dancers; they moved through my muscles, guiding me from one step to the next."

"That's amazing." Miss Holland looked as if she were imagining that sensation. "Your mom told me that the artistic director wasn't supportive."

"Madame Cosper? You could say that. She's a perfectionist. She didn't like me even though I worked hard so she'd respect me. Damien Black led most of our classes. He was easier to work with and gave me practice sessions while I prepared to return to the company."

"How's your ankle now?"

Marta shrugged. "It's improving. I still have lots of pain and stiffness, but when I massage it and exercise cautiously, the pain lessens. That's one reason I wanted to see you. I'd like to use a practice room when you have open hours. I'll pay as if it were a lesson."

"I'd be happy to have you here. For now we'll be sharing the large practice room since the physical therapist still rents out the small studio."

"I appreciate any space you've got available. I need to get back at it, maybe lose a few pounds and drop down to a hundred."

"You don't look like you need to lose any weight, Marta."

"I do. I feel bloated and sluggish. My old garage space is available when mom takes the car out, but I need to get back to a real *barre* with larger mirrors."

"No need to pay me anything. In fact, I'd like to offer you a job."

"Really? But I don't have mobility or strength for complex movements."

"That won't be a problem. I'm starting a Monday, Wednesday, Friday morning exercise class for women in mid-August to bring in more money and because women have requested classes since they have no other place to exercise. I'd thought I'd include *barre* exercises, stretching, and endurance movements you could handle in your sleep. And, since regular dance classes don't begin until early afternoon, you'd have the studio to yourself before and after the classes."

"Wow. That would be fantastic, Miss Holland." Marta felt a surge of energy just thinking about dancing. "The extra time and a larger space than my garage may speed up my recovery."

"Four other things, Marta. First. You need to stop calling me Miss Holland. Since you're going to be working with me, please call me Lindsay. Second, I'd like you to speak to the advanced class. Several families are looking ahead to their daughters beginning auditions. Your information will help them understand what they're up against."

Marta decided both of those requests were doable. "What else?"

"Third, feel free to say no, but would you consider leading a kinders class? The age range will be three to five. I want it to be playful games and movements with a focus on musicality and free expression. Any interest?"

"I'd love it. I worked with slightly older girls in Billings, so I can adapt what Lynne and I did and then add movement as they progress."

"Great. Number four is the most important way you can help me. I'd like you to work with Rosalia Marcus. She's arrived last September, and she'll be ready to audition next spring. Her drive reminds me of you; your help and knowledge about what she should expect at auditions would benefit her tryouts."

Marta flashed back to her string of auditions and letters of rejection. How does anyone prepare for that? For years you're the darling, the star of a dance studio. Suddenly you're one of twenty people in one of a dozen auditions, vying for one of two positions. No one cares where you came from as long as you stay free of injury and perform as needed. "Let me think about it for a bit. My ankle needs to support me. If it does, I'd love to work with her."

"Good," Lindsay said. "I just need to get her mother, Zandora, to take a giant step back and let Rosalia grow and develop in her own time and in her own way. Her mom's my first true stage mother. I shudder when I see her coming my way. She makes more demands than anyone I've ever known, so if that is a deal breaker, I'll understand."

Zandora sounded like a challenge. Couldn't be any worse than dealing with Madame Cosper, could she? "I'll consider it. Sharing what I now know about auditions might help Rosalia and any others as they take that leap. When do you need my answer?"

"Soon as possible. We'll be down to one studio so we'll need to workout scheduling."

On the walk home, Marta moved with a bounce in her step as she organized her windfall of jobs. So far they fit together like pieces of a jigsaw puzzle. She'd need diet pills to keep up her energy for the long days. No sweat. She seldom took more than one or two a day lately, so an occasional four or five a day wouldn't be a problem.

As she neared home she saw Mr. Dunbar rocking in his porch swing. He waved, so she stopped. "Hi, Mr. Dunbar. How are you today?"

"Can't complain. The sun feels good on my old bones. Haven't seen you lately."

Marta told him about working at the theatre and the dance studio.

"Remember to take time for yourself," he said.

"I will. I'm headed home to start dinner. I'll see you soon. Have a nice evening, Mr. Dunbar."

Marta prepared garden vegetables for a dinner salad for three, positive that Robert planned to show up and stay past dinner. Over the past few weeks she'd come to accept his presence, knowing he brought joy to her mom. She missed her one-to-one time with her mom from last year, but now she had her own interests and issues to keep her busy.

Her visit with Miss Holland had gone well; she wasn't embarrassed talking about her injury. But speaking with her former advanced ballet class, with dancers she shared classes with last year, could be uncomfortable. They might see her brief career as an omen for themselves. It didn't need to be the same for them.

The next afternoon Marta arrived at the community theatre in time to observe the committee assembled on the stage. Hal and Dennis, along with four strangers, three women and one man, stood looking at the sets. A fourth woman appeared at the side aisle. All eyes followed the graceful woman sashaying toward stage. Her long black ponytail swayed from side to side as she hurried to join the rest of the theatre committee. She moved with the assurance of a performer about to take center stage. Dennis certainly noticed.

"Lily Rose!" Hal said. "Glad you made it. We were about to begin."

"Wouldn't miss this for the world," she said. "This summer program is the talk of the town."

As Marta joined the group on the stage, Lily Rose stretched out her hand. "Hi. You must be Marta. I've heard a lot about you. Welcome to our little theatre group."

Marta felt a warmth radiate from Lily Rose through her handshake and her smile. "Nice to meet you."

"Ever hear of *Lil' Rose and the Sounds*, Marta?" Hal said. "This lovely woman sang lead in the group until the early '50s. She did a few dance moves as well."

Lily laughed and shrugged. "Can't deny it, but now I'm back to plain ol' Lily Rose. Let's get back to our tour for the play."

Hal led the committee on their walk-through. They examined the sets Dennis and the art team designed, then listened intently as Hal shared the story details of the play. Marta shared the progress the students had made and that each learned a few basic dance steps and animal movements to add humor to their roles.

"Marta's being modest," Hal said. "She's taught them so well many want to take dance lessons. This young woman also made many of the costumes, helped build and paint the sets, and took phone subscriptions."

Marta felt a rush of heat surge through her body at becoming the unexpected focus of the committee. She guessed she had done a lot, but being singled out and put into a spotlight of sorts confused her. Should she curtsy or nod or just smile?

The committee smiled toward Marta then wandered around the stage talking with Hal, Dennis, and Marta before saying their goodbyes. Lily Rose remained seated on the apron of the stage as Marta said goodbye and started down the steps, heading home.

"Marta?" Lily Rose said. "May I speak with you for a minute?"

"Sure." Marta returned to the stage and sat down.

"I need dance school information for Olivia, my dizzy dancing four-year old. I understand you work with the Holland Dance Studio. Do you have classes for kids her age?"

"We do. I'll be teaching the class."

"Thank heaven. Every time I turn on music, Olivia starts dancing and twirling."

"I did that when I was her age. But if you live out of town, another studio might be more convenient."

"I live on Pill Hill at the end of north Lafayette, so Callow Avenue is perfect. I'll call next week." Lily Rose checked her watch and hopped off the stage. "Got to pick up my darling daughter. I'll see you soon, Marta."

That evening at dinner with her mom, Marta talked about the meeting with the theatre committee.

"Do you remember hearing the music of *Lil'Rose and the Sounds?* Her pop group sang in the late '40s and early '50s."

Her mom shook her head. "I'm not good with music group names. Do you know any of her song titles?"

"Dennis told me a few that she wrote, sang, and recorded: *Tender Love, Sweet Brier Rose,* and *Love in the Air.* I've heard them on the radio. She sounded good. I might go down to Brown's Music and buy one of her long play records to listen to her music."

"So," her mom said, "we may have a celebrity living in Bremerton, huh?"

"She doesn't act like one. She asked me about classes for Olivia, her little girl, so maybe we'll see her around the dance studio."

Mom laughed. "Don't count on it. I've heard those Hollywood types often tell you what they think you want to hear. She could probably buy the studio without even looking at her checking account balance. It's great that she's on the theatre committee; maybe her rich friends will become patrons so Hal can continue to expand his teen plays throughout the year."

"She's excited about this one," Marta said. "Guess we'll know what might happen after opening night."

Dress rehearsals went well. The teens knew their speaking parts and danced with enthusiasm, so Hal made only a few tweaks.

"Keep your faces toward the audience when possible," he said. "George, try to jump up and down with your hands bent like kangaroo front paws. I'm afraid you'll fall off the stage if you don't find your balance. Pam, work with Marta. We need you to float like a butterfly rather than flap like a bird. Marta, do you have any suggestions?"

"Yes. Have fun," she said. "Remember, most of your audience will be young children, so don't speak too fast. We want them to hear every single line."

"So, see you tomorrow at six for your makeup," Hal said. "Performance begins at seven. Leave your costumes here each evening. Now, go rest."

After Marta finished with Pam, the theatre fell silent. Marta walked to the back of the theatre and sat down appraising the sets. Looked good to her. Should be easy enough to sit on the side of the stage to help with costumes and coach the dancers during the first performance. That changed her plans to sit with Dennis, but oh well. At least she wasn't performing!

❧

Opening night: 6:10. The teens rushed in with excited chatter. All except Willis. Marta helped them into their costumes and started their makeup. "Have any of you talked with Willis today?"

"I did," George said. "He didn't say he had a problem getting here. We could have given him a ride."

"What do we do if he doesn't come?" Valerie asked.

"I don't know," Marta said, feeling only mild concern. As a young teen he probably forgot the time.

Just then Hal appeared in the dressing room. "No one answers when I called Willis's home. I'm worried. We can't rewrite the script at this late date. Any ideas, kids?"

"Marta knows the play and his dance," Pam said.

All eyes turned to Marta. She froze. Now she knew how it felt to be caught in a trap with no possible escape. Please come, Willis, she thought. Please get here in time. "Sure, I'll do it. But let's give Willis fifteen minutes before we make that decision."

Fifteen minutes passed. No Willis. Marta stripped down and stepped into the elephant costume. She walked around to feel the way it moved, then she painted her face gray with dark accents around her eyes. They still had time for Willis to arrive.

6:45. Still no Willis. "Places," called the stage manager.

Marta swallowed hard and became the plodding elephant, the character who danced on hind legs then mistakenly sat on the birthday cake. Certainly not as artistic as dancing in *Swan Lake,* but a performance just the same. Hopefully no one knew an adult played the elephant.

Laughter greeted the performers during and after the play. By the ending applause, Marta's ankle started to throb and swell, but icing would have to wait. She needed to remain in the dressing room, helping the teens remove their makeup and stow their costumes for their future performances.

"That was fun," Neil said.

"So much fun," Terry said. "And we get to do it two more times."

"Marta, you were so good," Pam said.

"Thanks, everyone did a great job. Did you hear all the giggles?"

Hal hurried into the dressing room. "I found out what happened to Willis. He had an asthma attack and went to the hospital."

"Is he okay?" George said. "Can we go see him?"

"He's resting at home and will probably be able to perform on Saturday and Sunday."

"That's good news," George said. "He's my neighbor, so I'll stop by his house tonight and let you know if he's coming tomorrow. If not, Marta can perform his role again."

"I'm glad Marta is such a good sport," Hal said. "Filling in at the last minute shows lots of caring. You kids are lucky to have her."

The teens smiled and applauded Marta. She did a deep curtsy and trumpeted like an elephant. As she rose she spotted Dennis, the theatre committee, and a little girl watching her. Great, she thought. Another silly move, kind of like mimicking Madame Cosper and getting caught. Too late now to take it back.

The group applauded her, then personally thanked her for stepping in. This time she didn't curtsy or trumpet a response. She smiled and assured them that her stepping in created no problem for her.

Lily Rose and the little girl stood to one side, waiting for the group to disperse. When they stepped forward, each handed Marta a white rose.

"That was wonderful, Marta. Thank you so much for offering your dance talents and for being gracious enough to step in." Lily moved the little girl ahead with a gentle hand. "Olivia, honey, I want you to meet a real ballerina. This is Miss Selbryth. She's going to be your ballet teacher in a few weeks."

Olivia dropped her chin and tucked herself behind Lily Rose, taking sneak peeks toward Marta.

Marta knelt down beside Olivia. "I'm glad to meet you, Olivia. I hear you love to dance."

Olivia nodded.

"Good. We'll dance and twirl and you'll have other children in class with you. How's that?"

Olivia shrugged, then smiled.

Lily Rose shook Olivia's hand and called back as they moved toward the exit. "I'll talk with you soon."

The last person waiting was Dennis. Marta felt his eyes follow her as she straightened the costumes on the clothes rack. "I noticed that Willis had an accomplished understudy."

Marta laughed. "I muffed several lines, but I did a good job sitting on the cake."

"How about we toast your play debut with a drink?"

"Can't. I'm underage."

"Are you old enough for an ice cream at the Dairy Queen?"

"Yes. I believe I am."

Eating ice cream after performing brought up similar times with Steve in Billings. She enjoyed Dennis's company, but she'd need to get home and ice her ankle if she planned to walk more than a few steps tomorrow.

"Hey, Marta. You've slipped away. Where did you go? What were you thinking about?"

"How I did this very same thing after performances in Billings."

"Alone, with friends, or with your sorta boyfriend?"

"Both, but usually with Mister Sorta."

"Is he a dancer?"

"No, he's a college student who works as a part-time reporter. Why are you so curious?"

"Trying to get to know you. That was a great thing you did tonight."

"Tell that to my ankle. It's telling me to wrap it in ice."

"Let me grab a cup of ice from the attendant. Will that help? Or I could massage it for you."

Marta squirmed at his suggestion. "I'll be fine, but I need to get home."

Dennis scraped the bottom of his bowl of ice cream, and carried their empty containers back to the counter. He turned to Marta. "Ready?"

She nodded. As they backed out of the Dairy Queen parking lot she asked, "Are you still dating Alice?"

"Who?"

"Alice Marsden from my family's summer party."

"Oh, her. What made you think I dated her?"

"You looked fascinated by her charms." Marta stretched out "charms" with a southern accent.

"You must admit she's a beautiful woman," Dennis said. "But I prefer a woman who can swing a hammer and toss back my insults."

Willis returned for his elephant role, leaving Marta the task of assisting the teens and watching their performances from backstage. Dennis didn't return either night, perhaps because he wasn't needed or because of their Dairy Queen conversation.

She'd stammered as he hinted about his interest in her. She didn't know how to reply, so she'd said she needed to get home and didn't speak another word until they reached Rhododendron Drive and were stopped at the back gate.

"Well, Marta?"

"Well what?"

"Are you available, or is Mister Sorta hogging your dating life?"

Was she available? She hadn't heard from Steve for two weeks. Was he busy, or had he lost interest in her? Or was he following her cue of not writing? Where was Lynne when Marta needed her advice?

"I'm not entirely clear about that, Dennis. Can we be friends for now?"

Marta sensed a tension in him as soon as she finished speaking.

"No problem." He got out of the car and opened her door. "Have a nice evening. See you around." As he drove off he revved the engine as if to say "I'm outta here."

ॐ

Marta called Lynne on Sunday after the matinee, anxious to hear her friend's voice and catch up on her latest dating misadventure.

"So," Lynne said. "You were a dancing elephant? Wait until I tell the little girls. Did anyone take a movie of the play?"

"I imagine, but I haven't seen it yet."

"At least you wore a mask. Should help keep down your embarrassment. I, on the other hand, have had one embarrassment after another here in the wild west. These summer dancers all have two left feet."

"At least they're trying."

"I guess." Lynne laughed. "But then I was showing off. I completed a complex turn and ended up falling off the outdoor platform where we danced. Not one handsome, eligible guy around to pick me up!"

"Now that's embarrassing, even for you. Did you hurt yourself?"

"Just my pride. When I get out to visit you, I'll expect you to have found at least one hunk to introduce me to. He doesn't need to be as cute as Steve, but close would be preferred."

"There *is* one guy that meets your criteria. He's tall, funny, and likes to tease. He's a carpenter for the community theatre. We went out for ice cream and—"

"Hold it. You're dating a guy? What about Steve?"

Marta felt her face heat up thinking about Dennis. "We're friends. He reminds me of that Lenny you dated."

"You mean he flirts with other women while you're out on a date?"

"We're not dating; we're just friends, Lynne."

Lynne laughed. "Of course you are. You don't need to worry about his type, Marta. They never get serious. Now Steve, on the other hand, fell hard in your case. How's he doing?"

"I haven't heard from him lately."

"I'm sure he'll call soon. For now, forget about him and Dennis and concentrate on finding a great guy for me. Deal?"

"Deal."

Lynne always brightened Marta's moods with her outlandish comments. Marta needed to forget about Steve and Dennis and focus on things she could control. In three days she promised to speak with the advanced ballet class. Time to plan what she'd mention to her former classmates. Auditions and dancing with the ballet company, of course. Her injury as well. Would they think she'd thrown away her career since it ended so quickly? She'd know next Wednesday.

arta walked to the dance studio to allow extra time to rehearse speaking to the advanced ballet class that met year-round. Lindsay told Marta she'd invited parents to attend as well. She'd suggested Marta discuss strategies for tryouts, her daily routines at the ballet company, and other bits to encourage the dancers.

As Marta stepped off the curb, her thoughts focused on what she'd mention to the waiting girls. A car honked. The lady driver shook her head. Marta jumped back, stepping off-balance into the gutter. She stared after the car, then drew in several deep breaths as she watched it continue along Burwell. She stepped back onto the sidewalk, watching the traffic breeze past, waiting for her heart rate to slow to normal.

Her near-miss with the car jumbled her ideas about what she wanted to say. Hopefully she'd remember them once she started speaking. Right now she needed to pay attention to where she stood. She waited for a break in the traffic, crossed the street, and walked into the studio.

As she entered the practice room, she felt her heartbeat quicken. A large circle of dancers and parents sat chatting. One chair in the circle remained empty beside Lindsay Holland. Lindsay stood to greet her.

"Here's our Marta now. Right on time. Everyone, I'm sincerely proud to introduce Marta Selbryth, my first ever professional dancer."

The circle of parents and students clapped. Marta bowed her head and curtsied.

She recognized several classmates from last spring. Most were high school juniors from West Bremerton, a couple attended East Bremerton, and one drove in from Central Kitsap for classes. Rosalia was the only new student face. None of the dancers had become her close friends. Why was that? Was she hard to approach? She didn't think so. She'd easily made friends with her corps de ballet friends Lynne and Bartley.

Lindsay stepped toward Marta and took her arm, directing her to join the group. "I've invited Marta to give our young dancers a chance to reacquaint themselves with her and ask those burning questions they keep asking me."

Everyone chuckled.

Marta sat, crossed her ankles, and straightened her spine as she smiled, looking around the circle. "Thank you for inviting me. It's wonderful to be back in the studio."

"Let me start," Lindsay said. "Tell us the best part about performing as a professional dancer."

Marta nodded and bit her lip. Talking about dancing carried her back to the moments before the first time the curtain went up and she realized she'd become a professional dancer. Her stomach did flip flops. "All the practicing, the blisters, and the tiredness disappeared as I stepped onto the stage. You know how you feel when it's your birthday or when it's Christmas? Roll those two events together and you'll begin to understand. During every performance, the huge professional sets, the fancy costumes, the live orchestra music, and the choreography swept me up. As corps dancers we frame the soloists, but we also add depth and fill the stage with our dancing in the village and ballroom scenes. I was lucky to take lessons from Miss Holland. Learning famous choreography while I danced here gave me confidence, and it will for you too."

"How do you learn so many dances?" one parent asked. "I've heard that you only work a few weeks on a new ballet."

"That's true. At the ballet company we learned several dances at the same time to cut down on the amount of time we need for a new ballet. It confused me for a bit, so I suggest you tackle as much choreography as possible while you're here. That will help you become familiar with more ballet music as you prepare you for audition choreography."

Marta paused and noticed Lindsay's appreciative smile. "In Billings we danced on a wonderful stage. We had dressings rooms with lighted mirrors and—"

"Did you receive flowers on stage?" asked one dancer.

"Yes and no. Only the principal dancers, the artistic director, and the conductor receive flowers from the patrons. I was a corps dancer, but my mom and my friends brought me flowers like yours do after your recital."

"Did you perform with famous dancers or go on tours?" Rosalia asked.

"No famous dancers came last year, but Patrice who's our principal ballerina, is a wonderful dancer and is well-known in Montana. Our company does a *Nutcracker* tour each November and December. It was fun, but lots of the stages were not good for dancers. Some cement floors gave us shin splints; other turned out to be old wooden stages that ruined our *pointe* shoes with splinters."

"What ballets did you dance? And did you have any solos?"

"I danced in the corps in *Coppélia*, the *Nutcracker,* and *Sleeping Beauty*. I had two solos: Mother Ginger in the *Nutcracker* and the evil fairy, Carabosse, in *Sleeping Beauty.*"

Lindsay spoke up. "Tell the parents about your practices. They think I work their daughters too long and too hard sometimes."

Several parents nodded and whispered to each other.

"Lindsay's classes are exactly what dancers need to be prepared. We practiced five days a week, morning and afternoon, except performance days when times vary. We danced six hours a day, including warm-ups, learning and rehearsing our choreography, and attending meetings. I'd usually go back to where I lived and practice in the evenings as well."

Several girls looked to each other and grimaced. Many moms shook their heads; a few frowned. Lindsay shrugged.

"Did they *make* you practice on your own in the evenings?"

Marta smiled. "No. I chose to practice on my own because I wanted to show them I could be as close to perfect as possible. And I needed the extra time to work on my turns and extensions."

"So, you were allowed to do things in the evening if you wanted like go to a movie or on a date?"

A titter of laughter followed. The girls glanced at their mothers. Their mothers glanced toward them with cautious stares.

"Remember, you're not stepping into a dance academy. You'll live on your own and make your own rules when you're away from the company. It's important to be rested for each day's rehearsals, to eat properly, and to make good decisions every day. I signed a contract that said I needed to act professionally at all times, attend all practices and performances, and to not take any risks that would jeopardize my dancing."

Head bobs and raised eyebrows greeted any girl looking toward her mother.

Lindsay stood and walked to the record player. "Let's stop for a minute. I want you ladies to share your choreography from Bizet's *Symphony in C*. I'm excited for your mothers and Marta to see your leaps and turns."

As the girls lined up and began their dance, Marta sat back, enjoying the chance to watch them dance. Most performed passable leaps, turns, and footwork but weren't ready for professional auditions. Their crossing patterns needed work, except for Rosalia. No wonder adults raved about her. She commanded everyone's attention without trying.

The adults applauded as the girls reassembled at the circle of chairs. Each dancer looked to Miss Holland for her comments. She shrugged and smiled. "Not bad. I see improvements since our class earlier today. This is a lively selection, so we'll keep working on the crossing patterns and your facial expressions in hopes of being ready to perform it during our winter programs." She turned her attention to Marta. "So, did anything ever go wrong when you were dancing?"

Marta laughed. "Oh yes. Most performances we had little mistakes with footwork as well as dancing in unison. When I was Mother Ginger I wore short stilts. One boy pinched my leg to see if it was real. I almost fell. Then, when I was Carabosse in *Sleeping Beauty*, I had a quick costume change. My dark make-up got smeared on the back of my neck. I think my wig covered it; I hope so anyway."

"When are you going back to Billings?" asked Rosalia.

"'I'm not sure." Marta hesitated, deciding how to encourage the girls despite her problems. "Dancing in a ballet company requires long hours of practicing and performing. Since I broke a small bone in my ankle, I haven't been able dance in *pointe* shoes. I'm hoping to be able to put my full body weight on that ankle so that one day I'll dance *en pointe* again."

One younger dancer asked, "What are you doing until you can dance again?"

Marta read sympathy on her former classmates' faces, the last thing she wanted to deal with. She put on a stage smile. "For now, I'm home. I just finished working on the community theatre teen play last week. I'm beginning women's exercise classes and kinder classes for Miss Holland very soon. Both will help me continue my healing."

"How did you get injured?" Rosalia's mother asked.

"I fell off an icy porch and landed on rocky ground."

"You're a professional dancer and you fell? Wasn't that careless of you?" said the same mother.

Lindsay stood again. "I think that's enough questions for today. You'll see Marta here over the next few months. She may even drop in on your classes. If you promise not to bug her to death, we'll meet again as fall session begins, okay? Now, for a surprise. Marta brought Intermountain Ballet programs. Follow her into the small practice room. The physical therapist is gone for the day so you can slip in there. Marta will answer a few more questions and autograph the programs she brought. While you girls do that, I'll speak with your mothers. See you all next class."

As Marta finished and gathered the extra programs, she thought all the girls and mothers had left. Hearing a strident voice as she approached the large practice room surprised her.

"True. But what does Marta know? She danced one season for that second rate ballet company. Billings? Really? I didn't put Rosalia in this ballet studio to receive guidance from a young, washed-up dancer. My daughter has real talent. She's on her way to becoming a star. She needs a real professional."

Marta scooted out of sight in the room and sat down on the stairs to the upper floor. Rosalia's mother sounded angry. Even so, why did she say such horrible things? Was she a washed up dancer, a has-been? Granted, Billings was not a premier ballet company like the New York City or the San Francisco Ballet, but they performed across a large region to packed theatres. She had lots to offer dancers starting their careers. But working with Rosalia might not be a great idea if her mom was so demanding. Marta sat in the darkened stairway until she heard her own mother and Lindsay talking in the studio office.

As Marta entered Lindsay smiled. "Thanks for coming down and for bringing the girls programs. I think it went well, except for Rosalia's mother just now. Did you hear any of the things she said?"

"I did. Sounds like she doesn't want me to work with her daughter."

Lindsay shrugged. "What can I say? She's a hard woman to under-stand. So, did you spot my most promising dancers?"

"Paige and Rosalia stand out," Marta said.

"Good eye, Marta. I'd like you to give them pointers and let them compete informally against each other to prepare for spring auditions."

Marta smiled. "I'd like that. I can start whenever you want. I'll need to work in ballet slippers if that's okay."

Lindsay laughed. "I guess you didn't notice. I always work in ballet slippers."

Marta puzzled over that for a long minute. "Hm-m. I never thought about that. So, any excuses for my not teaching aren't needed. I'll fit right in with my ballet slippers."

"You'll more than fit in!"

After overhearing the conversation, Marta asked the question burn-ing a hole in her confidence. "Will *both* families give you permission to teach their girls? I'm not really a teacher."

"You're better than a teacher, Marta. You've danced professionally, so you know what ballet companies are looking for in dancers."

Marta's insides twisted like a stomach cramp. She hesitated, then said, "But what about what Rosalia's mother said to you about me being washed up?"

"That woman," Marta's mom chimed in. "She's always stirring up things. I know a lot about her that she thinks is a secret. Cornish wanted Rosalia, but they didn't want Mrs. Marcus in their school. She's the first stage mom they've kicked out because she's so rude and inappropriate."

"Really?" Lindsay frowned. "She *is* difficult, but Rosalia's talented. I'm sorry you heard her latest rant. I'll work with her and try to explain how valuable you are to Rosalia's auditions. Again, I'm sorry. Mrs. Marcus was totally out of line. Do you want an apology?"

Marta shook her head. With any luck she'd avoid speaking with Mrs. Marcus all together.

A week later, Marta entered the dance studio and heard a familiar laugh. Lily Rose stood filling out paperwork.

"Marta! Are your ears burning? We're talking about you. I've signed up Olivia and just learned you're starting a women's exercise class."

"I am. It starts at nine next Wednesday. We'll meet every Monday, Wednesday, and Friday."

"Do you have room for four more women?"

"She does," said Marta's mom, tapping her desk calendar.

"Great. I'll have my friends call." Lily Rose passed her paperwork across the desk and picked up her purse. "Got to scoot to my haircut. See you next Wednesday."

Marta watched her breeze out the door.

"She's a bubbly person," her mom said. "I remember her now; she was a teen star. When she married her high school sweetheart, a lot of fans were disappointed. He's a baby doctor in town. Olivia is their only child."

"You learned all that from her paperwork?"

"No. She's chatty. You know that large home on north Lafayette, the one with the gray brick front and the huge sloping front yard? That's hers. Says she does all her own cleaning and cooking, but she lets her husband hire a lawn service."

Marta nodded and decided it must be nice to have your own home. Right now she could barely afford bus tokens. But after she took over dance classes, she'd have money and could start looking for a place to rent near her mom's so she could keep her ride to the dance studio. There was no way she could afford a car, even an old clunker.

August 19. The first day of kinder classes. Marta pulled her ponytail back and added a bright bow. She'd hung posters of baby animals as

inspiration for the young children and found kinder music in Lindsay's record collection. Now all she needed were the four little ones signed up for her class.

At 9:20 she stood in the entry, ready to greet her students. Today she'd allow the parents to participate. Once the kids became comfortable with her, the parents would have one day every month to watch class.

Three little girls and one boy arrived wearing shorts and T-shirts. Lily Rose smiled at Marta as she helped Olivia put on her ballet slippers. Marta smiled back, feeling comfortable about her first class. When all the adults finished assisting their kids with their shoes, Marta put on quiet music and sat on the floor

"Welcome everyone. My name is Marta. Today I'd like all students and parents to sit on the floor with me and listen to the music for a minute."

Three children sat tight against their parents; one sat pressed against her grandmother. Having their support was vital. Since she was unknown to the children, she'd start slowly. Soon enough they'd run in, put on their own slippers, and forget how shy they'd been early on.

"Today you and your grown-up partners will dance and play together. Let's start by sitting crisscross applesauce. Cross your ankles and pull your feet close to your body, then rock side to side so your froggy knees will stretch out."

Near the end of class, Marta brought out scarves as she and Lynne had done with their young dancers. "Now, when I start the music, I want you to move with the scarves. You need to stay inside this room, but you are free to hop and skip and jump as long as you don't run into anyone when you move. Stand up, and when I start the music, I'll say 'dance.' Then you may start moving around. When the music stops, you must stop as well."

After everyone stood, Marta started a recording of Tchaikovsky's *Waltz of the Flowers*. "Dance."

The room came alive as the children and the adults filled the room with waves of color as they danced, swaying, turning and waving the scarves. Lily Rose and her daughter danced and laughed as if they'd done this many times on their own. Even the grandmother joined in. Marta danced with them, watching for the perfect moment to stop them before things got silly.

Marta collected the scarves and said good bye to each red-faced child. "See you on Thursday. Your grown-up partners are invited to join us once again. Until then, keep dancing!"

Lily Rose and Olivia stayed after the others left. "That was so much fun, right Olivia?"

Olivia nodded. "Can we do scarves again when we come?"

"Of course," Marta said. "We'll do scarves many more times."

"You are a natural with young children," Lily Rose said as she helped Olivia pack her dance bag. "I'm so glad we found you." The pair waved as they left the room.

Marta heard them stop to talk with her mom as she put the records and scarves away. If she were to judge this first class, she'd give herself an A grade, something she seldom earned in high school.

Before she began her personal exercise session, she made a list of recordings she'd need to locate for the kinders. She wanted songs with simple movements: "Farmer in the Dell", "Muffin Man", "Old Mac-Donald", "You Are My Sunshine", and "Skip to My Lou". For the spring recital "The Bunny Hop", "Little Teapot", or "Twinkle, Twinkle" would make a cute dance. A wave of calmness spread inside her. She'd pass her childhood music onto these little ones. Hopefully planning for the exercise class would prove as easy.

After she completed her exercises, Marta turned her attention to the 90-minute adult exercise classes scheduled to begin tomorrow at 9:00 and continue every Monday, Wednesday, and Friday throughout the year. She'd use the class as part of her daily regimen, then follow it up with another hour of personal practice.

Marta planned to begin with her *barre* music, then follow that with current top hits like Sam Cooke's "You Send Me" for slow movements, Fats Domino's "I'm Walkin" for vigorous movements, and Elvis Presley's "All Shook Up" for crazy, fast movements. That should get every woman's heart racing, including hers.

She'd watched American Bandstand to observe the latest dance crazes: the Bop, the Chalypso, and the still-present Twist could be fun. Maybe she'd toss in ballroom dance steps as well. After she met the women she'd make that decision. She'd definitely make circle skirts or have them bring one from home for dancing to the modern tunes.

Wednesday, Marta and her mom arrived early and found the parking lot already half full. Eight women stood near the door as Marta unlocked it and turned on the lights.

"Morning, ladies," she said with a smile. "I'm Marta. Welcome to your exercise class. Follow me."

The entry fell quiet as the women stepped into the practice room and stepped out of their street clothes and stood waiting for direction. The original four women registered for the class wore shorts and t-shirts and ankle socks. Their orders for basic black leotards and ballet slippers were expected to arrive soon.

Lily Rose's friends, the Pill Hill ladies, folded their fancy sweat suits, stripping down to reveal stylish black leotards with spaghetti straps and black ballet wrap skirts, probably ordered from a specialty catalog, not the dance studio. Their ballet slippers had been dyed green, orange, blue, and hot pink.

Marta looked down at her basic black outfit feeling under dressed. She could only imagine what the ladies in shorts were thinking. But clothes didn't matter once they started class. Flexibility and rhythm didn't depend on their style of clothing.

From their information cards she knew her class consisted of the original four women, stay-at-home housewives, whose husbands worked in the shipyard, managed small shops, or worked in Callow-area businesses. Lily Rose's four from Pill Hill were the wives of a doctor, tax accountant, lawyer, and a dentist. If any of these rich women were expecting special treatment from Marta, they'd be disappointed. She inhaled and exhaled deeply and invited everyone to sit on the practice room floor.

"Welcome, ladies. This class will use basic *barre* warm-ups, plus we'll explore various dance forms to build up our heart rates and make us sweat."

The ladies chuckled and looked around, eyeing each other.

"We'll begin by standing about three feet apart at the *barres* with our left hands resting on the top metal bar." Marta waited as the women shuffled around to find a spot.

"Use the *barre* as support. Try to keep a light touch on it rather than a death grip. We'll do exercises working the right side of our bodies, then turn and do the same for the left. Your toes will always be pointing outward, and your heels will be touching or close together much of the time. "I'll demonstrate each movement, then lead you through them. Let's begin."

Marta started the warm-up music she used daily. She demonstrated each move in slow motion, then restarted the music and led the women through the basics: *plies,* a series of *battements, ronds de jambs, and developpés.* As they worked, she circled the group, adjusting sickled feet, poor posture, and static arms. Their quietness suggested they were deep in thought, much like she'd be learning new choreography.

"You are all doing very well. I want you to look in the mirrors and watch four parts of your body as I mention them. First, your spine. Keep your back straight. Pretend you have a marionette string stretching upward through your back and neck, pulling you as tall as possible."

"I think my string is broken," Trish said.

The women laughed, but Marta noticed immediate changes in their posture. "Don't worry, you'll get all of this figured out. Next, watch your arms. Keep them rounded like you're carrying a beach ball. We want our arms to look graceful, as if our elbows have disappeared." Marta walked around and adjusted their arms.

"This is harder than it looks," Frann said. "There's so much to think about."

Chuckles circled the room, but the ladies held their concentration on their arms.

"Now, third, keep your feet in line with your legs. Otherwise you'll have sickled, or curved, feet. Your hip to your toes should create a straight line. If you start to feel a cramp, relax your foot. When you're ready, check your face and head. Try to relax and not make faces as you move. Remember, you want to make everything look effortless."

"No wonder little kids dance with their tongues out!" Trixie said.

Marta laughed out loud, enjoying the fact that the ladies maintained their playfulness.

After twenty minutes Marta stopped the record. "Nice work, ladies. Now shake out your arms and legs and we'll move away from the *barres* and work in the center of the room. We'll repeat the same movements, this time using only our arms and feet for balancing."

The women wobbled and tipped as they worked to find their comfort and balance stances. All thought of conversation dropped away during this part of the class. Marta had forgotten how different center work is for people who have no dance training; she'd rethink this idea before they met again.

Next, she picked up the pace. "Let's work on dances you can use at your clubs or parties. We'll start with the fox trot." She walked them through the box step, then put on Sinatra's *Come Fly With Me*, letting them dance with broom handles.

"My partner is not usually this smooth," one woman said. "Maybe I married the wrong guy."

"Yeah," another woman said. "Plus, these broom sticks have great personalities!"

After a few minutes the women were red-faced and sweat covered their necks and shoulders, but they all kept dancing and chatting about their unusual dance partners. Marta loved their humor and willingness to be playful. She felt her body soften, allowing her to relax and enjoy the women and laugh at their comments.

"How's this working out for you?" Marta said. "Anyone need a break?"

They all shook their heads and kept moving. Their heavy breathing and the sweat running down their faces had ended their conversations. With ten minutes left in class, Marta stopped the music and announced, "Time for a cool down." She sent them back to the *barres* to repeat *plies,* then added stretching movements.

At precisely 10:30, she stopped the music. "That's it for today. Over the next few weeks we'll add other dance moves. Let me know when I push you too much. See you back here on Friday."

As she turned to put the records away, she stopped. "Oh, by the way, your clothing orders should arrive by Monday at the latest. Remember to bring a thermos of water for class and to drink lots of water after class as well. And if you have a circle skirt, bring it along."

"What are you planning, Marta?" Lily Rose said. "Are we going back to the high school sock hop?"

"I plan to take you ladies lots of places," Marta said.

The women filed out, wiping their faces and necks with the towels they'd brought. They'd kept to Marta's pace, and if they all returned on Friday, she'd know her planning worked. She'd need to stay one or two steps ahead of these active women to hold their interest.

Marta's Monday morning exercise classes warmed her up for her next challenge, her late afternoon time to work with Paige and Rosalia, if Mrs. Marcus allowed her to train with the "washed up dancer." Somehow Rosalia's mother had broken into Marta's confidence. Had she gotten thin-skinned? In the ballet company all dancers faced put-downs daily. Add to that Marta's problem with Madame Cosper. This should not have rattled her, but it did, almost as much as having the responsibility to prepare the girls for auditions.

Lindsay spoke with Mrs. Marcus before their first session and laid out the plan for Marta's coaching the girls before their spring auditions. "I told her you were the best possible person to help Rosalia prepare for auditions since you'd experienced several within the past year. She finally conceded that she'd allow you to work with Rosie. I told her this was her only option if she stayed with our studio."

"I'll do what I can to satisfy her," Marta said.

Lindsay shook her head. "Don't you dare bend to her wishes. You know what needs to be done. Do what's best for the girls. Leave Zandora Marcus to me."

Marta stood at the *barre* waiting for the girls to arrive. She'd discussed her plan with Lindsay, and after a few tweaks, the course of action was set. She'd adjust parts of their dance warm-ups and center work, plus teach them a short selection following the procedure she'd experienced during her auditions. She didn't plan to replicate the stony faces many directors presented, but she'd eventually tell the girls about the negative comments they might encounter. But that came much later.

When Paige and Rosalia arrived, Marta welcomed them into the practice room. She moved to sit on the floor and motioned for them to join her. "Let's talk before we begin."

Just then Mrs. Marcus stepped into the room and took a seat along the back wall. Marta watched as she smoothed back her black hair, propped her arms on her bowling ball bag of a purse, and leaned forward to listen to the conversation.

Nuts. Marta felt a sinking feeling in her stomach. Mrs. Marcus wasn't wasting any time being involved.

Marta stood and approached Mrs. Marcus, who straightened and squinted as Marta sat down beside her. "I'm glad you're allowing Rosalia to work with me. I want to remind you that our practice sessions are closed; the girls and I will work alone in the room."

"I wasn't informed of this situation," Mrs. Marcus said. "I'll speak with Miss Holland about it."

"Miss Holland requested it. I'm sure Rosalia will share what we do with you."

Mrs. Marcus stood abruptly and glared at Marta. "Rosalia, I'll be back in one hour. Be ready to leave when I return." She hurrumped, adjusted her shoulders, picked up her purse, and sauntered out.

"Mrs. Marcus? Excuse me?"

Rosalia's mother turned and looked at Marta. "What?"

"The session lasts two hours. Will that be a problem?"

"Two hours? You expect me to pay you for two hours twice a week?"

Marta paused and smiled. "No, ma'am. I'm certain Miss Holland told you the second hour is free. Do you want Rosalia to meet you after the first hour?"

"Rosalia, I'll be back in *two* hours and waiting outside. Don't dawdle." Her high heels clicked across the entry hall, followed by the door to the parking lot slamming closed.

Marta returned to sit by the girls, noticing Rosalia kept her head down and picked at unseen lint on her leotard. "All right, ladies. Let's get started. There are at least seven elements you'll be assessed on during an audition. Each audition may ask for different skills, but these seven will prepare you for most anything they ask. We'll take them one by one, adding each new part as you feel ready. Let's begin by standing in front of the mirrors.

"Auditions are about how you present yourself. Your hair, the tidiness of your costume, the way you enter the room, and so on. So look yourself over, make adjustments, then walk back to the door. When you enter, I want you to pretend you are entering an audition. Form a line standing in fifth position and wait for further directions."

Both girls giggled and did as they were asked. Before they'd moved more than a few steps back into the room, Marta stopped them.

"Watch me enter. This is what I saw." Marta walked into the room looking around and standing slightly slumped forward. "You've got to think about this as if it were a performance. It is. Your performance begins at the door. Go back and enter as a serious dancer."

Both girls retraced their steps and entered standing tall and looking straight ahead. They stood in fifth position and waited for Marta to speak.

"Perfect! Enter every practice this same way. In time it will become as natural as breathing. Let's move on to warm-ups. Now, I'm looking for elongated bodies, tucked *derrieres*, elegant arms, and precise footwork."

By the conclusion of the warm-ups, their practice hour ended. The quiet of the two girls surprised Marta. They looked tired and unhappy.

Paige let out a long slow breath. "That was hard. I'm exhausted. Are dance company practices this hard?"

"No, but close. Auditions are what we're focused on. I want you to make a strong impression so the judges will watch you throughout the entire audition. You want them to see you at your absolute best."

"Was your audition difficult?" Rosalia said.

"Absolutely. But don't worry. We have six months. You'll be ready by the end of March. Now, let's move on to your solos. Show me what you're planning to dance."

Minute by minute the girls looked more and more stressed. After the next half hour, Marta stopped them. "Let's slow things down. Two hours is a long time. You'll need to build up your stamina, so today we'll use our remaining time to answer your burning questions about auditions and whatever else is on your mind."

The girls peppered her with questions about weigh-ins, wages, solos, dance costumes, their hair, living alone, stage makeup, costumes, and dating. Marta answered each question as truthfully as possible, trying to allay their concerns but not color their future experiences based on her point of view. When they left, they appeared to be satisfied with what she had told them. Hopefully she'd not receive a call from Mrs. Marcus over some tiny detail that Rosalia shared.

As she straightened the room, Marta thought back to her various auditions. Lindsay had done her best, but knowing more about their expectations would have helped her prepare. The fourteen intervening months since her early auditions allowed Marta to share experiences she hoped would propel Paige and Rosalia to gain positions as professional ballet dancers. They'd need to understand how difficult practices could be and how lonely they could feel as dancers.

Stardom didn't occur magically, plucking dancers from the *corps*. If it arrived at all, it came after years and years of hard work and sacrifice, but she didn't want to discourage them before they had the chance to experience dancing as professionals if dancing was truly their dream.

*C*lasses rolled by smoothly. Lindsay suggested Marta add additional fall classes: two international character dances and drop-in evening exercise classes. The week after Labor Day, when schools resumed, she'd be juggling close to a full schedule if she counted the community theatre jobs she intended to continue.

Marta reached for the calendar, about to tear off August, when the phone rang. When she heard Steve's voice, a warm, buttery feeling spread through her. Marta curled the phone cord around her finger. "It's good to hear your voice again. I've missed you."

"It hasn't been that long, has it? I talked with you last week, Marta."

She laughed. "Actually, it's been two weeks. You must have been busy with school."

They talked about his busy schedule at the paper, his projects, and his December graduation from Rocky Mountain College. "I need ten hours fall term, a handful of small projects, and then it's the big wide world."

"Are you looking for jobs yet? Do you know where you'd like to work?"

"Honestly, I'll take what I can get," Steve said. "I'd like to go back to San Francisco. Would you consider moving there and getting a job dancing to be close to me? I miss you more than you'll ever know, Marta."

Would she? Marta stared out the window, seeing nothing. She'd yet to feel settled at home and discover if she was capable of dancing again. Could she uproot herself and move so soon?

"Marta? Would you consider moving?"

"What about Seattle? Are you interviewing here?"

Steve laughed. "They're on my list. I sent requests for interviews, but neither have replied yet. Would it be okay with you if I moved to Seattle?"

Marta smiled into the phone. "Are you kidding? It would be perfect."

The phone line hummed with their silence. "Marta? You feel like you're drifting away. Are we still okay? Are you wearing the necklace I gave you last Christmas?"

"Yes, when I'm not dancing." She adjusted the necklace, then slid the pendent back and forth, feeling the chain vibrate against her skin.

"How about the bracelet?"

"Yes, that too." The bracelet demonstrated her promise to not date other guys. "Maybe I should have given you something so you'd have a reminder of me."

Steve laughed. "I don't need a reminder. I think of you every day and wish you had stayed here for your recovery. How's the ankle lately?"

"It's fine."

"How is it being home again?"

Marta hesitated. How did she feel about being home. Did it matter? "Home's okay; I'm fine."

"It doesn't sound like you're fine. Is something bothering you? You know I want to be with you when things settle down, if you still care about me." He paused. "Do you, Marta?"

She hesitated again, thinking about her conversation with Dennis after the teen play. "I'll always care about you, Steve. I dream about you and I wonder what you're doing. It makes me feel content."

He laughed. "Good. I tell you what I'm thinking, but I'm never sure about what's going on in that head of yours. I hate having these miles between us. Right now I need to get back to work. I wish the textbooks provided as much enjoyment as shadowing reporters did last spring. I miss you, Miss Fluff."

"Miss you too." The words caught in her throat. She did miss him and the way he brought happiness into her days. "Who could I tease about ballet being fluff news if I didn't have you?"

He laughed. "I know. I've apologized so many times, and I'll probably need to apologize for years to come. Love you. I'll call again soon."

Marta pictured his face watching hers, looking for clues into her thinking, smiling as he did whenever they reminisced about meeting. She'd always treasure that moment, the stunned expression on his face when she confronted him about calling ballet fluff. "I'll expect you to remember that day, but maybe I can find a new way to torment you. I'll work on that. Guess I'd better go. I miss you."

When Steve hung up, Marta stood listening to the dial tone. What *was* going on in her head? She loved talking and joking with Steve, but what did it mean when visions of Dennis kept popping up?

As the afternoon light polarized, turning the grape leaves a brilliant green, Marta stepped into the backyard to sit and think. She plopped into one of the Adirondack chairs her dad made. She slid her hands along the smooth arms remembering the year she'd helped him sand and paint them. "These are my gifts to the yard," he'd said. "They'll probably out-last me." He didn't realize the truth in those words; he died six months after he finished them.

How did her mom know when she fell in love with her dad? Did she ever doubt that he was "the one," the person she'd spend her life with? And if she felt that way, how could she now consider loving Robert?

Just then Marta's mom drove into the garage, closed the large door, and joined her in the backyard. She collapsed in the chair next to Marta. "What a day! I should know better than to let Robert volunteer me for the shipyard's back-to-school party. Lots of fun, but I'm so tired I could stay right here all night."

Marta pushed herself out of her lawn chair. "Stay and relax. It's nice tonight. I'll bring out dinner." As she assembled dinner she continued to wonder about Robert. Her mom obviously enjoyed his company. Did her heart race when she held his hand? Did she have a sinking feeling when they kissed? Were her feelings the same as they'd been with her dad?

After they ate their chef's salads and discussed the dance studio and the vegetable garden, Marta took the opportunity to shift their conversation. "You really like Robert, don't you, Mom?"

"I do. He's a good man; he makes me laugh. We're planning a short getaway to Kalaloch Lodge next weekend. I want to drive to the ocean before autumn sets in."

"Good. You need a getaway. Kalaloch would be my choice too. Wish Lynne had come out. I wanted to share the beach with her, but I think she's finally found a special guy."

"Really? Lynne? Hm-m. Speaking of someone special, have you heard from Steve lately?"

Marta shrugged. "He called today. He's swamped with class work and looking for a job."

Her mom's face registered a question before she spoke. "You don't act excited like you use to when you talk about him."

"It's been so long since I've seen him."

"Distance makes a relationship harder, honey. Your dad and I never had to worry about that."

"So you always knew he was the one you wanted to marry?"

"I did. For us it was love at first sight. He was kind, thoughtful, funny, and romantic."

Marta saw her mother's face soften as she spoke. "So, did that happen with Robert too?"

"Our relationship started as friends; our love grew over time. True, it's a different kind of love than I had with your father, but it's still love."

Marta nodded as she collected their dinner dishes.

"Give yourself time, honey. You'll figure out how you feel. Right now I have news that I hope will excite you. Lindsay just learned that the moving company is leaving from the upstairs space. She plans to rent the rest of the building. When she adds more classes, you *could* become a full time instructor, if you're interested."

"Did you tell her I'd be interested?"

"No, honey. That's up to you. I think it would be wonderful, but that's me being selfish. I enjoy having you here and seeing you at the studio."

"I enjoy both places. Dancing at Miss Holland's, I mean Lindsay's, studio speeds up my recovery. Maybe I'll talk with her about adding more classes."

"Great! Lindsay will be thrilled." Her mom stood and stretched. "Thanks for dinner. Think I'll water the front yard before I head in."

Marta washed their dinner dishes and set the nook for breakfast. When her mom came in, she carried a flat package that she handed to Marta. "I found this by the front door. Hope it's fun mail."

The package's return address confirmed it was from Lynne. She'd sent a dozen notes and pictures from the four little girls they'd taught in the spring. Each brought an ache of sadness and a smile to Marta. She missed seeing Tracy, Brenda, Carmen, and Lucy. They started third grade this fall. She wondered how much longer they'd remember her.

Lynne's attached note promised to keep Marta's lightened mood intact.

Dear Marta,

The girls and I began lessons last week in your old basement space, much to Carol's dismay. When she started complaining about how noisy we were, I told her to get a life. She huffed away just like she did when you used the space.

Turns out Mr. Right was Mr. Oh-So-Wrong. The handsome liar's a married man with two kids. Oh well. I'm too busy working on becoming a soloist.

Mrs. B. sends you her best. As do I.

Lynne

Marta pressed the letter to her chest. She needed to surprise Lynne and write back to her before Lynne had time to call.

That next Monday she found a postcard with a talking fish on the front. The bubbles around the fish read, "Cut out fishing around for a compliment. I think you're special just the way you are."

On the back she wrote in tiny script:

Tell those sweet girls thank you. I love each drawing they made. I want them to give you huge hugs from me to replace Mr. Wrong's. (Sorry he was a jerk.) I'd hoped to see you before fall training, but now it looks like Christmas before we'll get face to face.

Marta

Marta's life settled into a repeating pattern similar to her recovery time in Billings: exercise, work, bake, sleep, and begin again. It made it easy to move along without thinking too much about Steve or Dennis.

But soon she'd be back helping Dennis with sets for the next play. The thought of seeing him excited and frightened her, leaving their relationship in an awkward place.

In mid-September the phone rang, startling her as she played another game of solitaire.

"Marta? This is Dennis. How are you?"

A flush hurried through her. "I'm okay." She brushed back her hair and felt her lips curve into a smile.

"I have good news and bad. The next play is *Our Town*. It has no sets, but Hal has given us the chore of rounding up furniture for the stage. Are you interested in helping me find what we need?"

"Sure." She paced to the window and back, pulling the phone cord taut. "When do we need to get started?"

"I thought we could do it Saturday. I have one source of '30s furniture, but if you have ideas, bring them along. I'll pick you up at ten."

Saturday morning Marta put on her best capris and a summer top. She brushed her hair, put on makeup, and stood watching out the kitchen window for Dennis to drive up. Her thoughts jumped from Dennis to Steve and back to Dennis. Was this a good idea? She paced the living room, then stopped in front of the mirror. She surveyed her outfit, raced to her bedroom, and changed clothes. Back in front of the mirror, she turned her head side to side; a skirt looked best. She removed the necklace and bracelet from Steve and put them in her pocket.

Dennis arrived in an old open-backed truck. The sunshine and the warm day lent itself to wandering on their way to Brownsville to meet his contact. They stopped to explore Illahee State Park's forest trails, then descended to walk along its beach. The sun glistened on Agate Pass.

Marta pointed across the waterway. "My family used to take the little ferry from Bremerton to that dock on Bainbridge to visit my aunt and uncle's home. I always remember the day after my birthday when I wore my new Mickey Mouse watch. I let my cousin wear it and between the two of us we over wound it and the stem fell out in the tall grass. That ended my watch."

Dennis chuckled. "Bet your parents were upset with you. Mine would have tanned my backside."

"Actually, they didn't say a word. That was worse than having them get mad. I can still see them shaking their heads."

They walked in silence until they'd reached the end of the fishing pier. As they turned back, Dennis spoke. "I'm glad you decided to come with me. This is my first break since the teen play. With so much carpentry work lately, I'll be able to afford a new truck before too long." He reached for Marta's hand and held it firmly as they walked backup the trail. "So, how's Mr. Sorta?"

"He's fine."

"Too bad." He grinned and slid his calloused thumb slowly across her fingers.

Marta felt heat travel up her arm. He didn't release her hand until they returned to his truck and he opened the door for her to climb inside. She looked away from him, hiding her reaction to his touch until they'd driven out of the park.

At Brownsville the owner of the small furniture shop loaded up two dressers, a floor lamp in need of rewiring, and several framed paintings perfect for *Our Town*'s sparse set. As they pulled back onto Wheaton Way, Dennis turned to Marta. "Are you hungry? Want to grab a burger at the Bay Bowl? We could stay and bowl a few lines if you have the time?"

"A bowing alley with burgers? Sounds good."

With the burgers finished off, they sat side by side and talked instead of bowling. Dennis asked about her dance career and how her recovery progressed.

"I feel like I'm making headway. Working on the plays takes my mind off myself. I've enjoyed learning about making sets."

Dennis studied her face and twisted his mouth to one side. "When you got all bothered that first time about the kind of nails I wanted, I almost laughed. You looked cute and so irritated with me." He paused and smiled. "I wanted to kiss you and see how you'd react."

Marta shook her head. "I'd have probably slapped you and left."

"And now?" He stared at her with one raised eyebrow.

Marta turned away. "We'd better get going."

All the way home, she said nothing. She felt Dennis watching her, but she remained silent, focusing on her hands, then the scenery, then her hands again to avoid his gaze.

As they stopped at her mom's, he turned off the engine and shifted to face her. "You're certainly quiet. Have I upset you?"

"No," she said. "You surprised me that's all. I don't know what to say."

"Say you'll let me take you out on a date." Dennis circled the truck to open the passenger door for her. He held her hand as he walked her through the back gate and to the base of the kitchen steps. "I'll call you later in the week. Right now I'm going to kiss you." He planted a lingering kiss on her cheek.

Marta felt his breath as he pulled back and smiled. She stared up at him, feeling her body react to his closeness and the touch of his lips on her skin. "Um...Thanks for the nice day."

Dennis ran his hand down her cheek. "Totally my pleasure."

She waved and watched him get back into his truck. As she turned toward the back steps, she noticed someone walking toward her from the front yard.

She reached for the back step railing as her knees weakened. Steve stood a few short steps away.

*S*teve watched the truck as it drove away. When he turned back to face her, his eyebrows were furrowed and he'd crossed his arms.

Marta froze in place, waiting for him to step closer or speak. He did neither. She swallowed hard. "I wasn't expecting to see you."

"Obviously." He walked to within reach, close enough for her to see the sadness in his blue eyes.

"I can explain, Steve. It's not what it looked like."

"Okay," he said. "Explain away."

Marta told him about the play and the furnishings they needed and about stopping for burgers.

"Plausible so far. What about the kissing?"

Marta gulped down her nervousness and reached for her necklace, the one he'd given her as a sign of their commitment. She wasn't wearing it. Steve's eyes followed her hand and she quickly lowered it. "That was my fault, Steve. He's a nice guy. He reminds me of you. I've worked with him for several months. We tease each other and he kissed me. It just happened." Marta looked away. "I know I shouldn't have let him, but I was flattered that he wanted to. It didn't mean anything."

"Really? That's hard to believe, Marta. If it meant nothing, why were you holding hands as you came in the back gate? I love you, Marta. I thought you loved me."

"I do, Steve, and I've missed you. I…I'm sorry." She watched his face through her blur of tears. Each second moved as slow as an hour. She pulled in her lips, pressing them together to keep from blurting out something, anything, to fill the continuing silence. She longed to hear him say he'd forgiven her, that everything was going to be all right.

But Steve didn't invite her to step into his arms as he'd done back in Billings when they had disagreements. He stood motionless, looking across the yard, breathing slowly, not speaking. Finally, when he looked toward her, she saw the damage she'd created.

"I think I should leave," he said, "before either of us says something we might regret." He studied her face as he backed away from her.

Marta followed him, reaching for his hand, but he moved away from her grasp. "Not now, Marta. We both need time to figure things out."

She nodded and stepped back as he opened the gate.

Marta watched him walk toward downtown without a single glance in her direction. When he'd disappeared from view, she closed the gate and sat on the kitchen steps. She stared at the space around her, hoping to feel his presence. A tightness lingered in her chest as she replayed the last moments over and over, wishing it had been a bad dream. It hadn't been.

Rocking and pacing through the remainder of the evening didn't release her or stop her from reliving the disappointment on Steve's face. All night when she tried to sleep, images of Steve hovered over her. Much as she tried to picture the way his hair flopped over one eye and the happiness that had always flowed around and through him, the images dissolved, causing her to relive seeing his sad face and the hurt gathered behind his usually bright blue eyes. How could she have forgotten the intensity of his touch? The comfort of his arms wrapped around her? The steady beat of his heart when he held her close?

She pictured his arms open wide, inviting her to step closer, but as she moved forward, his presence turned to fog and disappeared. She startled herself awake and lay in bed crying in the darkness.

As dawn arrived, she realized she had no idea why Steve had shown up at her doorstep. Did he have an interview, get a job, come on a whim? Yesterday's drive with Dennis got out of hand. She should have avoided him like her instinct suggested. Did she want his attention and his kisses more than she wanted Steve's? What would have happened if she hadn't come back in time to see Steve? Would she feel the same ache of emptiness she felt now, or would missing his visit have been easier? Her tears and confusion returned and replayed over and over and over, becoming as entangled as her bed covers.

All morning Marta paced, rocked and watched the clock, imagining what Steve might be doing. Surely his coming all this way for whatever reason proved he loved her, didn't it? His visit sent her onto a roller coaster of confusion. She owed it to him to figure out what she wanted from their relationship and to tell him how she felt. If he was "the one," she needed to stop spending time with Dennis and extinguish the embers of interest she experienced in his company.

After her restless night, Marta felt exhausted as she entered the studio to help paint the upstairs rooms. The previous tenant had left behind scarred walls and scuffed stairs along with her rental cleaning deposit. Lindsay's coaxing resulted in the owner agreeing to allow them to paint and install wall-sized mirrors and barres for warm-ups.

Lindsay stood in the entry beside gallon cans of paint, paint rollers, and brushes. "Thanks for giving up your Sunday afternoon, Marta. Not the best way to spend this lovely day, but I'm so glad to get this space painted. The owner's allowing my plumber to finish the roughed-in bathroom, and I'm asking to add a storage room and a small office space next."

Marta plastered a stage smile on her face as she opened a can of light green paint. "The owner is getting a great deal by us fixing up his building. It's not costing him a penny. If he's smart, he'll let you make lots of improvements."

"He did make me promise to not build any permanent walls, but you're right. He's getting a lot of benefits, but so are we." Lindsay smiled as she handed a paint brush to Marta. "I'm thinking the upstairs should be your space. How does that sound?"

"Wonderful. Thank you." Marta smiled and forced energy into her voice. She made a quick ballet turn and curtsied, covering her emptiness with silliness. "In that case, let's get busy!"

By eight that evening the entire upstairs smelled and looked refreshed, but Marta scrambled to find any energy she could to finish the task. The pale cedar green walls created a calm space. With the mirrors and *barres* awaiting installation the first of the week, Marta hoped to satisfy Lindsay's belief in her within hours of destroying Steve's. Not even close to an even trade-off, but it was all she could look forward to until she found a way to reconnect with Steve.

With Monday morning studio classes and household tasks complete, Marta spruced up her mom's house as a welcome back surprise for when she returned from Kalaloch and to keep herself busy. Had it only been a day and a half since she'd seen Steve? Why did it feel like ten? Maybe she'd start adapting clothes for the *Our Town* play, turning current day street wear into 1930s costumes. The black curtain backdrop meant no painting jobs and helped her break her connection with Dennis. Ah,

Dennis. She needed to talk with him.

For the rest of the week, her daytime overflowed with dance classes, not allowing her time to think about anything, including Steve. It was her evening hours that hung limp and suspended like the play's black backdrop.

Sometimes her loneliness clawed like angry hands squeezing the life out of her. Did Steve feel the same way? From his reaction to Dennis, she assumed he'd not dated anyone since she'd left. That meant she'd been the one who'd broken the promise. No more. She'd find a way to explain to Steve that she wanted to wait for him and to be with him. That's what she wanted, wasn't it? Why was life so complicated?

Maybe she'd invite Dennis over for dinner to talk with him. No. Bad idea. But she did need to talk with him about her commitment to Steve. She was committed to Steve, wasn't she? She needed to decide and call him. No, she needed to start by calling Dennis and clear up things so they'd stay on good enough terms that she could work with him on future plays. Or should she start by calling Steve? Neither conversation would be easy.

On Thursday as Marta sat down at home to sew, Lindsay phoned. "Rosalia must leave high school early on several days when she performs for events her mother's set up. The school wants a note from us before they'll allow her to miss P.E. Could you go to the high school and speak with the counselor to find out what's needed?"

"Of course," Marta said. "I'd like to see Miss Abbot again. She was supportive last year when I needed early releases for auditions. I'm certain she'll support Rosalia as well."

Walking the steep hill beside the cemetery reminded her of Steve's hasty departure. The ache of his walking away saddened her. The challenge of walking on her weakened ankle faded in comparison. Maybe she needed to walk more often to exhaust herself and chase away thoughts of

Steve. If nothing else, walking would build up her physical strength and maybe she'd not need to resort to icing her ankle on every return home.

Marta felt a warmth inside herself as she entered the high school office and saw the familiar face of Mrs. Blair, the secretary.

"Marta! What a nice surprise! How's the first year of your dance career going?"

"It's been a challenge, Mrs. Blair. I broke my ankle, and I'm home recovering."

"Oh, I'm so sorry. That must be difficult. I so enjoyed watching you dance at assemblies last year. Best of luck, my dear. Now, what can I do for you?"

"I made an appointment with the counseling office. I'm hoping to talk with Miss Abbot."

"Oh. She's been called away to a meeting. Let me check who's taking her appointments. One minute."

A tall young man entered the office. "Miss Selbryth?" He extended his hand when she stood. "I'm Sam Faris. Follow me." They shook hands then walked together down the office hallway. "So, do you have graduation questions or a problem in a class?"

Marta smiled at his query. "Neither. I graduated last year. I'm here about Rosalia Marcus. I'm one of her dance teachers."

Mr. Faris held the door for Marta and invited her to sit down. He rounded his desk and nodded as he sat. "Rosalia. Yes. I've spoken with her mother several times. The latest is that she wants Rosalia allowed early dismissals for a series of performances. As a recent graduate from this school, I'm surprised you don't know our policies."

"I do, Mr. Faris. The dismissals are for performances her mother's arranged. She'd miss P.E. class with Mrs. Taylor, who allowed my early dismissals last year. Dancing is definitely exercise. I'll gladly sign the forms you require."

Mr. Faris made a tent with his fingers. "I'm new this year, so let me check with Mrs. Taylor and Miss Abbott. I'll get back to you. The Holland Dance Studio, right?"

"Yes. I'll write our contact information for you."

"No need. My daughter takes classes there."

"You're Betty's father!"

"And you're the famous Marta. Betty loves to dance and wants to be a ballerina just like you. She keeps us hopping. Now she wants me to buy her scarves for entertaining us at home."

Marta smiled. "Have her ask me about scarves after her next class. I'll send one home with her."

"Thanks. She's excited to show us whatever you teach her." Mr. Faris stood and opened his office door. "As far as Rosalia goes, I'll talk with staff and call Mrs. Marcus with our decision, then let you know the outcome. If you have questions, please do not hesitate to contact me. We'll need a week's notice for any approved early dismissals."

When they reached the front entrance to the school, they shook hands again. Mr. Faris held the door open for her. "Thank you, Mr. Faris. I appreciate your help."

"No problem. Thanks for working with Betty."

On the walk home, Marta wondered about the Faris family. So this was shy little Betty's father. His work day partially explained why the grandmother brought Betty to class. His wife must work or else she's one of those women so absorbed in her own needs that Betty gets shoved to one side like Bartley did. Marta stopped herself. She sounded like Carol, the grumpy, judgmental boarder at Mrs. B.'s in Billings. At least Betty had a grandmother who helped out.

September's cooler weather reminded Marta she'd been home more than four months. In that time she had started her recovery, found the community theatre, begun teaching at the studio, and ruined her relationship with Steve. It had been over a week since she'd watched Steve walk away. He'd not called, so she'd need to call him in the next few days, while he'd still be thinking about her.

Lately Marta took solitary, hour-long walks to provide space and alone time for her mom and Robert and to work through how she felt about issues in her daily life. So far, she'd covered all the streets and roads around Rhododendron Drive and Callow. During this evening's walk she found herself strolling along Corbett Drive. She stopped at an open stretch of beach and sat on a log to watch the wind ruffle the waves as they splashed against the shoreline. She enjoyed the cool edge of autumn creeping into the air as summer faded.

As she turned toward home, she noticed a House for Rent sign attached to the front porch railing of a small house: She walked around the exterior of the wood-frame house, looking in the windows, gauging the space in the living room and kitchen, and wishing the bedroom curtains were open. The sign said $85 a month plus utilities. She could manage that if she budgeted her money. Wouldn't take much furniture to make it comfortable, and she'd sew any curtains she needed. Her day-to-day life was settling down. Now if only her dating life would stop being a moving target.

Marta smiled that evening when she sat down to figure her finances. If she saved all her wages, she'd be able to rent the little house on Corbett Drive by Thanksgiving. Hopefully it would stay available that long. She suspected Robert would declare his intentions to her mom during Christmas so her timing to move out might be perfect.

Before she went to bed, she needed to deal with the gnawing feeling that circled through her body. Contacting Steve. A phone call? Too soon. A postcard? Too impersonal. It needed to be a letter. She took out her mom's best stationary and sat at the kitchen table. Now the hard part.

Tap, tap, tap. She flipped the pen against the table, waiting for ideas to blossom.

Dear Steve,

I'm glad you took the time to come to Bremerton to see me. I'm sorry I wasn't here to meet you when you arrived. Seeing you at the door would have made my day perfect. As it turned out, I ruined your surprise in so many ways. I can never say I'm sorry enough but I am truly sorry.

I know you're upset with me and I don't blame you. I'm upset with me as well. In my defense I didn't realize how the day would end. I guess I was lonely and felt flattered Dennis noticed me. I'll give up my job at the theatre if you want me to. That way I'll have no contact with him. I certainly don't intend to date him if that is your concern.

After you left, I realized that I didn't know why you were here. I'm hoping it was because you had an interview. I know you're looking for a job at lots of different newspapers. Seattle or nearby would be wonderful. I hope you will still want me to be part of your life after you graduate. And I hope I'm still invited to your graduation in December. I want to share that special day with you.

Please write and tell me how you're feeling after you think about everything for a few days. I love you and hope I have not destroyed our love by my stupidity.

Marta

Before she lost her nerve, she slipped on her shoes, walked to Callow and dropped the letter into the mailbox outside the A&P grocery store.

The cool evening air soothed her face as she walked home by way of the far end of Rhododendron Drive. She sat on a driftwood log listening to the waves splash against the beach. The constellation of Orion hovered over the bay, tipping ever so slightly as it moved across the sky. Please, please, Orion, she thought. Help Steve understand how sorry I am over what happened. Help him forgive me.

*M*arta slept in spurts over the next few nights, hoping to hear from Steve, knowing she needed to allow more time before he'd consider answering her letter. Much as she thought she'd handled her personal conversations with her mom, she knew her mom noticed changes in her behavior. As she sat rocking, the phone rang. Maybe....

When she picked up the receiver and heard Dennis's voice, her heart sank.

"Hey, ready for that follow-up on the date you promised me? I thought we could take in a movie or drive out to see the fall colors along Hood Canal."

"I can't, Dennis." Marta paused and plunged into her dreaded conversation. "I've decided to try to rebuild my connection to Steve."

"Huh," Dennis said. "So Mr. Sorta won after all. I thought we had a good time."

"We did, Dennis, but Steve and I have shared several life-changing events."

"But, hey, I'm right here, only minutes away. He's in Montana."

Marta closed her eyes and drew in a deep breath, "It's complicated. I'm hoping we can continue to work together and—"

"Look, Marta, I need to go. See you around." *Click.*

Marta frowned as she stared at the phone in her hand. That was abrupt and interesting. It appeared she'd made one good decision. Even if Steve refused to listen to her and forgive her, not dating anyone would be better than getting entangled with an impolite Dennis.

The telephone party line remained open, so she dialed Steve's family home and held her breath. He answered after the third ring.

"Hi, Steve. Do you have time to talk with me?"

"I've got a couple of minutes."

Marta felt the sting of his abruptness and heard the somber edge in his voice. She swallowed and dove into her apology. "Did my letter arrive?"

"Yes. Is that why you called?"

"Partly." She paused. "Also, I miss you and I think about you every moment since you left. I know you're hurt and angry."

"No, Marta. I'm not angry. I'm disappointed."

"I'm disappointed in myself as well, but I can't go back and undo what happened. I was lonely and flattered by Dennis's attention. You know how I feel about you."

"I thought I did, but now I'm not sure."

Marta's tears gathered in her eyes. "You *do* know how I feel. You're my first love, my only love. You're smart, funny, and kind. Being with you and thinking about you…You stuck by me when I was grumpy and sad about my injury. You even flew home last Valentine's Day and took me to the mountains to cheer me up. I'm hoping you care enough about me to give me another chance. I love you."

The phone line remained a quiet hum. She heard Steve's breathing. He cleared his throat. "I've spent a lot of time thinking about you and about us. I want us to work, Marta. I do love you, but seeing that guy kiss you twisted something in my gut."

Marta stretched the phone cord as she stared absentmindedly out the window. "I'm sorry about Dennis. It was a huge mistake. How can I get you to believe me?"

Steve exhaled loudly. "Maybe if you'd continue to write to me instead of me always writing to you and never hearing back. Maybe if I felt your support and encouragement. You didn't even ask me why I'd come to see you."

"I realized that. I'm sorry. I assume you had an interview. Want to talk about it?"

"Not now. The interviews aren't important unless something comes from them."

Marta hesitated, deciding not to press him for information. "I'm realizing how selfish I've been. I'll sit down and write another letter tonight."

"Writing another letter isn't the point, Marta. I want you to *want* to write to me. I want to hear what you're doing, how you're feeling, and how your recovery is progressing. If our relationship is going to grow, we need to share our daily lives."

The phone line hummed in silence. "My life isn't interesting. I'm not starting a career like yours. Promise you'll not give up on me."

"I can do that. But, Marta, your life *is* interesting to me. I want to be involved in what you do, what you think, and how you feel." Steve paused. "It's just over two months until my graduation. When you're here we can talk and decide where we are. You're coming, right?"

"Absolutely!" she said.

When their call ended, Marta felt a lightness return to her body. By attending his graduation she opened the chance for their relationship to recover and continue. She took in several deep breaths, then walked into the living room where she selected a classical ballet album and started the stereo record player. As the first strains of *Sleeping Beauty* began, she closed her eyes and swayed, feeling the music awaken the emotions inside her.

❧

As the first weekend of October ended, the play *Our Town* ended as well, but not without a surprise. Hal invited Marta to the cast party so she could say goodbye to the people she'd worked with. He'd tried to entice her to remain assisting the theatre group, but she'd politely refused, using her dance classes as an excuse.

Marta stood talking with the actors when she spotted Dennis across the room. The young, blonde woman with him turned toward Marta, laughing at something Dennis said. Marta nearly dropped her glass. It was Alice Marsden, Robert's daughter. While Dennis turned to speak to a group of men, Alice walked over to Marta.

"Hi," Alice said. "I didn't think I'd see you here. Did you work on the play?"

"No, but I didn't expect to see you here either, Alice. Did you like the play?"

"Not really. Dennis, my boyfriend, dragged me here."

Marta tipped her head and bit her bottom lip. "How long have you dated Dennis?"

"Don't you remember? He was at our family picnic at your house. We hit it off and started dating that same weekend. We like so many of the same things: walking to the beach at Illahee, bowling, and going for long drives." Alice sighed. "He's so romantic."

Marta nodded and used her stage smile to cover her urge to wring Dennis's neck. "That sounds wonderful for you, Alice."

As Dennis approached Alice and Marta, his smile disappeared as Marta's grew wider. "Dennis, how nice to see you again. Alice has been catching me up. If you two will excuse me, I need to head home. I've several overdue letters to write this evening."

All the way home, Marta chuckled at her stupidity, believing anything Dennis said. Seeing his smile drop from his face gave her decision an enormous boost.

> *Dear Steve,*
>
>   *Thanks for your latest newsy letter. I'm not surprised your project earned an A. I know how hard you worked on it. I earned so few A's it's as if the alphabet began with C. (I'm joking but it's also true.)*
>
>   *Our Town was a great play. I'm no longer helping with their plays. It's best since the dance studio is keeping me busy. I'm counting the days until I see you so we can talk and celebrate your graduation as well as the holidays.*
>
>   *Miss you tons,*
>
>   *Marta Fluff (ha,ha)*

Remembering her promise to write to Steve, Marta was determined to keep her conversation light and sharing bits of herself. The more she wrote to him, the easier it became to find funny moments to share. She also realized Lynne had stopped writing or calling; another relationship she valued needed to be restored. She'd save any discussion of her problems with Steve for their face-to-face conversation.

> *Lynne,*
>
>   *Hope you are staying out of trouble without me. I'm taking on classes and enjoying the chance to create my own dances.*
>
>   *Looks like I'll be in Billings to watch Steve graduate and see you dance in the Nutcracker. Hooray!!*

Thinking about moving out to a place of my own. Yes, I'm going to act like a grownup, but I can't afford a car yet. And, no, I don't want to buy your clunker. It wouldn't survive a week on our hilly roads.

Marta

She attached a stamp to each letter and left them out in the mailbox for pickup. She hummed as she watched the pecan rolls rise in the oven, filling the house with the sweet scent of cinnamon and toasting nuts. They'd satisfy both her mom's and Robert's sweet tooth.

Marta spent the rest of her afternoon thinking about guiding Paige and Rosalia. She remembered how much effort it required to keep audition details straight in her mind. No faulting Miss Holland—Lindsay—but she hoped to make the experience for the two girls easier than hers had been. As she looked over her hand-written list, she organized her ideas as logically as possible. Each suggestion brought up memories from her personal auditions: the times she received praise for a graceful extension as well as the times dance directors barked out corrections for a sloppy turn or a late ending.

She walked down Callow to the Kress Five and Dime and bought a large sheet of poster paper to make a chart for the girls. Back home, she placed the poster paper on the kitchen table and drew faint lines to keep her printing straight. When she finished, the chart read:

Audition Suggestions
1. Know your strengths and make them stronger.
2. Know your weaknesses and make them your strengths.
3. Become professional the minute before you enter the room.
4. Show your best form during barre warm-ups and floor exercises.
5. Learn the choreography as quickly as possible.

6. Demonstrate strong rhythmic sense and interpretation of the music.

7. Remember: 2 practices then a graded performance.

8. Stand still in fifth position between elements of the audition.

9. Blend into the group performance but stand out thru your skills.

10. Perform your solo with elegance.

11. Thank the judges as you leave.

12. No matter what happens, be content knowing you've done your best.

The list looked long, but each suggestion mattered. She anticipated that Zandora Marcus would prowl around upstairs at the studio, so this would give her something to chew on. Poor Rosalia. If her mom backed off, she'd perform better. If this was the kind of pressure Bartley faced at her dance academy and from her parents, no wonder she took diet pills to boost her energy.

Marta stopped herself. Why was *she* still taking diet pills? Had they become a bad habit? Appeared so. She looked around as if someone were watching her, then she walked into her bedroom and took out her stash of pills. Seven pills left. Why did she hide them if she didn't feel guilty taking them? She'd flush them down the toilet then confess to Lynne that she'd been right saying Marta was addicted to them.

She stood in the bathroom, holding the diet pills, considering her next move when the phone rang. She stuffed the pills back in her pocket and hurried to answer the phone.

On the other end of the call she heard the perky voice of Lily Rose.

"Marta? Are your ears burning? We're talking about you. I'm at the dance studio with your mom. I need to talk with you about the women's exercise class."

"Is something wrong?" Her stomach lurched. She'd expected a call from one of the Pill Hill ladies, thinking they'd be dissatisfied about *something*, but not calling her at home.

"No, no. The gals wondered two things. Could we come five days a week, and would you make those extra days more of an adult ballet class?

"I could do that." Marta felt relief that the ladies weren't dissatisfied, but that they wanted more classes was a surprise. "Do you have something special in mind?"

Lily Rose laughed. "Not really. We love working with you and thought it would be fun to experience ballet choreography. Nothing too hard, mind you. Are we nuts to ask you?"

Marta shook her head as she answered. "Not at all. I'd be glad to share basic choreography. You don't want to wear *pointe* shoes, do you?"

"Lord, no! There's no way we'd survive the pain. We thought we'd like to push ourselves a bit, though. You're so gentle with us, we knew you're the only one we'd dare ask. Your mom says your schedule is free Tuesday and Thursday morning between ten-thirty and twelve. If you'll take us on, could we start next week? Feel free to say no."

Marta paused, running through how she'd organize the additional classes. What choreography could she use? Like a flash of light, the ideal selection presented itself. They'd be familiar with the music and...

"No, Lily Rose. I'd enjoy that. Let's start next week at 10:30. I know the perfect choreography for us to tackle. It will be fun."

As she hung up, Marta hoped she'd made a sensible selection. If so it would be a second monumental decision in less than ten minutes. They'd love the music. But could she reopen the old wound associated with that music?

When the phone ran so soon after Lily Rose called, Marta assumed she was calling back with another question. Why was her mom allowing parents to call their home? Couldn't they call and talk during breaks in her studio hours?

"Marta? This is Zandora Marcus. We need to talk."

Surprise followed her shock. "Did the dance studio give you this phone number?"

"No, but I need to know why you spoke with the school counselor about Rosalia."

Marta closed her eyes and dug deep for a calm answer. "Mr. Faris needed information from the dance studio before he'd ask the P.E. teacher to excuse Rosalia early for the performances you've scheduled."

"I've never heard of anything so preposterous. Have you signed off?"

Again, Marta reached for a calm voice. "No, but I'll send in the forms as soon as the school contacts the dance studio."

Zandora harrumphed. "Don't bother. I want Lindsay to sign them. Coming from the studio owner is more appropriate. In the future I'll expect you to stay out of our business." *Click.*

Marta shook her head as she hung up the phone receiver. Nothing pleased that woman, and now that she had her home phone number, she might be an even bigger problem, even though she said she didn't want Marta involved. She'd need to tell Lynne about Zandora's antics. At least the upcoming adult ballet class and planning their choreography promised an opportunity to take her mind off Zandora until the next crisis arose.

Excitement and performance butterflies danced through Marta as she thought about simplifying *Rhapsody in Blue*, the choreography that ended her career. Why did that selection pop into her mind so quickly? Why not something less emotional, something with fewer haunting memories, something that wouldn't showcase her weakened ankle? What did she have to prove at this late date?

Much as she tried to think of another ballet selection, her thoughts returned to *Rhapsody in Blue*. She'd mimic Damien Black's presentation ideas: listen to the music, then discuss the way the instrumentation moves the melody. Those memories were happy ones she'd revisit as she shared the music with the ladies.

The new adult ballet class pushed Marta's recovery plans forward. She worked every afternoon after her classes to strengthen her ankle and refine the movements she'd expect the women to make. Editing Damien's choreography presented a challenge she enjoyed. If this dance went well, perhaps she could adapt others for the women.

She found airy chiffon remnants on her mom's sewing shelves and purchased additional yardage to make each woman and herself ankle-length skirts. Practicing while wearing a skirt changed the way she moved; hopefully it would do the same for the women.

Today, as the first adult ballet class began, Marta felt a new bubble of excitement spread through her. Since this was a special class for the Pill Hill women, Marta wanted to fulfill their expectations. She'd noted their body builds during the exercise classes. Three of the women were lean and looked fit enough to run marathons. The fourth carried extra weight on her backside, tummy, and legs, but also appeared fit.

After leading the women through the barre warm-ups they already knew, she introduced two basic floor exercises. First she demonstrated *ports de bras*, stretches made by moving and balancing their upper body over their lower torso using elongated arm reaches. Next, she shared *echappés*, simple jumps made while changing the position of their feet while maintaining balance and erect posture.

"Watch my hands," Marta said. "I'll point to where you need to place your body weight. We're repeating our basic warm-up positions and moving your body weight from foot to foot."

When Marta stopped demonstrating and turned to watch them, she continued counting the beats by clapping. She saw the determination on the women's faces as they stumbled, then restarted their movements.

"Good focus, ladies. Two more and stop."

As Marta removed the record from the player, she applauded them. "Great effort, ladies. Before I share our ballet dance music, let's take a water break. Then join me on the floor."

The women bent over, breathing hard and headed for their thermoses of water without comment.

Once they were settled, Marta explained. "Since this is your special class and it's something you asked for, I want you to tell me your past dance experiences and what you're looking for in this class. Lily Rose, please start."

Lily Rose folded her hands in her lap and smiled. "As you know, I used to sing with a band. Did a little shuffling and swaying during our performances, but nothing I'd call dancing. I want to understand what it takes to be a ballet dancer. I want to dance to classical ballet music to enhance my trips to watch the ballet companies that perform in Seattle."

In turn, the ladies mentioned their background. Trixie danced with her high school drill team. "After beauty school I bought a small salon. I married Jeff last year, sold my salon, and now I want to try something new with my friends."

Frann shared that she was a high school jock, playing field hockey and basketball. Irene had been a cheerleader in high school and college.

Marta stood and shook out her legs. "Great. Now that I know a bit about your experiences, I think the dances I've planned for the two ballet days will meet your needs. Let's get started."

"Wait a minute," Lily Rose said. "Tell us a little about your career. Part of the reason we want to do this is to develop our understanding of what dancers do to prepare and dance."

All heads nodded.

"Hm-m. My career." Marta sat down on the floor and crossed her legs, giving herself time to consider what to share. "My ballet career was fun, hard work, and very short. I danced last year from August until I fell on New Year's Eve when I broke a small bone in my foot. I came home in May and here we are."

"Do you miss dancing?" Irene said.

"Sometimes. Working here eases that longing. I love teaching classes and watching students try new movements."

"Do you plan to return to dancing?" Frann asked.

"Maybe. To the Intermountain Ballet Company, no. That door is closed." Marta wanted to stop the trip down memory lane, so she stood and walked to the record player. "Okay, let's get back to our center work. Most ballet classes include a variety of runs, jumps, and turns."

A collective groan escaped the ladies' lips.

Marta giggled. "Don't worry. We'll start out easy. Stay in your line and spread out more than an arm's length. We'll work on your arms first. Pretend you're running your arms through water. In fact, when you take a bath or go to the club for a swim, practice moving your hands through the water." She demonstrated, letting her hand lag behind her arm movements. "Follow me. Forward, back, forward, back."

The ladies bit their lips as they mimicked Marta's movement.

"Nice work. Move one hand until you tire, then move the other arm. Forward, back, forward, back. When you get tired, shake them out and repeat again."

"I never realized how heavy my arms could feel," Lily Rose said. "I feel my body starting to lean when I move my arms."

"Good. Your arms provide flow, and they also help your body stay balanced. Do two more with each arm. When I start the music, I want you to move around the room, letting your arms sway and your hands trail behind your arms. Walk or run to feel the motion."

When Marta stopped the music, the women bent forward to rest.

"That was harder than it looked," Frann said as she shook out her arms.

"My hands looked like Frankenstein's," Lily Rose said. "I don't think I can walk and move my arms, let alone make them sway."

"That's surprisingly difficult, isn't it?" Marta said. "Over the next weeks we'll learn a variety of runs, then jumps, followed by turns, and soon you'll be dancing the choreography."

"Can you tell us what music you'll use?" Frann said. "I'd like to buy the record so I can practice at home in my basement."

"What are you trying to do, become the teacher's pet?" asked Irene.

"No," Frann said. "I'd like to listen to the music and practice."

Marta smiled. "If each of you want a recording, I'll ask my mom to order your first choreography, Gershwin's *Rhapsody in Blue*. My former ballet master and mentor, Damien Black, created the choreography. Let's sit and listen to the way the selection begins."

After everyone sat, Marta gave one final suggestion. "Close your eyes and feel the music. Move with it; let it soak into your core."

She dropped the needle onto the first groove and rejoined the women on the floor. As the clarinet slide began, she drifted with the music, letting it seep into her body like a deep ache followed by a pleasant release.

When the music ended Marta opened her eyes and saw the four women watching her.

"You really love that music, don't you?" Lily Rose said.

"I do," Marta said. "But I could find another selection if you prefer."

They shook their heads. "If you love it, we love it too. Would you dance it for us?" Trixie said.

Marta half-expected this request. Her butterflies began doing flips instead of flutters as she stood, put on a filmy skirt, and started the music. "This is my version for you. Let me know what you think."

Time and place evaporated as Marta moved into the music. She executed the exaggerated *developés* that matched the elongated clarinet slide at the beginning of the selection. She recreated the sweeping steps that led into the *adagio*, followed by graceful steps as she gathered up the hem of her long skirt.

For the ladies she simplified the *relevés* by substituting *balancés* and *arabasques*. Lifting to the balls of their feet then stepping into turns would be too complex; swaying side to side followed by graceful poses on one leg would provide enough motion and interpretation.

As she stopped dancing and curtsied, the ladies clapped.

"Brava, Marta," Irene said. "That was beautiful. Is it even possible for us to dance like you just did?"

"Absolutely! So stand up and let's get busy." Marta reached for the chiffon skirts she'd made. "Slip on a skirt to help you get into the mood. It's almost too light to feel, but it will change the way you move."

Marta demonstrated. "Think waltzing. I want you to circle the room moving your entire body. Let your arms and head float. Don't worry about what steps we might do later. Move your feet any way you wish."

Marta watched them and made mental notes on how she'd adjust the choreography she'd planned. It didn't appear she'd need to change much to meet their current skills.

After several repetitions, Marta stopped the *Rhapsody* music and led the class in a cool down. She relaxed, noting how the time had flown. Next time she'd begin teaching the dance movements one by one.

As the women packed up to leave, Lily Rose called across the room, "Marta, would you like to join us for lunch? We thought we'd go home, shower, and head to the country club. We'd love you to join us, our treat."

Should she go? Did they ask her because they thought they needed to include her? She wanted friends to talk with; these women could provide a starting place. They accepted her as their teacher; potentially being their friend as well was reassuring.

"I'd love to come, thank you."

"Great. I'll pick you up in one hour. Give me your home address."

Marta froze. These women lived on Pill Hill. Their husbands were professionals with lots of money and expensive homes. They'd be fun to get to know and she wanted to go, but should she cancel now and save herself the embarrassment of having them see the tiny old house where she lived and the out of style clothes she wore?

"How about I meet you here in one hour?" Marta said.

Marta drove home, showered, and returned to the studio wearing a plain rose-colored sheath under her gray winter coat. October was mild this year, but her other coat was a plaid car coat and totally inappropriate for a country club lunch.

The Kitsap County Country Club restaurant occupied the edge of a woodsy glen. The dining room overlooked the eighteenth hole. Golfers finished their games and stepped inside for a drink or a meal.

When the ladies arrived, a hostess directed them to a table next to the front window and handed them menus. "Nice to see you ladies again. May I get you something to drink before I take your lunch orders?"

The Pill Hill women ordered wine; Marta ordered iced tea.

Trixie looked up. "Don't you want a glass of wine, Marta?"

She shook her head. When the hostess left she whispered, "Can't. I'm only eighteen."

"What?" Frann said. "You're that young? My sister is older than you."

Lily Rose set her menu aside. "Tell us about your family."

"It's just my mom and me," Marta said. "My dad died years ago."

Irene shook her head. "That's tough. Same with my mother. Your mom is still alone?"

"Yes, but she might get engaged this Christmas."

"You must have a boyfriend," Irene said. "Who's the lucky guy?"

Marta felt her face heat up. "His name is Steve. He lives in Montana, works for his dad's newspaper. He'll graduate from college in December."

Trixie clapped her hands together. "Oh, a college guy. Best watch out for him. College men are so full of themselves."

"Don't say that," Frann said. "Her Steve is probably one of the good guys. You'll need to bring him around so we can check him out."

"Not if she's smart, she won't," Lily Rose said. "We'd scare the poor guy off."

"Before Steve you probably had a string of guys waiting for you at the stage door or lurking off stage," Trixie said.

"No, Trixie," said Frann. "That only happens in the movies. But what about now? Does Steve have any competition?"

"Keeping things going across two states and two mountain ranges makes it difficult," Marta said, "but we're still okay."

"Sounds like the door is open," Lily Rose said as she took a sip of her burgundy. "Steve had better get his foot in that door before it closes."

"Yes, but if the spark is there, it will last," Trixie said.

Marta smiled. She hoped being with Steve and talking things out would rekindle the flame they'd shared when they saw each other almost daily back in Billings. As the time to see him drew closer and closer, her resolve to figure out their relationship grew stronger, especially in light of her discovery about Dennis.

The waiter arrived with their seafood salads. Conversation raced around the table as they ate, laughed, and talked about their exercise class with Marta.

"I like learning different ballroom steps," Lily Rose said. "Would you consider teaching our husbands a couple of evenings a week so we can dance with real people? I'd rather pay you than Arthur Murray."

"I'll talk with Lindsay," Marta said, "and let you know at our next class. Are you sure they'll come?"

"Oh they'll come," Trixie said as she pointed her salad fork toward Marta, "if they want happy wives."

That evening Marta set the kitchen table anticipating three for dinner. Her thoughts drifted back to lunch. The Pill Hill women oozed energy and confidence. It must be nice knowing you have enough spending money to take dance classes, go to the country club, and enjoy relaxed afternoons with friends. Some day she hoped to have time to gather a group of friends together to talk and share a meal. Until then she'd continue teaching classes while working to build up her ankle strength. No sense in closing any doors just yet.

Marta wondered how she'd find friends with similar interests. Since she'd been away in Billings, she'd lost what few contacts she'd had in high school. Without a club or a group to belong to, it appeared today represented a first move away from being a loner. Too bad Lynne was so far away; she missed her brash, funny friend. Too bad Bartley had died. Oh, Bartley; she missed her so much.

Her mom had a small cadre of friends, mostly because of Robert. Where did she find time to be social? Marta's relationship with her mom had noticeably shifted since she'd left thirteen months ago. They loved each other, but using the upstairs dance studio rooms as her own space felt more comfortable than the time she spent at home. Robert naturally took a lot of her mother's time. One thing was certain: Marta needed to find her own place. She hoped that place would be the little house on Corbett Drive.

In mid-November Marta created a to-do list as the Holland Dance Studio shifted into preparation mode for winter programs at the local hospitals, service groups, and community events. The *Nutcracker* remained as popular here as in most small towns and cities across the country. Thank heavens orchestrating the nightmare of a dozen winter program commitments belonged to Lindsay and her mother. Marta's only responsibility centered on recording the performance music onto the tape recorder, helping Paige and Rosalia perfect their solos, and moving to Corbett Drive. On the fifth of December, she'd take the train to attend Steve's graduation, stay to watch Lynne in the *Nutcracker,* then return home in plenty of time to assist with the last few Christmas shows. Any more jobs and she'd need to take diet pills every day, not just when she needed a last minute boost in energy.

Diet pills. Why didn't she toss them? She didn't need them, did she? Lately her dancing and working with students boosted her energy naturally. As soon as the hectic season ended, she'd quit the pills and focus on building her energy through hard work.

Marta sat with Lindsay as she opened the small case that held the tape recording equipment. "It's really quite easy to transfer the dance selections from our long play records onto the reel of tape," Lindsay said. "Just be careful to avoid the red erase button." She connected the record player to the tape machine. "Be absolutely certain both ends of the plug are completely pushed in. Otherwise, you'll get messed up. I've had to re-record dances many times. It's no fun.

"Here's the order of the most popular program we dance. Once you have the reel fed through the tape head and connected to the blank reel, set the counter on zero. Record the start time, then push record. When the music ends, stop the recording and write down the ending time. Leave ten seconds between each selection. Any questions?"

Marta shook her head.

"Here's the order. Start with "Jingle Bells". I'll walk you through the first selection."

Marta watched the process, listened to the music, and wrote down the recording information. Lindsay sat with her as she organized the second tape recording, then left Marta to handle the task on her own.

Two hours later, Lindsay returned to listen to the replay of the recording. "Wow! You've done a great job. But, you know what? I'm feeling queasy. I think I have the flu or ate something that didn't agree with me. I'm heading home. Record program B the same way. Program C recordings are the solos for Rosalia and Paige. We can listen to everything tomorrow." Lindsay waved and rushed to the bathroom.

As Marta worked on tapings, she drifted into thinking about her performances last year and sharing her dancing with Steve. Not long until she'd enjoy his banter as well as spend time alone with him.

As she refocused on the tapings, she stared at the machine. She'd forgotten to reset the counter. She went back, listened to each piece of music, wrote down start and end times, labeled the tapes, and set them on the shelf. How did Lindsay and her mom manage to accomplish all of this with everything else they handled? She'd need to remember to thank them for making the chores at the dance studio appear effortless.

During their extra classes Rosalia and Paige polished their solos. The *Nutcracker* and popular holiday melodies provided entertaining music for service clubs and hospital visits. Rosalia danced to Tchaikovsky's "Sugar Plum Fairy" and "Winter Wonderland," while Paige danced to Tchaikovsky's "Dance of the Flutes" and "Frosty the Snowman." They partnered for "Waltz of the Flowers" creating a memorable finale as well as showcasing their skills as advanced Holland Dance Studio students.

Marta helped the girls refine their movements. "You'll begin with the Tchaikovsky and end with the popular holiday songs. Think of the composer's intent as you dance. What is the mood? Does the music suggest tiny flicks of your wrists or sweeping moves? Should your face look serious or playful? Each selection needs to show a different view of your dancing. Any questions?"

"May we borrow the tape recorder to use when we dance at school or for friends and family?" Rosalia said as she packed up her belongings to head home.

"Unfortunately, no," Marta said. "The tape recorder cost around two hundred dollars, so we can't lend it out. We need it for the winter performances. I suggest you use a record, or, if you have a portable tape recorder, bring in a tape and we'll record the music for you."

"But we can borrow the costumes from storage, right?" Paige asked.

"Of course. Come on, let's see which ones you might want to borrow. Rosalia, do you want to borrow costumes?"

Rosalia shook her head. "Mom's buying me my own costumes. She doesn't want me wearing hand-me-downs. But may I borrow a tiara?"

"No problem." Marta smiled. "Let's get it now to make certain it looks good as new."

The girls looked through everything in the meager closet. They held up costumes and tried on tiaras and a variety of hats and capes until Zandora arrived and whisked Rosalia home.

"Thanks for loaning me the costumes," Paige said. "Where did Miss Holland get them?"

"A friend of hers found them at an auction. They were in great condition and only needed to be cleaned and minor repairs made. Don't tell anyone, but the rumor is that a famous ballerina once wore these for her performances in South America."

Paige's eyes widened. "Really? Do you know who she was?"

Marta nodded and whispered, "I heard it was Alicia Markova, but I can't prove it."

"Wow. Have you worn any of these?"

"I have. I've worn the costumes you're borrowing. You may borrow these for the recital as well if you wish. Just promise to be extremely careful. We'll never be able to replace them."

"I promise," Paige said as she smiled and wrapped the selected costumes in white tissue.

༄

Renting the Corbett Drive house renewed Marta's belief in good fortune. The Monday before Thanksgiving she signed the rental forms, paid her deposits, and picked up her keys. The owner gave her a six-month rental agreement that ensured her current eighty-five dollar a month rent would remain unchanged until next May.

"And, miss," the landlord said, "I don't tolerate any wild parties or them college pranks. I expect your neighbors will let me know if you do."

Thanksgiving Day Marta packed her things while her mom celebrated turkey day with Robert's relatives. On Friday she used Robert's box trailer and, with her mom's help, loaded up a twin bed, a dresser, a table lamp, the mirror from the garage, her mom's extra kitchen dishes and supplies, plus her personal belongings.

The drizzly weather didn't dampen her sunny spirit. In one hour they'd unloaded *her* scant possessions and stowed them in *her* living room in *her* house. Thinking about it brought a smile to her face. Now, for the first time, she'd begin life on her own: cooking all her meals, cleaning, and not worrying about what hours she came and went or played her music. Of course she'd miss her old room and her mother's company, but she'd ride to the dance studio with mom and stop by often to use the phone. She allowed herself a quick dance from room to room before she got serious about unpacking.

The Corbett house had three rooms: a living area with a kitchen corner, a bedroom, and a bath. The paint throughout was fresh and the wooden floors had been polished to a high sheen. Marta carried her personal items into the bedroom. Her mom helped her assemble the bed and mattress and make up the bed. Marta fluffed up the flowered comforter and pillows and lay a blanket across the bottom of the bed.

Marta stood back and smiled. "Thanks, Mom. I can handle the rest. You go enjoy the rest of the weekend with Robert."

"Are you sure?" her mom said. "I can stay longer if you want help with the rest of the boxes."

"No. I'm fine. I'm probably going to be a moving mess, finding the best place for everything. Thank Robert for the loan of the trailer. I'll see you Monday morning."

Marta hummed as she finished in her bedroom. Clothes went into drawers and the narrow closet, her frilly lamp went on the bedside table, and the garage mirror hung in the tiny hall between the bathroom and the bedroom.

Kitchen next. Four plates, cups, and bowls on the open shelf. Pots and pans on the shelves under the counter. Silverware and utensils in the drawer. Towels on the swivel rack by the sink. Tea, cereal and sugar bowl in the cupboard. Milk in the fridge for morning. Done. Tomorrow she'd walk to Capps Grocery for further supplies.

The bathroom next. Marta hung her bath towels below the window and put soap and shampoo in the shower and her other supplies in the medicine chest. She tested the wall heater: only enough heat to take the chill out of the walls. Just like at home, she'd need to bathe, dry off quickly, and escape to the warmth of the bedroom to avoid freezing during cold weather.

Before dusk arrived Marta took a break from unpacking to cross the road and sit on a giant driftwood log above the high tide line. This horseshoe-shaped Phinney Bay was situated just a two mile drive from Bremerton, but also a world away from the shipyard and the hubbub of downtown. If she had a speed boat it would take her a good hour to motor to Sinclair Inlet, the main waterway near town. Maybe some day she'd think about a small boat, but it wasn't a top priority like having her own car.

She buttoned her car coat up to her throat and crossed her arms over her chest to fend off the dampness soaking into her body. Gulls glided back and forth, cawing, snatching stray oysters and dropping them onto the rocks in hopes of opening them to gobble up the juicy bits inside. She inhaled the salty air and closed her eyes, envisioning springtime on this beach with her shoes kicked off, enjoying the warming sunlight. She shuddered from the November cold and returned to the little house to complete her unpacking for her first night in her own place.

In an hour's time she'd arranged her furniture in the living room. A dresser served as her buffet. Once she had the money, she'd scour the second hand stores in hope of finding a small round table and two chairs. Until then a TV tray and folding chair would do.

She positioned the small rocking chair and the floor lamp on a rag rug her Gran had made and sat down to rock. Back and forth, back and forth. What was missing? A couch. She needed a couch. No, a daybed would be better for overnight company.

Marta took a quick shower, put on her chenille robe, took the blanket from the bottom of her bed, and wrapped up in the rocking chair. She closed her eyes as the quiet enveloped her. Much as she had enjoyed Mrs. B's boarding house, making her own schedule and having all the space as her own was truly exciting. No wonder Lynne and Bartley liked having their own places.

Sunday evening Marta returned to her mom's house to wait for Steve's call. Lately he'd sounded more like himself: happy, anxious to share his class information, and closer to being ready to talk with her about their future. After they discussed her move, he asked, "You're definitely coming to graduation, right?"

"Of course. It's too important to miss."

"Good. We're invited to lots of parties, so you'll be able to meet my friends. I'll send you a plane ticket. Can you stay the month?"

"I can't. Besides, I bought my train ticket last week. I'll stay for your graduation and one *Nutcracker* performance, then I need to get back home for the last of the Christmas shows and to be with my mom for the holiday."

The phone line hummed in the quiet. "Okay. My mom will fix a guest room. We'll spend time in town, then slip away to the mountains for our talk. I may have a job offer by the time you arrive. I'm hoping so, anyway."

"That sounds great. It will be good to see you and wander around Montana again like we used to." She took a deep breath, figuring what to say about their impending talk. The party line clicked. Saved by an incoming call.

"Oops! There's a call coming in. I need to get it. Talk with you soon."

"I'll see you here in Billings in exactly...twelve days. Night, Marta. Love you."

"Love you, too."

Click, Click. Marta double tapped the phone cradle to connect to the incoming call. "Hello? This is Marta."

"Hi, Marta. It's Lindsay." Her voice sounded quiet, more serious than usual. "I wonder if you and your mother might come in early tomorrow morning, say eight-thirty. I have something to discuss with both of you."

"Sure, Lindsay. Is something wrong?"

"Not really," Lindsay said. "It's complicated. I'll explain it when I see you."

Overnight Marta speculated on the news. Perhaps the older students had lost their chance to dance on KING-TV's winter extravaganza, or the regional Christmas show didn't invite the Holland Studio dancers to perform. What could be on her mind?

Lindsay smiled but looked ashen when Marta and her mom arrived in the morning. "Thanks for coming in early. I wanted to tell you that I've been to the doctor and I don't have the flu. I'm pregnant." She smiled and looked down at her belly.

"That's wonderful news," Marta's mom said. "When's the baby due?"

"Middle of June. I'm glad our recital is the end of May so I can make it. But being so close to forty, the doctor says I need to simplify my life." Lindsay looked to Marta and her mom and pulled her eyebrows together. "I'm sorry to dump this on you, but I'll need you to take over the Christmas shows and most of the recital."

"Of course we will, right, Marta?" Her mom answered without a glance toward Marta.

Marta found her stage smile as she visualized her plans in Billings shattering like a mirror. "Of course," she said but her answer lacked enthusiasm.

Lindsay handed each of them a stack of papers. "I feel I'm deserting you, but you two are the only ones I trust to keep things organized and moving forward. I've made up the lists of what needs to be done for the Christmas shows. I'll handle typing up the master programs and making sure the contacts are up-to-date, and the newspaper writes an article, but, Marta, I'll need you to rehearse the dancers, fit their costumes, and handle the tapes."

Marta wiped her hands across her face, then nodded.

"Elle, I'll need you to work your usual magic arranging for parents to drive the students and check out the facilities to ensure they allow enough space for our dancers to perform." Lindsay rolled her eyes. "Can't have another grange hall disaster; it makes us look bad even if it was their fault we only had a small corner for performing."

"Certainly. How are you feeling about being pregnant?" Marta's mom asked.

Lindsay rubbed her stomach and straightened her top. "I'm fine knowing Adam is indefinitely stationed here. He'll be around to help baby-sit when I'm working at the studio. But the rest depends on Marta. If you plan to stay here and teach, I'd like you to think about taking over all of my classes. Is that possible?"

Marta nodded. "I guess."

"Good. I feel better already. Well, almost. Excuse me." Lindsay stood and hurried to the bathroom.

Marta stared at the handful of papers she held. "Mom, how long do you think Lindsay expects me to stay and handle her workload?"

"I don't know. Until she's ready to return, probably next fall. Why? Is that a problem for you? I'd think you'd be happy to have additional classes."

"Is there someone she might hire to teach ballet classes?"

"Not that I know about, but she's talking with Veronica Osborne about starting tap and baton classes in the fall. If you're not sure you're staying that long, you'd better tell Lindsay right away."

"Tell me what?" Lindsay said as she reentered the room, wiping her forehead.

Her mom stared at Marta and pulled in her lips before she answered. "Marta's not certain…."

"Um, I'm not certain I can handle the classes as well as you do, but I'll try." Marta picked up her lists and turned to leave. "Congratulations on your baby. It must be exciting to start a family."

Lindsay sat down and curled her feet under her body. "It's exciting and scary. You'll find out one of these days."

As Marta backed out of the office, she kept an eye on her mom's face. Did her mom get the message to keep their conversation to herself? She hoped so. Maybe she should have told Lindsay that her plans to stay in Bremerton were unsettled. Being slammed into a corner and expected to decide her future on a moment's notice was not something she'd anticipated. Why did everything happen in such a rush? She hadn't returned home to take on the responsibility of a dance studio, yet here she was.

She'd made promises to Steve and Lynne. Both would be disappointed almost as much as she was to disappoint them. What lousy timing. But that was life, and Lindsay's taking care of herself when she was expecting outweighed the importance of attending performances and graduations.

∽

Marta stood in her mom's kitchen listening to the phone in her hand ring and ring. Where was Lynne? As she started to hang up, the receiver on the other end lifted. "Hello?" said a breathless Lynne.

"Hi," Marta said, "I don't know how to tell you this, but I have bad news."

"Did someone die or something?"

"Miss Holland—"

"She died? Oh my God!"

"No, Lynne. She's pregnant and needs my help. I'm taking over the Christmas programs, so I won't be coming to Billings."

"Ever?"

"No, but not before Christmas. She needs to take it easy during her pregnancy, so I'll miss seeing you dance the *Nutcracker*." Marta waited for Lynne's response. "Lynne?"

"I'm here." Lynne's voice lost its usual animation. "Too bad, Marta. You'll not only miss me, you'll miss the little girls. The local kids have the measles, so our young dancers will be in the Billings performances."

"That's wonderful news! Are they excited?"

"Yes, and I told them you'd be here. They'll be so disappointed."

Marta let the stab of sadness linger inside her. "I know, and I'm sorry, but I need to help Lindsay."

"Does Steve know you won't make his graduation?"

"No. I thought I'd build up my courage by telling you first."

"Did it work?"

"No." Marta felt the weight of the dance studio situation pushing down on her. "Anyway, tell me how the little girls got invited to dance."

"It wasn't a big deal. I told Madame Cosper I understood that three of the young dancers had the measles and that we needed children to fill in for them during the opening scene. I told her our four little girls knew the steps."

"Did Madame think that was too much of a coincidence?"

"Not when I told her we taught them the dances *last* year. Plus I shared our overhearing her secret kissing moment with Herbert."

"No! You didn't. Really? You said 'our'?"

"Yep, I did."

"Oh, Lynne. Why? Did you mention me?"

"Not really. Madame figured that out all by herself."

Marta sank onto the nearest kitchen chair. "Then what happened?"

"Madame scowled and asked if this was blackmail. I told her it could be but that the girls were ready. I reminded her about last December's *Nutcracker* when one girl tripped and fell and another exited the wrong side of the stage."

"What did she say?"

"Nothing until I said all we wanted was a chance for them to audition. She finally agreed. Isn't that great?"

Marta let Lynne's bombshell wander around in her head before she answered. "I wish you hadn't included me. I'm sure that caused her to think twice about refusing your offer."

"It was fine. Besides, there's a big payoff for the girls if they dance. Local children who perform with the company during the year get first chance at scholarships for the ballet academy that's opening soon. Won't that be great for the girls?"

Marta's surprise over Lynne's methods for helping the little girls silenced her long enough for Lynne to fill in the quiet phone line.

"Marta, do you realize how special this is for the girls? I was fourteen before I ever danced on a stage with professionals. Our girls may get a chance to dance while they are practically babies."

"I understand, Lynne. Just don't get the girls' hopes up in case Madame slips into one of her angry moments. Warn them about her cane and her thumping their feet."

Lynne sighed. "I will. But now you'll miss it all."

"I know." Marta slumped forward in her chair and sighed. "I'm so sorry. Hug the girls for me and let me know how it goes."

When the call ended, Marta sat thinking about how Lynne's trickery created an opportunity for the little girls to dance. Would they get a fair chance with Madame feeling cornered into giving them that chance? Funny—at the present moment she and Madame shared the feeling of being cornered. She never expected to share any feelings with her, let alone something like this.

Before she called Steve's home, Marta paced and rocked attempting to calm her nerves. How could she explain her disappointment at being unable to join him on such an important day? What if he didn't accept that she had no choice in the matter? What if this ended their relationship?

Her palms were sweaty as she dialed his family home. The phone rang several times before Steve answered. Marta repeated the news to him and waited for him to fill in the blanks. "Steve?"

"I'm here. Wow. That's disappointing in so many ways. I wanted you to see me graduate and to share my excitement with you. I wanted you to meet my grandparents and my friends. I guess I understand. Your dancing still comes first, huh?"

Marta sniffed up her tears. "It's not that. It's...."

"Hey, don't cry. I understand. It's just that I'm disappointed. Let me think a minute."

The phone line hummed in silence. No clicks on the party line to relieve the stress building inside Marta. She sat and waited.

"Marta? I have an idea. Maybe we can salvage the trip. If you come *after* Christmas, I'll send you a plane ticket. We'll go to the cabin and talk, maybe have a private New Year's celebration. Will you come then?"

Marta wiped her nose and eyes and nodded. "I'd like that. I need to ask a favor. Would you go to the opening night of the *Nutcracker* and take flowers to the little girls? They're dancing in the first act."

"Yes, if I'll see you the end of December. Promise you'll come?"

Marta dried her face. "I promise. Thanks for understanding."

The weeks leading up to the holiday performances were hectic. Marta barely slept or ate. The dance studio's dozen performances took up several evenings and weekends. Marta was exhausted and dropped into bed to sleep restlessly until the morning alarm jarred her awake. She resorted to her dance-day meal. Back in high school when she danced several hours a day and several days a week, all she could eat was fruit cocktail and 7-Up. In Billings and now, she added an occasional diet pill when her day stretched beyond her endurance.

Her dance classes felt under control, but inside she harbored a tangle of nervousness, worry, and excitement. If she survived these weeks, she knew she could handle most anything else the world threw her direction.

The classes at the dance studio remained calm until the afternoon a whirlwind named Zandora flew into the studio demanding to see Miss Holland.

"She's not here," Marta said. "May I help you?"

"I doubt it. Lindsay copied a tape for Rosalia's private dances and somehow, someone erased it last night. We need another copy immediately. Rosalia's performing for our church in two hours, and this tape is blank."

"Let me make you a copy," Marta said. "It won't take long. Wait here."

Marta walked into the large practice room and assembled the record player, tape deck, and the reel. Zandora followed on her heels. "How long will this take? I'm certain Lindsay could do it in less time than you'll take. Why isn't she here?"

Marta connected everything and started the recording process before she spoke. "Lindsay is resting today. Shall I show you how this is done?"

"No. I know how to run a tape recorder. I pushed the red button. We played the tape and it was blank. How could you not check your taping and know it was blank?"

Marta decided to play Zandora's game. She smiled to herself as she shared her best stage smile. "We did play the tape before we gave it to Rosalia, so this is a surprise."

Zandora stood silently watching Marta record each selection, but her right foot made a frenzied tapping on the floor.

When Marta finished the tape, she smiled and handed it to Zandora. "Here you go. All three dances are on the tape in the order we danced them at the naval hospital. Is there anything else I can do for you?"

"No, nothing." Zandora's high heels clicked as she hurried from the practice room.

"Mrs. Marcus?"

Zandora looked back.

"This time push the white button. The red one erases everything on the tape in the blink of an eye."

Zandora narrowed her eyes and pursed her lips, then slammed the entry door on her way out.

Marta shook her head and started laughing. Maybe she could handle more than she thought she could. Wait until Lindsay heard about this.

The evening before Steve's graduation, Marta called and spoke with his mother. "Please tell Steve I'll be thinking of him tomorrow as he graduates."

"Yes, I will," she said. "He'll be sorry he missed your call. It's been hectic around here with family in town. I'm sure he'll call you when he gets a break."

Marta stayed near the phone the next day, but he didn't call. Was he mad or busy? They'd not confirmed a specific flight for her coming after Christmas, so maybe he had second thoughts.

୨

Holiday dance performances continued over the next two weeks as the dancers entertained for social clubs, grange functions, and on the KING television special. Events provided great publicity for the studio. Marta planned to share the news with Steve, but the phone didn't ring. Should she call him or write a letter? What if he didn't want her to come to Billings? If Lynne heard all Marta's fussing about Steve, she'd tell her to "get a grip" and "be patient," and she'd be right. Marta went back to her little house and kept busy making and wrapping Christmas gifts.

At eight o'clock in the morning on December 22, the doorbell rang. Marta looked out and saw the mailman impatiently looking around. "Morning," she said.

"Miss Selbryth? I have a special delivery letter for you." He handed her a clipboard. "Please sign after the X."

The letter was from Steve. Inside was the promised ticket and a note.

> Marta,
>
> Graduation was great. Parties were fun. Sorry you missed both. Went to the cabin with friends for several days. Out of town family members are staying to celebrate Christmas so I'm hosting them at the cabin as well.
>
> Dad's driving back and forth to work so he picked up your ticket and mailed this for me. I'll pick you up at the airport.
>
> Hugs,
> Steve

Each day, Marta had waited for his call at her mom's house. Now she knew why he'd not phoned her. Today she relaxed and helped her mom decorate the family Christmas tree, counting the days until she'd see Steve.

While Marta and her mom shared a dinner of navy bean soup and fresh baked French bread, they listened to holiday music. Then they returned to decorating the Christmas tree.

"Your Dad loved this album. He said it hustled him into the spirit of the season."

Marta nodded. "Perry Como can do that." She set down her handful of tinsel and stepped back. She flopped down on the couch.

Her mom watched her, then sat down beside her. "It's been a busy season. Thanks for helping at the dance studio. You've made lots of kids and servicemen in hospitals very happy this year."

"The article in the paper will generate more new students, I imagine," Marta said.

"I apologize for assuming you wanted to stay, honey. I thought you liked working for Lindsay. You'll need to let her know if you're staying or not to help until the recital is completed. You haven't spoken to Lindsay about it again, have you?"

Marta ran her fingertips over a tree branch, feeling the bristles and adjusting an ornament. "No, I haven't talked with her. Too many of my personal decisions need to be made and I don't know what to tell her yet." Marta tipped her head to one side, surveying the tree. "But you know what?" She bent and picked up a tiny box. "I'm not okay until I find out what's inside this box from Robert. An engagement ring?"

Her mom smiled and shrugged. "Maybe."

"If it's a ring, what will you do?"

Her mom returned the tiny box to under the tree before she spoke. "I don't know. I'm like you. I'm unsure of my next step."

Her mom's answer surprised Marta. She'd never thought of her mom needing to make life changing decisions at her age. But if she planned to marry Robert, that was a major adjustment.

Christmas Eve found Marta and her mother sitting in the dark with the tree lights on. They played carols and drank Crème de menthe from small wine glasses. About nine, Robert rang the bell and came in carrying an arm load of gifts.

Her mom helped him unload his arms. "Hey! You already brought plenty of gifts. You're spoiling us!"

Robert laid the gifts under the tree and stood back. "You two are easy to spoil. You never ask for anything." He stood, removed his coat, and kissed her mom's cheek. Happy Christmas."

The three sat quietly for some time until Robert hopped up and started handing out presents. "Okay, these six need to be opened tonight."

Marta and her mom unwrapped several boxes each, exposing a new set of individually wrapped pots and pans. Their shiny copper bottoms reflected the tree lights when they were placed under the tree.

"Hey! Put those in your respective kitchens, not under this tree. We need to leave space for Santa's gifts, you know!"

When he left at eleven, Robert had given her mom the ring, promising to not rush her into making a decision. Marta experienced a twinge of envy as she watched them exchange a kiss, but mostly she felt excited for her mother. She'd been alone for so many years, scraping by and never complaining. Now she'll have someone to share her days and nights.

Christmas morning after a breakfast of Jul Kaga, scrambled eggs with mushrooms, and steaming mugs of peppermint tea, Marta and her mom sat in the living room listening to Christmas music while waiting for Robert to stop in before joining Alice and their relatives for Christmas dinner.

Holiday happiness bubbled inside Marta. In three days she'd be in Billings, attempting to smooth over ruffled feathers from missing Steve's graduation and the little girls' dance debuts. Being home for Christmas felt better than last year when her mom surprised her by showing up in Billings. Home with family still trumped friends.

"Mom, let's each open one gift before Robert arrives, okay?"

Her mom laughed. "Okay, but I get to choose the one you open." Her mom laid a soft package on Marta's lap. "Happy Christmas."

Marta gently squeezed the gift and looked quizzically at her mother. "Hm-m-m. Feels like a sweater or a new bed pillow."

Her mother smiled. "Just open it."

Tears filled Marta's eyes as she opened the gift. Her mom had interwoven her *pointe* shoe ribbons, creating a decorative pillow cover. Most of the ribbons were pale pink; others were black, rose, and white to match her ballet costumes. All shared their worn spots, a sure sign they were her original ribbons.

"I hope it was okay that I took them without asking. I want you to have a happy remembrance of your year dancing."

Marta clutched the pillow to her chest. "Oh, Mom. It's wonderful. I, I feel so, I don't know, so strange when I see them; like my dancing never happened. This is a wonderful gift, and I'll cherish it forever."

"I wanted you to think about all the ballets you've performed, all the roles you've danced, and all the wonderful experiences you've had. I hope you'll think of your successes when you look at the pillow."

Marta wiped away her happy tears and smiled. "I will. I just thought I'd have many more years to dance. It was silly to expect to earn a solo after collecting eighty-four ribbons. I'd need twice that number at least."

"Maybe you *have* reached one goal, honey. It may not be a goal you'd thought much about. You've become a mentor to two young dancers; that keeps you involved in ballet. And look at your kinder classes. You're introducing music and movement to little children. Your other classes allow you to share your love of dance."

Could that be true? Was she missing the lights and performing, or did she miss the music and choreography? Could teaching satisfy her dreams, or would returning to the stage provide the only way to realize her deepest desire. She'd need to make her decision before too much time away from performing intervened and ended that possibility.

10

Marta looked out from her window seat, mid-plane. Her flight last spring she'd hardly known who she was or where she was headed. She'd flown to visit Bartley in the private clinic in Pennsylvania. How had Bartley allowed her diet pills to overtake her life? Seeing her so frail and unable to overcome her problems made Marta shiver. She missed her every day. Such a waste. Marta thanked herself for not allowing those same pills to ruin her life.

Despite her disappointing Steve, this trip to Billings promised to be a happy experience. She'd make time to see Lynne, Mrs. B., and the little girls and then talk things through with Steve. She might visit Madame as well, once she heard how the little girls danced during the *Nutcracker* performances.

The flight through clouds and rain provided time for Marta to consider her future. Steve looked ahead to his career as a newspaper reporter. She needed to decide how long she'd stay with Lindsay or if she wanted to leave. What if Steve ended up on the east coast? Would she move to be near where his plans took him? Maybe.

Deplaning, she moved with the crush of passengers into the small terminal and toward the baggage claim. She spotted Steve standing as close to the gate doorway as possible, holding a small bouquet of daisies and roses. His smile reassured her their relationship survived her slip-up with Dennis.

Her knees turned to gelatin as she stepped into his embrace.

"Finally." Steve held her tightly, then released her to arm's length before pulling her back into a hug. "I didn't think you'd ever get here. I've missed you."

"I missed you too." Tears slid down her face and onto his overcoat.

He handed her the flowers, then grabbed her free hand and towed her through the terminal.

The crush of people waiting around the luggage pick-up area provided time for them to stand to one side to exchange guarded smiles, warm embraces, and gentle kisses.

Steve whispered in her ear, "God, you're beautiful, Marta. I look at your photo ten times a day, but seeing you here, I realize I've missed you."

Marta remembered the comfort of melding into his hug and nodded in fear that speaking would break the spell or that she'd wake up and find everything so far had been a lovely dream.

When Steve had snagged her bag, he pulled her hand, dragging her through the airport at a near run. "Let's get back to my folks' place. I have a surprise waiting for you."

"What surprise?"

"You'll find out shortly. Just hurry!"

A blast of arctic air hit Marta in the face as they exited the terminal. She buttoned her gray winter coat, the one Steve gave her last year, and tied her red scarf around her neck. As they crossed the parking lot, she spotted Steve's trusty Chevy. When he landed a good paying job he'd be able to afford the Thunderbird he'd always wanted—if he still wanted it.

Once they reached his family's home, he whisked her inside and shouted, "We're here! Where is everyone?"

As Marta removed her coat and scarf, the double doors to the living room opened. She turned to see everyone she treasured standing there: Lynne, Mrs. B., Shorty, and James, as well as the little dancers: Tracy, Brenda, Carmen, and Lucy.

Marta gasped.

"Surprise!" A group shout erupted, followed by wild clapping.

Before she could react, Steve guided her toward his parents, standing to one side. "Mother, Father, you remember my special friend, Marta."

"Welcome, Marta," smiled his mother as she extended her hand to Marta. "We're glad to see you."

"Thank you for inviting me," Marta said.

Steve's father stood with his hands clasped in front of him and a smile on his face. "Welcome, Marta. I appreciate your helping Steve write about the ballet last year."

Marta felt her skin prickle as they shook hands. Last year she'd called him the grumpy guy in the glass office before she knew he was Steve's father as well as the editor of the paper. "Helping Steve was fun. He did all the work. I just filled in a few details."

The room hummed with expectation as Steve's parents greeted her then stepped aside. In the next instant tears and laughter filled the room. The little girls wrapped her in hugs and chatter, all trying to speak to her at once.

Lynne grabbed her next. "Finally," she laughed. "It's been so hard to not spill the beans. Welcome back!"

Marta hugged Lynne and saw Mrs. B. standing nearby, smiling. She reached out to her, inviting her to join in the hug. "Mrs. B., I'm so glad to see you. How are you?"

"I'm fine, dear. So glad you've come back. Bet you're finding our weather much colder than you remember."

"You're right. It's like stepping into the freezer lockers on Callow."

Shorty and James hung back, waiting for Marta to seek them out. When they pushed their hands forward, she grabbed them into hugs. Everyone laughed. "How are my two handymen doing?"

"Fine, fine," James said. "But it's awfully quiet without you."

"Not always," Shorty said. "When Lynne and those little dancers are in the basement, it feel like you're there too."

After the hugging and crying ended, Marta surveyed the living room. A massive Christmas tree filled one corner. Its lush ornaments and bubble lights gave the room a silken glow. Couches and chairs had been arranged to accommodate the crowd of people and focused on the tree. Once everyone was seated, hot beverages and mid-day sandwiches were served, followed by conversation ricocheting from one topic to another.

Lynne signaled to the little girls and led them from the room. When she returned she stood near the tree. "Ladies and gentlemen, the newest members of the ballet academy have a surprise for all of you. They'll perform their dance from the *Nutcracker*. It's the opening scene where children enter and dance around the Christmas tree. May I present Brenda, Tracy, Carmen, and Lucy."

The girls wore ball costumes as they danced and smiled at their audience, giving Marta's heart another wonderful surprise. Lynne had taught them well. Madame should be proud to include them in the new ballet academy.

After their curtsy and the clapping ended and the girls accepted compliments, a flurry of gift giving commenced, covering the plush carpet with knee-deep remains of Christmas paper. Marta had filled her luggage with loads of presents: a book of Swedish recipes for Mrs. B., colorful socks for James and Shorty, a blue sweater with seed beads on the collar for Lynne, and white silk fans with trailing gold tassels for the little girls. She'd tucked in books about the northwest for Steve's parents and passed around snapshots of the sets and costumes she'd made. For Steve she'd selected a gray and blue silk tie and a note: *Good for one briefcase of your choosing.*

Hours later, well after a sit-down dinner and more conversation, the guests headed out, promising Marta that she'd see them again before she left. Steve's parents said their good nights, leaving Marta and Steve alone to enjoy the Christmas tree.

Steve sat with his arm around Marta. "Were you surprised? I hope so because everyone was so excited to see you."

"This was a marvelous surprise!" Marta leaned into Steve and kissed his cheek. "Thank you for this and for understanding about earlier this month. I acted foolishly."

He tightened his arms around her. "I'm glad you're here now. We have a lot to talk about, but I want to save most of it for our time at the cabin. Your friends want to see you again, so Lynne and I have worked out a schedule." He handed her a paper from his sports coat pocket. "Ready? It's a work of journalistic genius."

Marta looked over the list and shook her head. "You've filled every waking minute."

Steve grinned. "Yes, and I'm your chauffeur. I've saved a couple of meals for you to get to know my parents, so we'll have dinner Tuesday and Thursday evenings." He studied Marta's face and continued. "We'll change anything else you want, but I'm keeping New Year's Eve and Day for us to talk."

৵

On Monday Marta slept in, then spent the afternoon with Lynne and the little girls at the boarding house. They danced and talked together followed by dinner with the boarders. Being back, sitting at her place at the table, made the intervening time shrink to feel like days instead of months since she'd lived here.

When she returned to Steve's family home, she begged off staying up and talking. After Steve kissed her good night, she closed the guest room door and stood looking out the window, savoring her return to the boarding house and the simple life she'd lived there before her injury. Could she build a calm, peaceful life with Steve? Could she find enough energy to become part of a couple? If she made a commitment to him, she'd need to find a way to keep a part of herself alive and not become lost in his world like she did last spring. So far on this trip he had organized everything. Did he also plan to organize her life if they became a couple?

Tuesday belonged to Lynne. Steve drove her to Lynne's apartment at Lake Elmo. "I'll pick you up at four o'clock so you'll have time to get ready for dinner with my parents." He kissed her and waved to Lynne as he got back into his car and drove away.

"Marta, Marta," laughed Lynne. "That man loves you. He organized everything for your visit, right down to asking me to bring the record so the little girls could dance for you."

Marta sighed and flopped down in one of Lynne's chairs. "I know. He's intense about things, especially since he saw me kiss Dennis. I don't know where we're headed. His future is unsettled; so is mine. If we resolve things, I'm afraid he'll ask me to become engaged again. I can't say yes. But I don't want him to give up on me, and I don't want to give him up either. I've had so many changes, and I'm just now feeling like I know who I am by myself. I don't want to lose my identity in his world."

Lynne played with a loose thread on her chair. "Give it time. I doubt you can have it both ways, Marta. Don't analyze everything. Try to go with the flow like I'm planning to do." Lynne laughed and sat down. "My aunt is considering moving back east next spring. I'm thinking I'll ask Mrs. B. if I can rent your old room if it's available while I figure out what I'm going to do."

Marta giggled. "Thinking about you and Carol sharing any space is too funny. Do you think you could share a bathroom without strangling her?"

"Maybe. Or perhaps she'll graduate and be gone before I need to move. I think the college should have a time limit on students like her who act like prima donnas but slog along at a snail's pace."

Marta studied Lynne's face. "You're planning to stay in Billings to dance, aren't you?"

Lynne shrugged. "I'm not sure. Madame Cosper is on my case ever since you left. She's ignored me for solos even though I'm stronger than many of the other dancers. I feel in my bones that she's written me off, and I'm not going to stay here and be ignored. She's never acknowledged that the little girls were capable of stepping in to dance in the *Nutcracker,* so maybe she's holding a grudge against me like she did with you. I'll be able to tell more once classes resume."

"Where will you dance if you leave?"

Lynne broke off the thread with a quick snap. "How should I know? She'll probably refuse to give me any letters of recommendation, so I may need to start over. Going back two years isn't too bad. At least I'm not fighting injuries like you are." Lynne grimaced. "Oh, sorry, Marta. I didn't mean anything, I…"

"It's okay. I know I'm losing my dance edge, but I'm not ready to give up yet."

Lynne popped up to her feet. "Good for you. Now, let's go shopping or do something before it snows."

Lynne and Marta ate lunch at the Bison Cafe to relive their old times before they wandered the shops of Billings for after Christmas sales. Both returned empty handed. Lynne didn't really need anything; Marta lacked spending money.

૭௦

Tuesday evening dinner with Steve and his parents challenged Marta to track several conversations: the upcoming Presidential election, the trouble in Venezuela, the opening of the new Air Force Academy in Colorado, and the NASA projects. By the time Steve walked her to the guest room door, she felt as drained as if she'd danced for hours.

"Well, what do you think about my parents?"

She smiled. "They're kind to let me stay here but are they always so intense?"

"Being in the newspaper world makes for lots of discussions about world issues." Steve kissed her nose. "But you held your own, especially when we talked about the arts." He encircled her in a loose hug as they leaned against the door to her room. "Tomorrow we have lots to talk about, so get a good night's sleep."

As Marta got ready for bed, she replayed tonight's conversation. It worried her. If she and Steve ended up together, would they engage in such intense conversations? Would she be expected to know about political unrest in Africa, the value of the franc, and the upcoming World's Fair in Seattle? Why didn't she know about the fair? It was an hour ferry's ride from where she lived. She needed to subscribe to the *Bremerton Sun* or a Seattle paper when she returned home.

The morning drive through the valley and into the mountains brought back impressions from February, the last time she'd traveled the road. This year less snow surrounded their drive. "It's been a dry holiday season," Steve said and smiled. "What snow we have is buried under dirt and sand on the sides of the road, but who knows? We could get snowed in."

Once they pulled into the driveway, Marta stood next to the car staring at the cabin railing and the drip line of the eaves. "When we visited last February, the snow covered everything. Now I can see where I landed when I fell through the railing. I was so frightened I'd die here alone in the dark during last New Year's weekend."

Steve stepped behind her and wrapped her in his arms. "I wish things had been different, that you'd called to tell me you and Lynne were coming up early. I should have been here for you. Maybe your career wouldn't have been ruined."

Marta turned around and leaned her head against Steve's chest. "Maybe. But something else might have happened, a different accident." She reached for his hand and pulled him toward the steps. "Let's head inside and start a fire."

The large open room comforted her seeing with the same tan leather couches and green overstuffed chairs facing the river rock fireplace. Blankets and quilts lay draped over the furniture ready for wrapping around chilly bodies. Marta looked at the game board shelf remembering their wild Valentine's evening game of Monopoly when Steve washed her hair to remove the stickiness from the spilled soda pop. He'd kissed her. That wonderful evening was soon overshadowed by the horrible nightmare. It still sent chills through her body. What a strange combination of events. That's when she first realized she loved Steve.

"Marta?"

"Hm-m?"

"You looked as if you moved a thousand miles away. Are you okay?"

"I'm fine. Just replaying our last trip. I enjoyed being here with you, getting away from being a captive in the boarding house. I hope I never need another cast." She walked to the wood storage bin and lifted the bin. "After we refill this and build a fire, I challenge you to a Monopoly rematch, if you're up for it."

"Sounds good." Steve flexed his arms as though preparing for a boxing match. "Expect another thrashing from Mr. Monopoly."

As it turned out, they never played Monopoly. Instead they spent hours wrapped in blankets seated close to the fireplace talking, cuddling, and taking turns feeding the fire. They tiptoed around a conversation of Steve's unexpected visit and her kissing Dennis.

"I'd like to move on, Marta, if you're sure the Dennis incident was a momentary lapse."

"It was. I've thought a lot about you since then," she said.

"And?"

Marta looked around the cabin, then back at Steve. "It feels so good to be here with you. I love the cabin and the quiet."

Steve tipped his head to one side to look at her face. "And me? Do you love me? I'll gladly take third place after the quiet."

Marta played with a curl of hair, kissed Steve's cheek, and laughed. "Hm-m-m. I put you higher than third place. Maybe second. Now, are we ever going to discuss your plans? I know you've been interviewing."

"I have a job offer in Sacramento. I'd do investigative reporting on migrant worker issues. It could be fine, but I'm hoping to find work covering state and national politics. I have two weeks to give them an answer." Steve turned to Marta and trailed his fingers down her cheek. "Would you consider moving to California? I'm sure they need dancers and dance instructors."

"I'm committed to help Lindsay until she returns from having her baby. That means staying in Bremerton until the end of summer or longer."

Steve nodded. "That could work. I haven't heard from Seattle or other papers I'm interviewing with, but I hope to know this spring. But you'd consider moving?"

She shrugged and slid her fingers along Steve's shoulder. "I might. It's hard to guess what may happen between now and then." Marta stopped moving her hand. If she wasn't careful in what she said, she'd slip into a corner or maybe a box and lose her chance to pursue her dance dreams, if her ankle recovered. "I'd consider lots of things once we both knew where we might end up."

At midnight Steve opened a bottle of champagne and served Marta's drink with an engagement ring resting in the bottom of her glass.

Marta stared at the glass. "What's...?"

Steve kissed her cheek and slid around to kiss her lips. "Happy New Year. I thought I'd try asking you again." He took her hand and led her to a couch and stared at her eyes as though expecting a reply before he asked his next question. "May I ask my burning question again? I don't want to lose you, and I don't think we should wait any longer."

Marta felt gears grinding in her head and a chill trace her spine even though sweat beaded on her upper lip. She shivered.

"Marta?"

She put her hand on his arm and smiled but shook her head. "I think we need to wait."

Steve looked stunned. He pushed himself to his feet and walked to the log bin where he grabbed a log for the fire and tossed it in. He stood with his back to Marta for several moments, then turned. "Why? What's your excuse *this* time?"

Marta pulled in her lips. She closed her eyes before she answered. "We need to wait until both of us have jobs, so we know where we're landing. I have my recovery to continue working on and...what's the rush?"

For a long moment the only sound in the cabin was the crackle of the fire. Steve stared at her. "I'm twenty-three and I'm ready to settle down. I don't want to lose you to some carpenter or a young lawyer. I don't want you to look around and decide you can do better than me."

The sadness she heard in Steve's voice ripped through her like an icy wind. If he'd gotten angry or shouted, the effect wouldn't have been so strong. Could she convince him once again to wait while she pieced the rest of her life back together?

When she started to speak, Steve slid his fingertips down her cheek, sliding them over to cover her lips. "Don't say anything more, please."

She closed her eyes and inhaled slowly before looking at Steve again.

"You might be right, Marta, but I love you and I want to have you in my life every day. A few minutes ago you said you loved me."

"I do, but Steve—"

"Sh-h. No buts. I know you think we need to wait, but what if I find my career in California and you find yours in Washington? How will we ever get together? Can't you marry me and be content taking care of me?"

"Take care of *you*? I can barely take care of myself, so how could I take care of you? If it weren't for the diet—" Her eyes widened.

Steve's head whipped up. He grabbed her wrists. "Wait. You're still taking those damn diet pills after what they did to Bartley?" He gave her arms a violent shake. "Marta? Tell me!"

Tears slid down her face. "I only use them when my life is too busy to rest or eat like these past weeks working on the Christmas shows. It's okay, Steve."

"No, it's not. Stop with the pills!" He walked away from her as she reached out to touch his face. He stopped and turned. "Do you have any pills with you tonight?"

She shrugged.

"Show me what's in your purse."

Marta's hands trembled as she rummaged through the pockets in her purse. She pulled out two pills. She watched as Steve's eyes trailed from the pills to her face and back to the pills. He shook his head, grabbed his coat, and disappeared out the door.

The silence in the cabin felt as heavy as the quilt she'd wrapped up in earlier that evening. She stared around the empty room. When she heard Steve's car start, she raced to the window in time to see him backing out of the driveway.

Marta watched the large sunburst clock on the river rock wall as the minutes passed as slow as hours. She sat by the fire, paced the room, looked out the window, and paced again. Had Steve gone for a drive, or had he driven home? Would he return for her or send Lynne to pick her up? If she'd chosen her words more carefully—

Two a.m. Three a.m. Marta saw lights trace the row of trees lining the driveway. A car door slammed. When the cabin door opened, Steve entered, his face somber.

"Where were you, Steve?"

"Do you care where I was? Really?"

"Of course I do."

He sat down in a nearby chair keeping his back to Marta. "I went to town to an all-night café to think." He stood and started pacing. "Sometimes you upset me so much I want to walk away and erase you from my life."

The comments felt like a slap to her face. She didn't know what to say or do, so she stood silent.

His pacing stopped several feet from Marta. "Even though I'd like to think I could walk away from you once and for all and never return, I can't. For some crazy reason I love you and want you to be with me."

"I love you too, Steve, but—"

"Then stopped taking those blasted pills."

Marta lowered her face and felt herself trembling. "I can try."

"No, Marta. Trying isn't good enough. I don't want you to end up like Bartley."

"I've never taken as many pills as she did. I only take a couple a day once in a while."

"Listen to yourself! You're rationalizing." He looked around the room as though searching for an answer. Marta watched and waited.

He shook his head. "I'll make you a deal. You stop taking pills, and I'll stop asking you to marry me."

Marta grabbed a chair back for support. "So you're giving up on me?"

"No. I'm asking you to stop because you need to stop. I'll quit hounding you until I have a permanent job and you've recovered. Deal, Marta?"

"I guess. I'm beginning to manage more than a few days at a time. When Lindsay needed me to take over the Christmas programs and the upcoming recital details, I tried to avoid the pills, but that responsibility put a lot of pressure on me."

"I get that, but you need to make a change. I'd hoped you'd do it for me, for us, but that didn't happen. Just do it for yourself." He checked his watch. "It's after three. When I came in it started snowing, so the temperature is dropping. I suggest you sleep on the couch by the fire. I'll be in the loft if you need anything."

Steve disappeared up the ladder without giving her a kiss or hug. She watched him step off the ladder and disappear into the bedroom. After she turned off the lamps, she stood at the window watching it snow. She touched the spider frost on the glass with her finger; their twist and turns resembled twists and turns in lives. She saw Bartley's life like the short finger of ice. The diet pills she had taken over several years destroyed her. Marta saw herself as a long trail of ice. Sure she'd taken pills, but only when she needed a boost of energy. That made a difference, didn't it?

At dawn, Marta watched Steve climb down the ladder. "Hi," she said.

"Hi." Steve's voice sounded mechanical. "Did you sleep?"

She closed the blanket she had draped over her shoulders. "Not much. How about you?"

Steve shrugged. "I think I slept, but not for very long." He stepped toward the kitchen, then stopped and turned to face Marta. "We should pack up and head back to town. How long do you need?"

"I'm ready now." Marta loosened the blanket she'd wrapped up in and folded it. "Can we stop along the way so I can call Lynne? Maybe I can stay with her until I fly out tomorrow."

Steve nodded but didn't look at Marta. "Sounds good."

Neither spoke during the drive down the mountains, making the trip long and sad. Should she have lied and taken the ring? Maybe the diet pills would have never become an issue if she had. Their relationship was rocky, but it always ended up sorting itself out. Would that pattern continue this time?

Marta phoned Lynne from each small town on their way back to Billings. No answer. Fidgets circled inside her; the longer they drove, the more her options shrank.

After a final call to Lynne from a phone booth in Laurel, Marta shook her head as she returned to the car.

"Stay at my parents' house. They're gone for the day. I'll make up an excuse for you if you want."

Marta shook her head. "Just drive me there to pick up my clothes, then drop me off at the Rim View Inn. I can get myself to the airport in the morning."

"That's not necessary, Marta. Stay at my parents."

Tears puddled in her eyes. "No. Please, just do this one simple thing for me."

An hour later Marta stood in one of the motel's rooms, gazing at a thin orange bedcover, same as when she'd first arrived in Billings. Only the view was different. This room overlooked the parking area.

She sat down on the bed and stared at the wall, seeing and feeling nothing beyond the draft of cool air slipping under the door. She pulled the bedspread around her shoulders and paced the small area. *Step, step, step, turn. Step, step, step, turn.*

She opened the curtain. Snow filtered down, caught a breeze, and drifted upward. She closed the curtain and returned to pacing: *step, step, step, turn.*

Darkness crept in around the edges of the curtain. When she looked out, the drifting flakes from earlier in the day swirled like mini tornadoes and covered the cars parked in the lot, making them appear like rumpled blankets under a white coverlet.

The bar and restaurant she'd remembered from last year were gone, replaced by a near-vacant room with vending machines offering potato chips, candy bars, and pretzels. Marta opened her purse. Two dollars and two bus tokens; she'd need to save them to get all the way home. She'd wait for the breakfast on the flight home in the morning.

Marta dialed Operator and placed a collect call home. No answer. She tried Lynne; still no answer, so she returned to her room and paced. *Step, step, step, turn.*

When she tired of pacing, she looked out the window one more time, then climbed under the bedcovers. The trip that began with happiness and reunions shifted to confrontations and hurt feelings. Perhaps it was just as well she'd not seen Madame Cosper. Why open herself up to any further confrontations? She closed her eyes, waiting for sleep to arrive.

Darkness. Coldness. A strange sensation shivered through her body. She dreamed she stood on The Rims as she'd done in dreams so many times before. Suddenly a hand reached out and pushed her. The loose gravel beneath her feet propelled her forward. Falling, falling, spiraling like a helicopter, she twisted toward the rock-strewn base. Crash!

She fell off the bed, grazing her head against the sharp corner of the bedside table. A trickle of blood stained her hand. She allowed her tears to flow, hoping they'd stop the deep ache tearing at her heart. 1959 was not beginning as she'd hoped.

૭

Evening had settled in by the time Marta landed at Sea-Tac airport, caught a bus into Seattle, and took the ferry back to Bremerton. She rode the nearly empty city bus to Lafayette, then walked along the narrow, twisting road to Corbett Drive, feeling the weight of her suitcase pull through her arms while the weight of her conversation pulled at the rest of her body.

Her little house sat in darkness as though the trees wanted to protect her. Inside the house a dampness swept through every room, matching the icy coolness of her mood. She dumped her suitcase inside the door, took off her coat and crawled under the bed covers. She expected to drop into an exhausted sleep, but the way she'd left things with Steve kept her awake much of the night. She couldn't erase the expression on his face when he challenged her about the diet pills and the way he turned away and left her standing in the cabin. Had she broken their relationship beyond repair over a couple of linty pills?

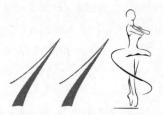

B ang, bang, bang.

"Marta? Honey? Are you there?"

Marta woke with a start. Morning light filtered in around the edge of her bedroom shade. She threw back her bed covers and hurried to the front door. When she saw her mom's anxious face, she realized she'd forgotten to call her.

"Hi, Mom. Sorry I didn't call you from the terminal. It was so late I didn't want to wake you."

Her mom frowned. "Are you okay? You look exhausted."

"I am. Guess I'm not a good traveler." Marta ruffled her hair and turned toward her bathroom. "Give me five minutes."

"How was everyone? I hope you got to see Lynne and the others."

Marta emerged carrying her dance tote. "I did. They're all fine. Steve's family had a party for me and invited the boarding house renters, plus Lynne and the little girls."

"What a wonderful surprise! And how was Steve? Excited to have finished school?"

"Yes. Now he's job hunting." Marta grabbed her purse. "Let's go. I'm sorry to keep you waiting." She held the door for her mom, then stopped to lock it.

In the car Marta yawned and closed her eyes. "I'm still tired. Have you spoken to Lindsay since Christmas?"

"No." Her mom tapped her fingers on the steering wheel as she drove along Fifteenth and turned onto Callow. Marta felt her mom scrutinizing her. "Marta, is there some reason you've not mentioned Steve?"

She nodded and looked away. "Sorta. We're taking a break. I really don't want to talk about it right now."

For the rest of the drive to the dance studio, neither spoke. As they entered, Marta headed upstairs rather than saying anything else to her mom. Lindsay wouldn't be in until afternoon, so that gave Marta time to compose herself to face her first challenge, the eight women in the exercise class due to walk in any minute.

She stood at the *barre* doing *pliés* as the women chattered their way up the stairs. Their expected energy presented a challenge today. Best for her to paste on a performance smile until she'd managed her changing situation with Steve.

"Marta! How was your holiday?" asked Tricia.

"Great," Marta said, smiling. "How about all of you?"

The consensus was everyone had great family times, the kids liked their gifts, and the dances at the country club were a success. "You should have seen our husbands dancing," Trixie said. "Everyone wanted to know where they took lessons. We did as you requested, saying it was a special holiday offering from the dance studio."

"Lot of good that did," Lily Rose said. "Zandora Marcus hovered nearby, and when she heard us talking ballroom, she quickly hinted that her friend's Arthur Murray studio offers ballroom dance lessons year round. She even passed out business cards for her friend."

"That sounds like what I'd expect." Marta winced at the mention of her ballroom classes in front of the four women who'd not been included. Too late to do anything about that now. She'd need to do something special for them soon to keep things even among the women. For now she put on the *barre* music. "Let's get started."

After a two-week break in classes, the women moved as stiffly as Marta felt. Their center work lacked energy, and their dancing to Buddy Holly's "That'll Be the Day" didn't have its usual pizzazz. Thank heavens their need to concentrate helped Marta hide her fuzzy focus.

"Looks like we're all a bit tired today." Marta removed the record from the turntable and smiled. "Rest up. Dance around the house. See you Wednesday."

As the women grabbed their towels and bags and exited, Lily Rose lingered. "Sorry. We forgot the other exercise class women and their husbands weren't included in our little dance lessons. Let us make it up to them and you. At our next exercise class, I'll suggest all nine of us go as a group to the country club to lunch. We want to hear all about your visit with your boyfriend."

Marta clenched her jaw to hold back the tears that threatened. "Thanks for noticing and offering, but I've got several projects due for the dance studio. Could we do it another week?"

Lily Rose tipped her head and watched Marta's face. "Sure. Whatever works for you. See you tomorrow when I bring Olivia to class." She grabbed her exercise bag and left.

A sigh escaped Marta's lips. She walked to the counter and unwrapped the 1959 calendar from *Capezio*, the dance shoe and clothing company. The dancers in the photo atop the calendar wore long white *Swan Lake* gowns with white feather headdresses cascading down the sides of their faces. Their white *pointe* shoes drew her eye to the advertisement. It read *Capezio: perfect fit every time.*

Marta exhaled. Once she believed in perfect, but no longer. Nothing perfect about her life. The issues with Steve weighed on her, pushing aside any thought of returning to dance or working for perfection. She knew Lily Rose saw something wasn't right, but Marta didn't want to talk about it. By next week all might be back to normal, but she doubted that. At least she'd attempt to pull her life back into her usual routine and delay talking with the Pill Hill ladies even longer.

In the early afternoon Marta went downstairs to speak with Lindsay, who sat in her office looking through dance costume catalogs. Marta knocked on her open door.

"Hi, Marta. Welcome back. Come in and clear off a chair."

Marta moved the stack of catalogs to the floor and sat, waiting for Lindsay to start the conversation.

"I am so sorry about the Christmas programs. I really thought I had the flu. Guess it's a common mistake for first pregnancies. But now you know what it takes to manage a dance studio. When you have your own studio someday, you'll be somewhat prepared."

Marta looked down at her hands and swallowed hard. "Lindsay, I'm not certain that's what I want."

"I know." Lindsay put her hand on Marta's. "Selfishly, I hate the thought that you might go back to performing, but you know I support you. It's just that you are such a thoughtful teacher. Paige and Rosie are making great strides with your help."

"Thanks for letting me work with them. I'm enjoying myself, except when Zandora sneaks up the stairs and thinks I don't see her."

"I can speak to her if you'd like."

Marta shook her head. "It's fine. I ignore her."

Lindsay walked over and closed her office door. "Strange that you mentioned her. I don't want her to know I'm trying to buy this building. I've mentioned this to your mom, so I want us to be careful where we talk about anything related to my plans."

"Got it." Marta's enthusiasm came from her sincere interest in the studio. "This is such a great location. I'm excited for you."

"It is. Adam thinks Bremerton is a good place to settle down, and if we buy the building, we'll have a permanent home for the dance studio. I'm tired of the owner raising our rent every six months. That's also news I don't want Zandora knowing since I've heard she wants this space for her friend's ballroom studio. I'm certain she'd try to interfere in our plans. Has she said anything to you about pulling Rosalia from classes?"

"No. She doesn't often speak to me, since I'm that has-been dancer."

"You're anything but a has-been, Marta, and you know it. Anyway, the carpenter will start adding storage shelves upstairs and finishing the small apartment area after hours. I'm telling everyone it's being done by the owner, which might be true very soon."

Minutes later, Marta started her practice session, which usually erased any unresolved issues. But thinking about Zandora's attitude toward her hung like a heavy cloud over her dancing. Could she have done anything to reverse Zandora's opinion? Probably not. She could work harder to befriend her, ignore the digs, and keep a smile ready when that was the last thing she wanted to share.

Marta returned home and brought in the mail. She read the reminder note about having a phone installed next week and carried a postcard from Lynne inside to read with her afternoon cup of tea. She'd never caught up to her during the rest of her visit to Billings, so she expected Lynne would be mad or at least irritated by Marta's not saying good bye.

Marta,

My Dad had a heart attack so I made a quick trip home on New Year's Eve. He'll be fine if he takes it easy. I know your days with Steve were all lovey dovey. Call me with the latest scoop on you two, if you ever install a phone!

Lynne

Marta dropped everything and rushed to her mom's house to call Lynne. No answer. Of course she wasn't there. She'd be at practice at the ballet company. She wished there was a way to leave her a message, but there wasn't, so she'd need to wait until evening and try again.

At home she put the postcard in her bedside table and returned to her living room to sit and rock. When she closed her eyes, she replayed Steve's face as she turned down his proposal. Add to that his reaction when he found out she continued to take diet pills. Would he ever forgive her for her decisions? Did he mean he'd wait only if she gave up the pills? Could she give up the pills? Of course. Did she want to give them up was a bigger question. They provided an easy solution to her stress. Seeing Steve's reaction, she knew she needed to stop taking them if she wanted him to continue to be in her life.

A memory from kindergarten crowded into her thinking. She'd been watching a man ride his horse past the house on Rhododendron. In five minutes she needed to leave for school, but the ties on her dress hung loose, waiting to be tied.

Her mom had said, "Hold still a minute. Let me tie these into a bow."

When she'd pulled away to watch the man on the horse, she'd ripped one tie from the dress. By the time she'd changed clothes, her mom had to walk her to school to explain to the principal why she was late. For the next few days, Marta put up a wall of silence with her mom and wouldn't apologize even though she knew she was wrong to disobey her. Did the bow incident show resolve or her stubbornness?

Was this incident with Steve like that? Had she erected another wall of silence? Or had he? Was she stubborn, or did she show resolve? Had she hurt his feelings and now *she* needed to apologize? It didn't feel like she should; after all, she had the right to speak up, didn't she? But what if he was her true love like they talk about in books? What if no one ever wanted her? Marta rocked and rocked, waiting for answers. None arrived.

After dinner Marta returned to her mom's and called Lynne again. The phone rang and rang. A distracted Lynne answered.

"Hey, it's Marta. I'm sorry to hear about your dad. How's he feeling?"

"He's better, thanks for asking," Lynne said. "He needs to rest, but they say he'll have a full recovery if he follows orders. I was afraid we'd lose him."

"I understand how that feels," Marta said. "I was seven when my dad died. That's probably different, but I'm glad he's going to be okay."

"Me too." Lynne cleared her throat. "So, tell me about you and Steve. Did you have a great time together in the mountains?"

Marta closed her eyes and inhaled as if those actions would change what she was about to say. "No. He offered me a ring. I refused. He asked about diet pills and got furious when he discovered I still used them sometimes. He—"

"Marta? I thought you stopped using them!"

"Not yet, but I've thrown my last few pills away. I'm trying to handle my stress without them." She paused. "It's harder than I thought."

Lynne sighed. "You can do it. Just stop. Get more sleep, eat better food. Those pills will ruin your life if you don't ditch them."

"I know, but Lynne, I feel so listless without them. And now that Steve and I are taking a break, I—"

"Marta! Listen to me. Stop...taking...them. Promise me!"

"I promise. Maybe when I—"

Lynne tapped on the phone, startling Marta. "No maybe. Just stop! Look. I need to go. My aunt is having guests and I promised to help her. Call me whenever. I'm glad you've finally gotten a phone so I can call you. What's your number?"

"It's being installed soon. I'll call you. I miss you, Lynne."

ର

January rains blanketed the days; chilly mists arose during the nights. Marta had quit the community theatre but stopped in one last time to return sewing materials.

"I'm sorry to lose you," Hal said. "Our door is always open if you find you have time you want to fill."

"Thanks," she said. "I enjoyed helping out, but my dance classes at the studio are multiplying like bunnies. I'll need to help out even more since Lindsay expects her first child this spring."

The next day the phone company arrived and installed her phone, but now she really didn't need it. She'd simplified her life to teaching dance classes, period. No dating, no calls from Hal or Dennis. The new void allowed sadness, excitement, and disappointment to roost inside her. The sadness increased because she'd not be hearing from Steve. Of course, she could contact him, but she didn't and wouldn't for now, so what did she expect? What could she say to soften their New Year's confrontation?

Excitement blossomed as Lindsay gave her more young student classes with permission to create dances whenever she wanted. She listened to recordings, played tapes, and read instructor magazines, looking for the perfect dance for each class. In two or three weeks she'd begin mock auditions for Paige and Rosalia. Not a great Valentine gift for them, but practicing for auditions provided valuable lessons, one she wished she'd had. Recently Zandora had stepped back, letting Marta share her expertise from her string of auditions last year, so maybe the Zandora storm had passed.

Disappointment arose when she did her private practicing. Much as she tried, her ankle consistently failed to support her. One *relevé* was fine, two or ten okay, but more than ten caused strains and cramping, stopping her instantly. After the past eight months of daily exercising and practicing, she needed to face reality: professional ballet company doors were closing to her. She'd give herself two more months, then decide her next step. Would Steve step back into her life by then? She didn't know, but she did care.

Two weeks later at the dance studio on another rainy January afternoon, Marta started to pack up to head home. Lindsay called her into the office. "Do you want a full time job?"

"You're buying the building?"

"Yep. We signed the papers. I have so many plans I'd do cartwheels if I wasn't pregnant. Finally we'll be able to upgrade everything! I'll ask the carpenter to start opening up the two small rooms upstairs to create a large walk-in storage room, add a visitor seating area in the west end, and rough-in a small office area for you next to the apartment, which we'll keep intact. With the upstairs construction closing off your space, we'll be a bit crowded for a while. Elle will manage the temporary schedule changes."

The news seeped out, spreading through the dance classes like a wild fire. Every class bubbled with energy. Lindsay sent out information about adding more ballet classes and providing tap and baton classes next fall. Lindsay hinted that they'd consider adding modern jazz and gymnastics if experienced instructors could be found and hired.

This change, this potential influx of classes, nudged Marta to view her future in a new light. Maybe teaching *could* fill her need to dance. After all, she'd still dance when she demonstrated choreography to others. Was that enough to keep the music flowing through her? She looked at herself in the wall mirror as if expecting an answer to suddenly appear when a bigger, more personal question jumped out. Could she or would she give up everything to be with Steve, if he still wanted her in his life? She needed more time to consider her answer to that question.

After her last class that week, Marta dashed to the nearest drugstore on Callow to pick up personal items as her mom finished up her day's tasks. The storefront window display stopped her. A sea of red hearts and naked cupids floated above heart-shaped boxes of chocolate. A large scrolled banner read: "Valentine's Day is February 14. Find Everything for your Special Someone."

Special someone. She'd not heard from Steve since their New Year's debacle. Lynne didn't call much; she appeared to be focused on her dad's recovery and her career. Didn't mention wacky boyfriend stories anymore either.

Marta bought a funny Valentine's card for Lynne and one for the little girls, then hurried to pick up necessities. As she walked to the counter to pay, she passed the aisle with the diet pills and stopped.

*M*arta stared at the pills, debating. She'd avoided taking diet pills over the past weeks, but with the studio's final remodel and extra classes stirring up her life, she missed the jolt of energy the pills provided. Nothing worked as well as the pills to mask the confusion that threatened to disrupt her thinking.

Her hand hovered over the selection of pills before she picked up two packs of Slim-Eze Diet Tablets and walked to the counter to pay. Next month would be a better time to permanently quit.

Upgrading the studio included hours of shifting boxes of costumes and morning cleanup from the carpenter's nightly work. Today before the young kinder students arrived, Marta swept construction debris into a dustpan. It wouldn't be long now until she'd have a permanent space. Beginning next month she'd have daily classes between nine and twelve, then afternoon classes from four until six, followed by Paige and Rosalia from seven to nine. This fragmented day, typical for most dance studios, left her pockets of free hours. She'd bring her mom's sewing machine down and use the little apartment to work on costumes as well as clothes for private clients as time allowed.

Clomp, clomp, clomp. She smiled; the young dancers were arriving. Marta hurried to greet the boys and girls as they arrived for kinder class. Each child, except Betty, raced to sit for their opening circle. Betty arrived late most days. But if Marta didn't begin class immediately; she'd run the risk of losing control of the session. It had almost happened once when the record player quit working. She'd discovered that little kids easily take over a space if left to their own devices.

Betty's grandmother climbed the steps, shooing the cute little girl ahead of her. "Sorry, miss. Betty couldn't find her ballet slippers. We had to go to the high school and get them from Sam's car. He says you've met and he apologizes for the shoe mix-up."

"Tell him it happens to all of us. Try your best to get here on time."

Betty ran to her place and sat down. Marta put on their music and sat with them to begin their stretching routine. She might mention the evening class to Mr. Faris as a better fit for Betty. Plus, it would give him the chance to watch her dance during parent visitation week.

February 12th was a Thursday and President Lincoln's birthday, a holiday on the calendar, but just another day at the dance studio. Today, like every Tuesday and Thursday, the chatty kinder classes brightened her mood. She enjoyed watching them twirl around and try to hop and skip to the music. In a couple of months they'd know their right foot from their left and their cute awkwardness would vanish. She'd continue encouraging their love of music and dancing. After all, who didn't love nursery songs with funny words to sing and movements to dance?

Today as the little dancers met their parents at the back of the room, they huddled around Lily Rose. Suddenly they rushed forward, each carrying a white rose, curtsied and handed their roses to Marta.

Olivia hopped and jumped around Marta as she handed her flower. "These are for you."

"It's for Balentime's Day," Betty said. "Olivia's mom said you are our balentime."

"Oh! What a beautiful surprise." Marta curtsied. "Thank you for the lovely roses. Each of you are my valentine too. Let's show your parents and grandmother our favorite dance. Make your circle."

Marta placed the roses in a vase filled with water that mysteriously appeared on the counter. When she saw the children were ready, she put on the "Muffin Man" music and led them through their hand and body motions to their final bow.

The adults clapped and clapped, then whisked their children out of their dance shoes and into their coats. Marta smiled and listened as they chattered and clomped down the stairs. She turned off the music but continued to hum the tune.

The lovely surprise had Lily Rose's touch written all over it. She'd need to thank her and schedule the lunch with the country club ladies now that she'd reconciled herself to life without Steve. These past weeks she'd found her balance, pushing thoughts of Steve aside until she returned to her cozy Corbett Drive nest to enjoy her solitude.

Dennis called her Thursday evening, inviting her to a non-Valentine's party on Saturday. "It's a last minute party. Just a bunch of friends having a game night. You like games, don't you?"

"How did you get my number?"

"Alice gave it to me. I told her it was an emergency, so she asked her dad. Well, do you want to come to the party or not?"

Why did Alice give Dennis her home number? Marta held her breath to calm herself and finished the phone call. "I've made plans," she said. "I appreciate being invited, but I'd like you to stop calling me."

After a long pause, Dennis replied. "Got it." He hung up before she could say anything more.

She closed her eyes and sighed as she hung up the phone. She didn't tell him her plans were sitting and rocking in her living room with a cup of tea and a quilt tossed over her legs. Or that there was no way she wanted to be in the same city, let alone the same room, with him. Hopefully Alice would wise up and dump him very soon.

On Saturday evening after a quick dinner and hot shower, Marta slipped on her chenille robe and set the teakettle on the stove. She grabbed two chocolate chip cookies and an apple and stood waiting for the water to boil when someone knocked on her front door. A glance at the clock told her it was 7:30. She peeked through the front drapes and recognized her mom.

"Marta? Are you home?"

Marta unlocked and opened the door. "Hi. I thought you were on your way to Kalaloch for the long weekend."

"We were, but Robert got called in for some emergency. I was on my way home from the studio and thought I'd see if you might want to go to the coast with me. We could drive down tomorrow, wander the beaches, and come back late Monday. Since classes are cancelled for the building inspector's walk-through, there's no pressure to hurry back. What do you say?"

"I say it's just what we need. I haven't had a weekend with you for a long, long time."

The next morning they drove through Aberdeen and Hoquiam before turning north to Kalaloch Lodge. After they checked into their cabin, they bundled up and walked to the overlook. Wild, smoky gray mustang waves crashed against the shoreline, making conversation difficult.

"I love this beach," Marta shouted. "Let's head down."

The wind blew against their bodies as they navigated the higgledy-piggledy trail cut through the wall of driftwood that lay pushed against the hill like a giant's discarded matchsticks. They crossed the soft taupe sand, their rubber booted feet sinking out of sight.

Once they reached the open beach, the wind buffeted them again. They leaned into it and walked with their chins buried in their coat collars. The ground shook with each wave that crashed ashore.

The Kalaloch Lodge Dining Room provided a break from incoming sheets of rain and blustery wind. They sat at a small table overlooking the ocean, finishing hot drinks while watching high tide drift in to fill the estuary and merge salt water with the fresh water of Kalaloch Creek.

"This was a great idea, Mom. I'm glad we had this chance to come down. I've missed the ocean more than I imagined. It feels good to spend time on the beach and have you all to myself."

Her mom inhaled deeply and poured the last of the tea into their cups. "I'm glad we came. It's been too many years since you and I stayed here. Do you remember the time we waded into the surf looking for clams?"

Marta laughed and placed her hands over her mom's. "I do. The water was so cold it took hours to get over the shivers. Dad made that beach fire for us and you brought down hot dogs for us to cook, but we couldn't find any sturdy sticks, so we ate them raw."

Her mom stretched and stood to put on her coat. "Let's unpack and get out the cards. You need to learn to play Canasta."

Outside, the ocean's roar resonated through Marta's body. The thunder of the waves vibrated as if she stood beside a track when a train passed. She helped carry in supplies and stopped to look around the cabin. Nothing had changed over the years. Two beds in one corner, two chairs, the stinky oil stove, the tiny bathroom, a basic kitchen, and her favorite spot, the kitchen nook.

After they finished dinner, Marta sat in the kitchen nook and watched the lighthouse beacon on Destruction Island cut through the fog as dusk turned to night.

Her mom sat down across from her and reached to cover Marta's hands with her own. "We haven't had time alone together for so long. I'm almost glad Robert couldn't come."

"Me too." Marta felt the warmth of her mother's touch and smiled. "It's hard to believe the last time we came down with dad was over eleven years ago. Do you think of dad often?"

"Of course I do, honey. He's an important part of my life just like Steve is for…. Do you think you and Steve will get back together?"

Marta slid her hands free, stood, and paced the cabin. "I have no idea. I feel more settled now that I'm teaching dancing, but I still don't know what I want to do with my life. Steve needs to find a job, but he hasn't yet, as far as I know. He expects me to drop everything and be ready to go wherever he lands, without any thought of what I want or need. It's not fair to expect me to give up my dreams, is it?"

"No. You need to decide your own future. I know dancing is important to you and you've experienced a huge setback; you need to figure out what you want and need to live a happy life. If Steve's important to you, if you love him and want to be with him, you may need to compromise."

Marta played with a strand of hair as she spoke. "Doesn't *he* need to compromise as well?"

"Of course. Compromise means everyone involved makes a change. Maybe he has. Wasn't your last conversation around New Year's? Maybe he's come to realize that you need to figure out your next step. Have you called him lately?"

Marta curled hands into fists as she paced. "No, and he hasn't tried to contact me."

"A relationship is made up of two people. Both of you need to make an effort. Robert and I spend time getting caught up on changes in our lives most every time we're together. We're separate people, but we love each other, so we work and listen to each other. It was like that with your dad too."

Marta shrugged and sat down. "I don't know what I want to do, so how can I call him? I don't know what to say."

"Yes, you *do* know what to say. Last year you had the courage and drive to leave home and move to Billings to join the ballet company. Now you need to use that same courage to share how you feel."

"It's hard for me to share my feelings."

"I know, honey, but he can't read your mind. If you love him, you need to talk with him, ask what he thinks and help him understand your needs."

Marta sat down on her twin bed and closed her eyes. "I know I'm not ready to give up my dream to dance again. I need to test my ankle and make that decision very soon. I also know I miss Steve, but I'm not ready to get engaged or married. But I think he is ready and wants to settle down once he lands a job. Also, I worry that if we get married, his goals and dreams will overpower mine and I'll disappear." Tears filled her eyes. "I don't want to disappear."

"Marta, honey." Her mom rushed to sit beside her and hug her. "You won't disappear. You're a strong young woman. You've proven that over and over."

"I'm not strong, Mom. I'm...I still take diet pills sometimes."

Marta felt her mom's arms tighten around her. "Oh, Marta. No. Why?"

"They help me when I'm stressed or exhausted. That's what Steve and I fought at New Year's. Well, that plus he asked me to get engaged again."

Her mom released her grasp and sat back. She wiped her own tears away. "That explains a lot. Why didn't you tell me before?"

Marta shrugged. "I was too embarrassed. I hate disappointing you. And Steve. So you see, I'm not strong, and I don't make good decisions."

"Stop talking nonsense," her mom said as she reached to pat Marta's hands. "You can make any changes you truly want. I'm hoping you'll start by getting rid of those damn pills."

"Me too. I admit I've taken a couple from one pack and thought a lot about taking more, but I haven't taken any this past week." Marta reached for her purse and rummaged through it. "I have been meaning to toss them out," she said as she pulled out her stash of Slim-Eze and handed it to her mom.

Her mom pushed them away. "Don't hand them to me, honey. You need to take care of this yourself. I'll do whatever it takes to help you, but those pills are your responsibility."

Marta looked at the pills. Should she keep them as a reminder of her bad decision, or toss them to get them out of her sight? She walked to the bathroom and flushed them away.

"Do you feel better now?" her mom said as Marta returned to the main room of the cabin.

Marta shrugged. "I don't feel *better*, but I do feel relieved to tell you about them, and to toss them out. If I get all crazy and exhausted, may I come talk with you?"

Her mom smiled. "Any time. You do realize that all of us have stressful moments. It's part of life. You need to find ways to handle stress that won't cause you any harm."

"What do you do, Mom?"

"I sew, play cards, and share my concerns with Robert. He's a great listener."

Marta took a deck of playing cards from their travel box and moved to sit in the kitchen nook. She shuffled the cards with a quick riffle and looked up. "So, how *do* you play Canasta?"

They played cards and talked until both began yawning. Then they climbed under their twin bed covers, spread their sleeping bags over the top, and lay listening to the wind drive the rain, splashing it against the windows and under the door.

In the morning they drove to Trail Four. The rain passed, so they took the forest path to the shore and stood looking at the stretch of beach below the log bridge.

"This is my favorite beach in the whole world," Marta said. "I can't believe any beach is this unique or beautiful."

Her mom stood next to her. "It might be, but you have lots of years ahead of you to explore the world."

That was true; she did have time to visit other beaches once she knew the direction she wanted her life to move. For now, she was content to step from the bridge and scramble down the outcropping of rocks.

Tiny black pebbles covered the upper beach where a hillside spring trickled into the ocean. Incoming waves crashed, then disappeared into the beach as though dropping through a sieve. A sluicing sound announced each wave's disappearance. A quiet moment followed, then the next incoming wave repeated the sluicing.

They walked north toward the curve of the beach, then turned back when rain clouds threatened. Back at the top of the trail they sat with their feet outside the car, stomping off the sand and pebbles their boots collected during the walk, before the drive back to the cabin and another evening of cards and conversation.

Monday afternoon they returned to Bremerton. Marta waved and smiled as her mother drove out of the driveway on Corbett. Having the time alone with her made this a perfect Valentine's weekend. They'd needed time since their last togetherness happened in Billings while Marta was recovering from her injury. The stress she felt at being in leg cast after leg cast didn't allow them to share quality time, at least from

Marta's point of view. Thank heavens that event in her life ended almost a year ago.

The remodel moved closer to completion every day. By next week the storage shelves and the upstairs bathroom would be finished. After a final inspection by the bank, the studio would belong to Lindsay and Lieutenant Commander Adam Holland. They'd requested a loan for the entire building including the warped stairs and the weeping windows. Amid a difficult pregnancy, this realization of their dream excited everyone.

The celebration promised to be remembered for years. Students, their families, and community guests were invited to the party scheduled for three on Sunday afternoon, March 8th. The studio rooms looked festive. Marta and her mom worked into the night on Saturday hanging a rainbow assortment of balloons and streamers on doorways, around windows, and on the walls.

Music hosted by the local radio station greeted every visitor and dancer's family as they entered. The A&P donated cookies and napkins. Kitsap Sporting Goods printed a "reserved parking" sign for Lindsay, and Callow Drug brought a gift basket of aspirin, Bandaids, and Ace bandages. McGavin's bakery sent a gigantic "Welcome Dancers" cake decorated with black musical notes and pink *pointe* shoes. They also sent along fliers for free cookies to dancers who stopped in during March while wearing their dance costume or lesson attire. A dozen other local businesses sent cards, flowers, and promotional handouts to welcome Lindsay as the newest Callow building owner.

Hour after hour the building vibrated with music and activity. Dance studio students performed, then rejoined their families to explore the normally off-limits nooks and crannies. Upstairs, Marta supervised dance exploration by the guests. She invited everyone to take turns dancing with scarves and ribbons and laughed as they circled, moving to classical waltzes and current hits. One parent took 8mm home movies, promising to share them with the studio after they edited their film.

When the event ended at 7:30, the studio enrollment had increased by a dozen new families, and the one hundred dance studio brochures had been eagerly snatched up by prospective dancers. After a quick clean-up, Lindsay, Adam, Robert, Elle, and Marta turned off the studio lights and sat in the newly de-cluttered office with their shoes off.

"Quite a party," Lindsay said as she propped her feet up on an empty chair. "I'm amazed at the turnout. Thanks to all of you for making this evening possible. I'm so sick of bed rest. Coming here tonight gave me a wonderful chance to see everyone and meet new people."

"I knew Lindsay worked hard," Adam, her husband, said, "but this is amazing. I'm glad we're staying here to raise our family." He rubbed Lindsay's bulging front side. "Not long now."

Lindsay struggled to stand. "I'm counting the days. I'm grateful to Elle and Marta for keeping things running smoothly since Thanksgiving. All the painting and working around the remodel, my being gone." Lindsay rubbed her eyes, blinked, and sniffed. "Thank you. This was wonderful; you're both wonderful."

"Bremerton needs this studio," Marta's mom said and hugged Lindsay. "Considering the trouble getting loans these days, this is a miracle."

"I'm happy you two are staying around. That's some of the best news I've heard all week. Now, if you ever want to buy into the studio, I'd gladly share the headaches with you."

Everyone laughed.

Marta's mom shook her head. "There's no way we'd ever pull off a loan. Who'd loan to a widow and a nineteen-year-old dancer?"

Robert waved his hand. "Hold on, Elle. Remember, you're about to become Mrs. Marsden so we'll be sharing our resources. Besides, who wouldn't help a beautiful woman and her lovely dancer daughter?"

"Have you set the date?" Marta asked.

Her mom blushed. "We set it this afternoon. I guess he knew I'd be too distracted to argue. You're all invited to join us on July twelfth. It's the second anniversary of when we first met."

Marta leaped up and hugged her mom. "This is great news! I'm happy for you, Mom."

The rest of the group shared their congratulations as well.

Adam moved to take Lindsay's arm. "We need to get you home, hon. When I saw the doctor here tonight, he reminded me that you needed to get home, put up your feet, and give you and that baby a rest."

While Marta and her mom stayed in the office to talk, Robert excused himself to do a quick double check of the clean up and to take out the trash.

"Robert is a great guy," Marta said. "I'm glad you've set a date."

"Me too. We'll keep it simple. July in his yard will be the perfect setting. He'll have flowers in bloom that are better than any florist's."

"What will you do with our house, Mom?"

"I'd like you to have it, if you want. It takes a lot of work with the garden and lawns and fruit trees, but if you want to move back after the wedding, I'd be happy to arrange it." Her mom picked up her purse. "Think about it. My loan is almost paid off, so you'd pay about the same as the Corbett house each month, plus utilities and taxes. If you don't want it, we'll probably rent it out rather than sell it. I'm sentimental about keeping it as long as I can."

Marta knew she needed a plan. What did she want if she planned to stay in Bremerton? What about Steve and his plans? Marta rotated her shoulders to loosen their tightness and yawned. "I'm tired. Let's head out. We're about to become so busy we may never sit down again."

Marta and her mom closed the classrooms and headed home. Minutes later, Marta sat in her rocking chair reliving the event. Working with the amazing families and dancers might change her mind about her goal. Teaching others allowed her to share her love of music, encouraging her to seek additional ways to enhance the studio. She'd stay, for now, until both her future as a dancer and her decision about where her heart belonged settled into place. Good thing no one asked her where that place might take root. She had no idea.

Marta called Lindsay two days later to begin planning their spring schedule. Her mom listened in on the extension.

"How are you feeling today?" Marta asked.

Lindsay sighed. "Ready for this baby to be born before my due date. So distract me. Let's nail down the details for our scheduled performances. Just in case you need to be reminded, I'll be at the recital even if I have to arrive in a wheelchair."

They started their discussion with the most immediate performances and the Armed Forces Day parade. Providing year-long opportunities for the students to dance served two purposes: entertaining at social events and the local hospitals, but also practicing their dances and routines before recital season.

"I have most events handled," Lindsay said with a sigh. "All you need to do is rehearse the students and arrange transportation from our parent helpers." She paused. "The recital is another matter. Brace yourselves."

For the next hour they discussed the details for the recital, scheduled for May 22. The list went on and on: programs, sponsors, tickets, posters, lighting, sets, sound system, taping the music, ticket takers, hostesses, clean up, scheduling parent meetings about the recital, and costumes and organizing the order of dances during the program.

Lindsay yawned. "I think I'll need a nap after this. I'm so glad you two work together so well. I can't imagine having a recital if I'd had to hire a new ballet instructor before next fall."

"I expect the costumes to arrive April tenth so we'll avoid last year's fiasco," Marta's mom said. "Now it's just a matter of keeping the classes running smoothly, right, Marta?" She turned to look at Marta.

Marta momentarily let herself drift back to last May when she returned home. The months disappeared at lightning speed since starting her work at the studio. Her days leading dance classes and practicing were just what she needed to move her recovery forward. But, by the time they completed the recital, she'd need to decide how she wanted to spend the next years: dancing or teaching dancing, or maybe some yet-to-be-determined possibility she had not uncovered.

"Marta?" Lindsay said. "You'll keep the classes running, right?"

"Of course."

"Good. Now, I'll keep Elle on the line to discuss the new *Capezio* catalogs and ordering for fall. We'll get a special discount if we order before May twelfth."

Marta took her list and returned upstairs to sit at her desk while she wrote notes about the classes. Her brain spun from all the details to be handled over the next two months. Whoever held her position next year would have a time consuming job, especially if they ran a full spectrum of classes expanded to include tap, baton, and gymnastics classes.

These past few weeks Marta avoided taking diet pills. When she felt herself reaching for them and remembered she didn't have any left, she put on music and danced or helped her mom downstairs in the office. At home she took herself for a walk, baked cookies to give away to parents waiting for their children to finish their classes, or she'd clean another drawer in her little house. Slowly the cravings for diet pills diminished, but the urge to reach for them remained strong.

When the mail arrived today, Marta received a personal letter from Betty and her father:

Miss Marta,

   Pleze cum to my spring progam. My Dad will pik you up. He says we can git ice cream after. Pleze cum. It's March 26th.

Betty and Sam

Such a sweet invitation. She encouraged all her students to invite her to their programs; Betty was the first to actually do so. Should she go? Of course. Things at the studio continued to be busy and she went home exhausted, but that was no reason to turn down the invitation. She wanted to support Betty and repay Sam Faris for arranging early release times for Paige and Rosalia. Somewhere she'd find the energy and attend the program.

At the next kinder class, Marta spoke with Betty. "I'd love to come to your program. What is your class singing?"

Betty looked at her feet. "A song about a bear with tennis shoes." She looked up. "It's a silly song."

"Will your mother be there?"

Betty looked down to her feet again. "No. She's in heaven."

Marta didn't know what to say. If only the floor could open and swallow her. She wished she could take back all the nasty things she'd thought about Sam's wife being self-absorbed. Why didn't anyone tell her that his wife had died? She glanced at Betty's grandmother, who smiled briefly then whisked Betty down the stairs.

March 26, Thursday. Marta rushed around deciding what to wear. Nothing matched the current fashion or fit well. How had she let this happen even as she'd cleaned out her closet so many times lately? She selected a floral print skirt and a rose-colored sweater thinking that when Lynne came for a visit this summer, they'd make a day of it and shop in downtown Seattle.

Marta stood on her porch waiting for Sam and Betty to arrive. With early spring flowers popping up and daylight hours lengthening, Marta enjoyed the funny-faced primroses she'd planted in pots on her steps, reminiscent of Mr. Dunbar's plantings. Oh, no. She should have invited him to the studio celebration. Her slip up troubled her. Was her forgetfulness from a lack of focus since she'd stopped taking diet pills? Had she taken on too many tasks? Or maybe she wasn't organized enough to handle things for the studio. Too late to do anything about it now.

Soon she'd have been home an entire year. Instructing wasn't anything like dancing, but the planning and helping Paige and Rosalia prepare for upcoming auditions stirred a different happiness inside her. With the recital close at hand, then summer, maybe she'd find her stride by then.

Sam drove up and waved as Marta hurried to his car. "Hello, Betty, Sam. Thank you for inviting me to the program." She slipped in next to Betty in the front seat.

Betty smiled. Sam grinned and nodded as they headed out Kitsap Way to the program.

"I see you're all dressed up, Betty," Marta said. "The flowers on your dress are beautiful. Your hair looks special too."

Betty twisted her finger in one of the curls that hung down beside her face. "I know."

Sam pulled into the Chico School driveway and followed the line of cars that parked in the field behind the building. As soon as they entered the hallway, Betty broke free of Sam's hand and raced to her classroom. At the auditorium entry, they followed the crush of parents and relatives to the bleachers, choosing to sit up high to catch a view of the entire space.

Most of the parents knew Sam, stopping to shake his hand and wait for him to introduce Marta. She smiled and nodded but remained quiet while he spoke with one, then another.

Seated in the bleachers, Marta laughed. "You know everyone!"

"I do. My wife worked here. They've been helpful since Ginger died."

"It must have been encouraging having their support. How long has she been gone?"

"Three years. She had a massive stroke at the age of twenty-five." Sam looked away before he spoke. "It's been hard, but I've got Betty."

"She's is a wonderful little girl. She acts shy, but she loves to dance."

"It's fun to watch her twirl around in the living room. We've had to move the coffee table to make space for her. Her grandmother says she's always off in her own world."

"Sounds like me when I was her age," Marta said.

After the program, Sam drove them to the Silverdale ice cream shop, now crowded with families from school who had the same idea. Marta felt uncomfortable being with Sam and Betty in such a personal way. She noticed stares that averted quickly when she made eye contact. As they left, she felt people watching her back.

Eating ice cream after a musical performance triggered the memory of her evenings after dancing. She and Steve crowded into the Billings ice cream shop with dance patrons looking for a way to extend their evening. Would images of her time with Steve ever fade?

Sam finished his sundae and turned to his daughter. "Betty, tell Marta about the book you made in school last week."

"My book was about a ballerina," Betty said. "She had a magic wand, and she made the trees and flowers dance. She turned the stones into raindrops, too."

"That's quite a story," Marta said. "Did you create a dance to go with that story?"

Betty took a bite of ice cream, and nodded. "I just did."

Sam drove to his home near the school, tucked Betty in bed, and said good night to his mother who lived with them. Marta sat in the living room, watching all the hugs, kisses, drinks of water, and more hugs until Betty disappeared into her bedroom. It was her first time watching a family outside her own. It stirred a new sensation inside her that she couldn't name but that she enjoyed.

When Sam drove into Marta's driveway, he turned off the engine and turned to face her. "Thanks for coming," he said. "Betty was so excited to think you'd come."

"I enjoyed it very much. Betty is so sweet."

"She thinks the world of you, Marta. She's always saying, 'Marta would do this,' or 'Marta says we should do that.'"

Sam patted Marta's hand as he got out of the car and walked her to her door. He cleared his throat. "Ah, I was wondering...Do you think you'd like to go out for dinner or to a movie some time?"

Marta pressed her lips together as a rush of heat reached her face. "Maybe."

"Good." Sam backed away. "I'll see you soon or call you about that dinner. Thanks for coming tonight."

Marta stood on her porch and waved as Sam backed out. When he was gone, she walked across the road to sit by the bay. Tonight the light from the waning full moon vibrated on the water's surface, marking a path straight toward her. Maybe that was why she felt such a tugging from deep inside. Or was it from being with Sam and Betty? Sam had a calming effect on her. His patience as well as his loving ways with Betty reminded her of her father and how he handled day-to-day situations. She looked forward to talking with Sam again, to learn about his hopes, dreams and interests.

When Marta climbed into bed and closed her eyes, she imagined warm lips pressed against hers. The kisses continued on and on until she woke with a start. Was she kissing Steve or Sam?

While Paige and Rosalia packed up and prepared to leave for the evening, Marta scanned the audition information chart she made for them. She'd covered everything she could think of based on her personal auditions. She'd taught them short bits of choreography like they'd be expected to commit to memory during their real auditions and shared her suggestions for improving their performances.

"Tomorrow when you return for the mock audition, please wait downstairs until I call you. I want you to experience the tension you'd feel at a real audition. It's important to be confident regardless of any mistakes you make and to keep a soft smile on your face to show your confidence."

Both girls nodded.

"Who'll be our judges?" Rosalia asked.

Marta wiggled her finger at the girls and smiled. "Ah, that's a secret. They'll fill out long forms of information about each of you, so prepare to stand and wait. I suggest you call each other and ask questions you think they'll ask to help you prepare." Marta hugged both girls and shooed them from the room. "Now go home, practice your solos, and be here and ready tomorrow evening at 6:50. Do your best and stay confident. Good luck."

The practice audition judges arrived at 6:30. Lily Rose and Veronica Osbourne, the prospective new instructor, smiled as they hung their coats on the coat rack and seated themselves at the long table beside Lindsay.

Marta handed out the forms and pens. "When the girls arrive, I'll introduce you formally, then explain the judging system. The girls will go through the first part of the process together, then they'll dance alone and answer questions. Take lots of notes; I'll share your information with them during a future class. We want them to have every advantage possible when they step into real auditions. Also, don't smile your encouragement to them. The audition judges will keep their faces as neutral as possible. Remain objective and assess each girl using the criteria I've created on the forms."

Marta called down to the girls, "Please come upstairs, ladies." A sudden memory of her own audition experience flashed through her. She relived the pulsing tension she imagined they felt as they reached the top of the stairs.

Paige and Rosalia entered the room dressed in black leotards, black practice skirts, pink tights, and *pointe* shoes. Marta handed them audition numbers to pin onto their leotards. Neither dancer smiled as they moved to stand before the judges in fifth position awaiting directions.

"Good evening, ladies. I'm Marta Selbryth. Your judges tonight are Mrs. Holland, Mrs. Costello, and Mrs. Osbourne. We'll begin shortly."

The judges started writing, appraising the girls for body proportions, posture, tidiness of their dance costume, and their stage presence. When they completed their assessment, they looked toward Marta and nodded.

"We'll be judging you on seven elements including your basic style during *barre* exercises, your form during floor exercises, your ability to memorize new choreography, your rhythmic sense, how you interpret and perform the group selection together and as a solo, plus how you dance your prepared solo. Please move to the *barre* to begin warm-ups."

Marta watched both girls as they moved to the *barre*. So far so good. They looked calm, but she noticed Paige's legs trembling and Rosalia squeezing the *barre*. Both probably felt as if they'd swallowed jumping beans. That's how she'd felt. Warm-ups and the center work, both well known procedures, would relax them—hopefully not too much.

Instead of dancing with them as she usually did during class, Marta directed them by speaking her commands and clapping the beat much like Madame Cosper and other dance company directors did. It provided one more chance for the judges to observe how they handled themselves in an unfamiliar situation. The girls performed without hesitation once they adjusted to the change.

For the group dance, Marta shared her choreography for *Rhapsody in Blue,* a flowing choreography to showcase their skills. Both Lily Rose and Lindsay knew the music and choreography, providing them with the background to judge the performances artistically. Veronica represented a fresh perspective since she'd never met the girls or seen the choreography.

After instruction and two practices, the girls danced together, then performed the selection as solos. Marta relaxed her hands, realizing she was holding them as fists. Both young women continued with strong skills, filling Marta with a confidence that she'd provided useful training they'd take with them as they advanced to real auditions.

As they danced, she noticed how much Paige reminded her of herself: tentative at times, but also graceful with flowing arms and good finishing detail. Rosalia, technically the better dancer, moved mechanically. Her amazing memory became obvious early on, but her lack of finesse filled Marta with concern. During future practice sessions she'd address the skills where they needed to improve their focus.

Marta dismissed the girls to wait downstairs to allow the judges time to complete their forms. In a few minutes she brought them back, one at a time, to perform their individual selections. Rosalia selected her "Sugar Plum" solo; Paige chose her "Dance of the Flutes." After each girl danced, the judges asked their individual questions, wrote comments, and dismissed them. *Poof.* Their practice audition ended abruptly just like real ones did; harsh, maybe, but true to form.

As the girls left the room, Marta refrained from following them to check in with them. After all, this was a mock audition. In real auditions, judges never spoke to the dancers once they left the room.

Tonight the judges would score the girls and give Lindsay the results to share with Marta. When the girls heard the comments, they'd know what skills to work on to prepare for real auditions coming up between April's spring vacation and the end of July. Marta would build on their strengths, then work with them to improve sections in their audition that would increase their total scores.

The mock judges completed their forms, then stayed after to discuss their scores and comments. "It looks like we agreed on their average scores," Lindsay said. "Paige is more prepared than I anticipated she'd be. With one more year to develop, she'll be a lot like Marta."

"I agree," said Lily Rose, looking at her notes. "They are both strong dancers. Paige lacks confidence at times, but she's graceful and finishes each movement before she begins the next."

Marta kept her head down, listening to their comments, gauging how to share their thoughts with the girls while maintaining their confidence.

"Rosalia has great focus," Veronica said, "and accurate skills, but I wish she'd flow from one step to the next and appear to enjoy what she was doing. Her face is tense and expressionless."

"She has amazing strength and agility, but you're right," Lindsay said. "I don't see her passion. Maybe she's feeling pressure from her mother."

"Or she's nervous," Veronica said.

"I'll work with her on both her flow and her facial expressions," Marta said. "Her needs will take priority since her upcoming auditions will determine if she'll receive a professional ballet position this fall."

The mock auditions inspired Marta to stay after the others left and work on her recovery exercises and think of how to help the young women improve their chances for garnering a ballet company position. For Paige she'd offer more detailed praise to encourage her self-confidence. She'd also push her to think ahead and to plan her next move before she began the movement. That would eliminate her occasional jerkiness.

Helping Rosalia took a more delicate approach. Since Zandora pushed her daughter so hard, Marta didn't want to add to her stress. She'd adjust the speed on the record player to slow down the music in hopes of helping Rosalia relax, anticipate her next move, and soften her facial expressions.

Relaxing. Marta laughed to herself. Lately she'd been a tense person herself, so maybe she needed to heed her own advice. She adjusted the rotation speed of the record for her practice session and began dancing. Within a few seconds she felt her movements soften and meld together. This tactic would work for both girls.

While she felt mellow, she decided to place a call to Steve. It was time for her to make a move. The phone rang several times before Mr. Mason answered, "Mason residence."

He wasn't there. Should she leave a message? What could she say? Her plan to stay relaxed disappeared. "No, thank you." She hung up and leaned against the wall. That was stupid, she thought. Why didn't she say who she was? What was wrong with her?

Lindsay called Marta a few days after Marta shared the mock audition scores with the girls. "Zandora called me yesterday. She's spitting pins about the judging and wants to know how each judge scored Rosalia. I told her we averaged our scores and she'd get no further details. I'm so glad I took the forms home and burned them. How is Zandora behaving toward you?"

"More frowns than before, but she hasn't approached me directly. Mom's overheard her bad-mouthing my mock audition, saying I favored Paige even though I've offered to spend extra time with Rosalia and she flat out turned me down. Paige told me Rosalia is excited about going to a handful of early auditions, all around her spring break."

"Oooh. That's a lot," Lindsay said. "Traveling to so many cities over so few days puts immense pressure on Rosalia. I'm glad Paige has a year before she decides if she wants to pursue a career."

"Paige's mother will pay the thirty dollars for the Seattle evaluation, but she isn't certain she'll get time off work, so I may accompany her. It would be great if I took both girls, but Zandora will undoubtedly want to handle Rosalia's auditions."

༄

March 3. For Marta, returning to auditions in the Olympic Ballroom in Seattle felt like returning to the scene of a crime. True, that audition had gone well and she had become a member of the Intermountain Ballet Company, but her nervousness flooded back as she entered the ballroom corridor with Paige. "Just remember, do your best. Give it all the energy you have, and thank them before you leave."

Paige nodded. "Thanks for coming with me. I feel so funny inside. I can't imagine doing this without your help."

Marta pulled Paige into a hug. "It's been my pleasure. I'll be in the waiting area. When you finish, they'll hand your scores to you since you aren't being considered for a real position. We can look them over on the ferry ride home. Good luck, Paige."

As Marta returned to the waiting area, Rosalia and her mother entered. Rosalia smiled and waved. Zandora looked the other way and nudged Rosalia ahead of her to the ballroom corridor. This could be an amazingly long afternoon.

Zandora didn't return for several minutes. When she did, she chose a seat far away from Marta and pulled out a cigarette case. A member of the hotel staff approached her and told her the smoking area was further down the hall, away from the kitchen and banquet rooms. Marta pretended she'd not heard or seen the confrontation. Zandora put away her cigarettes, pulled out a pack of Juicy Fruit gum and a *Reader's Digest*, checked her watch, and settled into her seat.

Half an hour later, Paige returned to the waiting area carrying her evaluation notes. A smile spread across her lips.

Marta stood as she approached. "So, it went well?"

"I think so." Paige nodded and handed the evaluations to Marta. "I can't wait to call my mom. Can we stop before we catch the ferry?"

"Absolutely!" They exited through the door furthest from Zandora and stopped to make Paige's call.

"...and, I think I did a good job on my solo. When they asked me questions about myself, I looked at each judge the way Marta suggested we do.... Yes, it was hard, but I did okay. I'll share everything with you when I get home—Love you."

On the hour-long ferry ride, they discussed the judges' notes. "Fifty-seven points out of a possible seventy is a good score from the San Diego ballet group. Their comments are consistent with what we wrote at the mock audition. You'll need to work on refining your *barre* and center movements, and maybe we'll add more difficulty to your solo to lift those sevens to eights or nines. You have plenty of time to decide. You told mom you enjoyed the audition. What made it enjoyable?"

Paige's face wore a smile that extended far beyond her lips. "I enjoyed the challenge to push myself to relax when I danced the new choreography. I didn't enjoy answering their questions. Maybe you can help me with that before next year?"

"Whatever you want and need. Now, let's relax, enjoy the view, and think about where you want to insert more challenging choreography into your solo."

❧

Rosalia attended the first practice session following the audition. She participated in discussing and working on skills suggested by Paige's evaluation, but had not yet received her results. Now, as Paige exited the practice room, Rosalia lingered, slowly packing her dance tote. Marta sat next to her on the floor.

"Is everything alright, Rosalia?" Marta said.

Rosalia shrugged. Her clenched jaw and pulled in lips told Marta how she felt. "Marta," Rosalia sighed. "What if I don't get invited to join the San Diego Ballet?"

"That's why we all do multiple auditions. We never know what they are looking for. We use their evaluations to improve our dancing, we make changes, then we move on to other auditions and perform our best. It's seldom a dancer earns a position after one audition."

"Can you help me with my flow between steps? I think it's a problem."

"Of course. I'll help you with anything you need, Rosalia." Marta stood and pulled Rosalia to her feet. "For now, go home, forget about auditions, and get your school homework done. You're a strong dancer. I wish I'd had your memory when I auditioned. It's a marvelous skill most dancers need to work on over time, and here you are, owning that skill already."

"You really think my memory is a special skill?"

"Yes," Marta said. "Now go home and try to relax. Over the next weeks, we'll work on whatever the ballet company recommends and whatever concerns you."

Rosalia hugged Marta and finished packing up just as Zandora arrived at the practice room doorway. "Rosalia. I've been waiting for you in the car. Hurry along." Rosalia scurried out the door. "Marta, I'd appreciate if you'd keep track of the time. We can't follow your whims in ignoring the posted schedule with our busy lives."

"Certainly, Mrs. Marcus," Marta said. "Have a nice evening."

Rosalia missed the next two practice sessions. Marta's mom shared what she knew. "Rumor has it that Rosalia didn't receive an offer from the San Diego Ballet Company. It's my understanding that Zandora hired a private instructor to train Rosalia. You won't see Rosalia except during her regular ballet classes, which she says she's considering dropping if the new instructor she's hired proves worthy."

The uprooting of Rosalia didn't surprise Marta, but it created a sadness inside her. Why did Zandora think Marta was of no value when she shared her professional experience and knowledge to help Rosalia? If she pulled Rosalia from the dance studio, that would be a loss to both sides. The mock judges agreed with Marta, so maybe this was Zandora's, and ultimately Rosalia's, problem.

As March downpours changed to April showers and spring blossoms, Marta answered the dance studio phone and recognized Lindsay's voice. "I'd like to come in to talk with you and your mom after hours today. Can you stay?"

"Of course we'll stay. What's it about?"

"Our favorite topic these days: Rosalia and Zandora Marcus."

Lindsay arrived and locked the doors. "Follow me. Let's meet in my office."

"Sounds serious," Marta's mom said.

"It is. I've received a string of calls from Zandora. San Diego didn't offer Rosalia a position, plus she received similar results at all of the auditions she's heard back from to date. Now she's sent the Holland Dance Studio a letter saying she was suing the studio for negligence: failure of performance of an implied contract."

"What?" Marta heard herself shouting. "We had no contract."

"I know. My attorney, Mr. Harris, is looking into it. He imagines it will be tossed out, but I wanted you to know what was happening. Mr. Harris says we're not to speak with either Rosalia or her mother. That way we'll not say anything Zandora can use against us if it goes to a trial."

Marta's mom shook her head. "To trial? Could she sue you? What would she gain from that? The ballet companies won't change their minds about hiring her."

"I know," Lindsay said. "She wants someone to blame and doesn't realize or want to believe she may be the problem."

One afternoon a week later, Marta answered the dance studio phone and heard, "This is Anna Cosper of the Intermountain Ballet Company. May I speak with the studio owner?"

Marta nearly dropped the phone as she sank down into a chair. Her hands shook as she cleared her throat to speak. "She's out of the studio today. This is Marta Selbryth. May I help you, Madame Cosper?"

A long pause hummed along the phone lines.

"Yes. How are you Marta? Has your ankle healed?"

"Not quite, Madame, but I'm teaching ballet for Lindsay Holland to enhance my recovery. How may I help you?"

"I'm calling about Rosalia Marcus. She auditioned with us in Portland. We felt her dancing was strong, but we want to know more about her mother. The woman demanded entrance to the judging room and had to be removed by security. We'd like to offer Rosalia a contract, but I need more information about her mother."

"Of course," Marta said. "Let me give you Lindsay Holland's home number. She'll be glad to speak confidentially with you." Marta gave her the number.

"Thank you, Marta."

"Is there anything else I might do to help you, Madame Cosper?"

"No. That is all."

Marta sat staring at the receiver in her hand, then placed it back onto the phone cradle. Madame Cosper, her former company director, called and she spoke with her. She shared information that should have been reserved for Lindsay. Maybe Madame trusted her.

Should she have asked Madame about her dismissal and if there was any possibility of her returning to the company? No. Today's conversation was about Rosalia. Talking about her personal issues demanded a face-to-face conversation.

Madame Cosper *did* share an interesting piece of information. If Zandora pursued her lawsuit, the fact that she'd interrupted the Portland audition could be useful to Lindsay. Marta grabbed a piece of paper, wrote out what Madame had said, dated it, and placed it in Lindsay's office desk for safe keeping.

Marta sat in Lindsay's office replaying the conversation. Oh my good gracious! Madame's call might prove a disaster. If Zandora ever got wind of Marta's conversation with Madame, and if the Intermountain ultimately rejected her, Zandora would certainly blame Marta. She needed to call Lindsay right away.

Each time she dialed Lindsay's number, the busy signal buzzed and buzzed. Then, as Marta finished sorting the mail, the phone rang. "Marta, This is Lindsay. I hear you spoke with Anna Cosper."

"I did."

"I just got off the phone with her. Can you join me at my home tomorrow morning before classes? I'm asking my attorney to join us to be certain we only share appropriate information."

Sleep eluded Marta that night as she considered what she'd say to Madame about Rosalia. At 4 a.m. she untangled herself from the twisted covers, took a shower, and straightened her house to keep busy until time to meet with Lindsay. She dressed with care, as if Madame could see her through the phone lines.

She borrowed her mom's car and arrived at the door at the same time as a middle-aged man carrying a briefcase and a portable tape recorder.

Lindsay let them in and made introductions. "Mr. Harris, this is my assistant, Marta Selbryth. She danced with the Intermountain Ballet Company last year. Marta, Mr. Harris is our attorney for studio issues, including our concerns about Mrs. Marcus. Let's sit in the living room. I expect Madame Cosper's call at any moment."

The three sat in an impatient silence. When the phone rang they all straightened.

"Hello, this is Lindsay Holland." She leaned forward as she spoke. "Yes, my attorney is here. I've also invited Marta since she helped train Rosalia. I'm putting you on a speaker phone and taping our call for future use as needed."

Introductions were made all around. Damien and an attorney joined Madame in Billings. Madame also recorded the call.

After greetings were exchanged, Madame began the conversation. "Thank you for meeting with us. After speaking with counsel, we're not offering Rosalia a contract with the Intermountain Ballet Company. She's a strong dancer; our issues were with her mother at the Portland audition. It precludes our extending her a *corps de ballet* position. We've instructed our attorney to send you, Miss Holland, and your attorney, our letter and other pertinent, confidential information for your records."

Marta's shoulders drooped thinking about how Rosalia would feel when she received another rejection letter from a ballet company. She understood the company's decision. But the wrath of Zandora had new fuel for its fire. She'd find some way to use it against the dance studio and Marta.

Madame Cosper continued. "We appreciate the training Rosalia received from your studio. Like Marta, she had excellent skills, but we can't take the risk that Mrs. Marcus poses for our company."

"I understand," Lindsay said. "Thank you, Madame."

After the phone call ended, Marta left the attorney and Lindsay to work out their response to her earlier suit for negligence and to prepare for any further action from Zandora. Marta drove to the city park to walk along the pebbled shoreline letting the sound of the waves erase the sadness she felt for Rosalia. She'd never thought much about what a stage mom did to earn the unwanted title. Now she understood too well.

Thank heavens her mom never interfered. She'd supported Marta through her successes and low moments, her injury and her returning home. Tonight she'd prepare a special thank you meal and tell her mom how grateful she'd been and still was to have her unquestioned support.

She took a moment to savor the small compliment Madame made to Lindsay and indirectly to herself. That meant Madame didn't disrespect Marta's skills as a dancer, so she must dislike Marta as a person. That perplexed her even more.

When Marta returned to the dance studio, she took her mother upstairs and into the little apartment to discuss the phone call at Lindsay's.

"Brace yourself. The Intermountain didn't offer Rosalia a contract, so Zandora will probably attempt to stir up trouble."

Her mom sighed and shook her head. "That is so sad."

"It is. Rosalia deserves better. Lindsay and her attorney are working out a reply to Zandora's earlier suit. Our conversation today is never to be mentioned to anyone, but I thought you needed to know. I ache for Rosalia. I doubt we'll see her or Zandora again."

Marta startled every time the phone rang over the next days. Zandora had already started spreading stories about how the Holland Studio was in cahoots with all the ballet companies to deny Rosalia a position. Most parents and dancers never mentioned hearing the information, but enough shared their conversations with Zandora that Lindsay, Marta, and her mom were aware of what was said. Zandora's cousin withdrew their children from early ballet classes, but most families shook their heads and began providing treats, notes of support, and friendly smiles of condolence.

Paige didn't speak of Rosalia to any of the dancers in the class she'd shared with her. She did talk about her audition saying, "Marta helped me prepare. It took a lot of hard work and extra classes, and I haven't decided if I want to become a professional."

Marta sensed that Paige wanted to talk, so she lingered after class, waiting as Paige packed up. "How's everything going? Anything you want to discuss?"

Paige shrugged. "I keep thinking about the audition and how hard it was and then how Rosalia just gave up coming to class. I miss her. Can we still do the extra classes? I want to keep working with you on several things."

"Of course. Have you decided if you want to pursue a career as a dancer?"

"Not yet. I know Rosalia is a stronger dancer than I am, so I wonder if it's worth my time to keep dreaming about it."

Marta smiled. "Dreams are important. We should reach for them as long as they remain important in our lives." As Paige left, Marta realized she needed to take her own advice and follow her dream until it faded or reshaped to a new vision.

Within a few days the dance studio settled back into their regular days. The phone calls returned to questions about classes and the upcoming recital. Marta still could not figure out what Zandora thought she would gain by pulling Rosalia and hurting the studio—besides making herself look petty.

When the studio phone rang Tuesday afternoon after classes, Marta absentmindedly picked it up. "Holland Dance Studio. This is Marta. May I help you?"

Sobbing tumbled along the phone lines.

"Hello?" Marta waited. "May I help you?"

"It's me. Is you mother there?"

"Lindsay? What's wrong?"

"I have terrible news."

arta heard Lindsay Holland's voice continue to break into sobs.
"Lindsay, tell me what's wrong. Are you and the baby okay?"

"We're fine. But,..." More sobbing. "Adam's been reassigned to San
Diego. He must report by July first."

Marta sank onto the closest chair. "What about the studio and your
loan and everything?"

"I'm not sure. Could you put your mom on the phone?"

"She's at the bank. Do you want her to come to your house?"

"Maybe. Yes. Tell her—thanks, Marta."

Marta paced as she waited for her mom to return. When she walked
in the door, Marta rushed to meet her and tell her the news. "I'll handle
things here. You head over to her house right away. Call me if there is
anything I can do to help."

"I'll call in my friend to cover the desk," her mom said. "This could
be a long afternoon."

Students entered as her mom left. Marta enlisted a parent to handle
phone calls and messages until her mom's friend arrived, then she started
classes. "Hello, everyone. Find a place at the *barre* and let's warm up."

Marta watched the clock hands slowly circle as though covered in molasses. When her mom stepped in to Marta's last dance session and shook her head, Marta knew the news was not good.

After the last family exited the studio, Marta locked the door, then she and her mom entered Lindsay's office to talk. "Lindsay is so upset," her mom said. "She feels like all her hard work is lost. Adam is excited about the move, but he understands how distressing the news is for the dance studio. He's promised to help her talk with the bank. They'll figure out how to deal with the new loan she took out. I doubt they can undo it now that the papers are signed."

Marta shook her head. "What will happen to the studio?"

"They don't know, Marta. For now we'll keep things going as usual."

The phone rang, jarring Marta's thinking. As her mom answered the phone, Marta returned upstairs to be alone until her last evening class with Paige, which was to be more of a celebration than a class. As she prepared, a gnawing sensation interrupted her focus. Lindsay filled an important part of her life, but now she'd be living over a thousand miles away. Her ten years of teaching, being an important community asset, and being Marta's staunch supporter would end. And if the studio closed now…. There had to be some way to allow the studio to continue without Lindsay.

After her class with Paige, Marta rejoined her mom in Lindsay's office where they shared a sandwich. Her mom shook her head and closed her eyes. "I guess we always knew there'd be a chance Adam's orders would change, but I hate to see ten plus years of Lindsay's hard work disappear. It feels so wrong."

Marta doodled on a pad as they spoke. "I agree. This could be our last recital unless Lindsay finds a buyer, or…what if we found someone to buy the studio? I know it's a harebrained idea, but maybe we could make that happen."

Her mom's eyes widened. She stood and looked around the office as if sizing up what she saw. She turned toward Marta. "I don't know. Maybe. Do you think we could work with a different owner?" Her mom's face registered a look of surprise. "Wait. You said we. Does that mean you'd stay and teach? You'd be giving up your dream to dance again."

"I know. I'd stay for awhile, anyway. Over the past months I've let my plans and friendships slip away. This afternoon my mind spun through so many things: Steve, Lynne, dancing professionally, working and dancing here, Lindsay's support, and of course your support and love of this place. I'd stay here and help until the studio's future became clear. I owe that much to you and Lindsay."

Her mom smiled and sat down. "Honey, you can't base any decisions on owing something to people. Caring about someone doesn't mean you need to pay them back. Hopefully, a buyer will emerge. Just so long as it isn't that friend of Zandora's who's had her eye on the building for an Arthur Murray studio. If Lindsay or if we find someone to buy the studio, it needs to happen quickly. Perhaps we could try to buy it. I don't know if we'd qualify, or how much this dance studio is worth, but we could check into it. Let's see what Lindsay figures out before we get too worried about details."

Marta waved as her mom backed out of the Corbett driveway. She closed the door and stood with her back against it. An unexpected stillness flowed through her. If they did buy the studio, she'd be tying herself to staying in Bremerton for an unknown about of time. That affected her future as a dancer, as well as her future relationship with Steve, if it still existed. She decided to stop worrying about what *might* be and focus on something that *could* be decided very soon.

As Marta and her mom drove to the studio the next morning, they continued brainstorming.

"If all else fails and I try to get a loan for the studio," her mom said, "I may have to sell the house. That would mean our family home would be gone. If you had to pick one to save, the dance studio or our family home, which would you choose?"

Marta smiled. "All my memories of growing up are tangled inside both of them. I've laughed and cried, worked through problems, and found happiness in both places. It's hard to choose. I hope I'll know what to do if selling our home becomes necessary."

When they'd parked the car and gone inside, her mom hugged her. "Maybe we can salvage both. I'll call Lindsay when we have a break between classes to learn what she's thinking."

A loud chattering at the door startled Marta. She shook out her arms and legs and twisted her head side to side to release her tension as she welcomed in the kinders. She glanced at her mother before she led the children upstairs. "How is everyone today? I hope you're ready to dance and sing. I've found a new song for us. Let's sit down and get started stretching."

During their lunch break Marta and her mom locked the door again and resumed their discussion. "Lindsay called to say she didn't have any information yet, but that she and Adam were working on it."

Marta circled the waiting room, straightening the cushions and picking up loose bits of paper. "The waiting around is hard. It's like standing in the wings, dressed to perform, waiting to see if the dancer you're understudying can go on or not."

Classes began and ended as Marta struggled to stay focused. By the end of the day, she'd exhausted all her reserves thinking about so many things. Would Lindsay expect Marta would take over teaching *all* the classes permanently? What about auditioning for a professional ballet company? Marta hadn't even figured out if she was going to tryout again or not. Besides, how was she expected to know what she wanted? She was nineteen, not twenty-five or forty. And what about Steve? What if they did end up together and she moved for his job? What if the Holland Studio hired new instructors and then his job fell through or they broke up? She'd need to start over yet again.

The warm spring day faded to dusk as Marta heard her mom call her downstairs. She looked around the upstairs thinking of all the recital decisions to be finalized over the next few days. She needed to stay focused on the details of the recital and stop thinking about any plans beyond kids, music, and costumes.

They called Lindsay. "We've been thinking about keeping the studio open once you move to San Diego," her mom said. "The dance studio is important to so many people. We want to try to keep it running if possible. We...."

Her mom's eyes widened. Something had distracted her. Marta turned in time to see Zandora Marcus standing in the doorway with a large box in her arms. She dropped it with a thud, crossed her arms, and smiled as she turned and left.

Marta gasped. They'd forgotten to lock the door.

Marta opened the box to find the capes and hair ornaments Rosalia had borrowed. Of all the times to return them, she thought.

"Lindsay," her mom said into the phone. "We might have another problem. Zandora overheard our conversation."

By the following morning, dance school patrons began calling and stopping in, worried about the studio. "Where will we go if you leave?" "What about the recital? I paid good money for this year's lessons and costumes." "Are you buying the studio and the building?" "I just called Lindsay and she said...."

When Adam called the dance studio, his voice sounded strained. "I'm worried about how this stress is affecting Lindsay and the baby. Why did you give out our private phone number?"

"We didn't give out your number," Marta said. "Believe me, we never intended for any of this to get out. We're so sorry. We're hoping this all works out."

Now Marta paced and rocked and wished she knew what her future held. Her mom and Robert had plans, so they'd be staying in Bremerton at least until Robert retired, and that was years away.

Marta's decision about sticking with the studio would affect her life for years to come. What if she made the wrong choice? What was the wrong choice? What was the right choice? Should she flip a coin? No. She'd need to give it serious thought, after she attended Betty's early evening school talent show as she'd promised her last week.

The program was short and lively. Betty borrowed a blue, sparkly costume from the dance studio to perform her class dance to *Twinkle, Twinkle Little Star*. She made every turn, waved her star wand on cue, and bowed as though she'd been dancing for years rather than less than seven months.

Marta and Sam met Betty in her classroom afterward and handed her a bouquet of carnations. "We enjoyed the program, Betty. You danced like a lovely fairy," Marta said. "I loved the way you waved your wand and smiled."

"That's what I was 'pose to do," Betty said.

Sam laughed. "I think we can thank Marta for that new confidence. Now more than ever she wants to become a dancer."

"Yes, but Daddy, I *am* a dancer," Betty said, "and I want to be a teacher and a doctor and a taxi driver. Can we get ice cream now?"

By seven thirty, they'd eaten ice cream and tucked Betty into bed. Now Marta and Sam sat for a minute outside in the porch swing. Sam took her hand and absentmindedly rubbed his long fingers along her knuckles as they spoke of their dreams. "I love my job," he said, "but I hope to scrape together enough money to go back to school and get my doctorate so I can open a counseling service for kids. There's a need for counselors to help kids through crises like the death of a parent, divorce, or debilitating injuries."

"I went to a counselor after I broke my foot," Marta said. "She helped me deal with the stress I experienced not knowing if I'd dance again. She was kind and didn't push me to make a decision until I had time to heal. I've kept up my exercising, and now, after almost a year, I'm close to making that decision very soon. Steve helped me...."

"Who?"

"A friend of mine in Billings." There it was: Steve crept into her life when she least expected it.

"A boyfriend?"

"Yes, and a good friend," Marta said. "He took me places to distract me during my recovery."

"Is he a dancer?"

"No. He's a reporter from the local paper. Over time he understood how much I missed dancing."

"Do you still miss dancing professionally?"

"Yes. I used to imagine it every moment of every day. Now it's only when I play certain recordings or I watch professional dancers perform on television. The longer I'm away, the more my chance to return fades away."

Sam nodded. "We all have things like that in our lives. What if dancing again doesn't work out? How do you feel about staying here to teach?"

"I'm giving it serious consideration. I imagine you've heard about Lindsay moving to San Diego."

"I have, and that you and your mom want to manage the studio. I know Betty loves her time there, dancing and being with you. As you saw tonight, she's become confident. I attribute that to you."

"Thanks. I try." She stood and pulled him to his feet. "But right now I need to get home. The studio decisions could happen any day, and I want to be as rested as possible."

Once she returned home, Marta didn't think about the situation at the studio. She focused on how Steve popped into her conversation tonight. Why didn't she tell Sam about her on-going relationship with Steve? The fact he kept stepping forward in her thoughts told her it was time to pick up the phone and dial Steve's home to address their relationship.

The phone at Steve's family home rang and rang. Marta held on for a dozen rings, then hung up. She'd made a step toward talking with him, a kind of challenge to herself to break through her stubbornness. For now she'd try to stop thinking about Steve and Sam and Betty and focus on events surrounding the dance studio.

Pacing didn't help. Neither did rocking. Did she need to restart using diet pills? No. She'd promised to stop, and she'd handled the pressures without them. No reason to slide back now, although who'd blame her in light of all that was happening?

Could she stay in Bremerton, teach at the studio, and feel content creating dances for children? Possibly. She led classes and made children laugh when they danced. She'd helped Rosalia and Paige, sharing her experiences. But was teaching enough to hold her interest? If she didn't give professional dancing another try, would she always regret that decision?

Morning classes and warm-ups began and ended. Recital dances were practiced throughout the day. Still no news from Lindsay. When the students left for the evening, Marta felt jitters run through her as she walked downstairs to meet with her mom.

"I think we need to call Lindsay and find out what we can," said her mom. "Neither Lindsay nor us need any added stress right now. Do you know what you'll do if the studio continues on with a new owner?"

Marta closed her eyes and nodded. When she opened her eyes, she wiped away a single tear. "I can't leave knowing I caused the studio to move backward or close. I love it here. It's my dance home. I'll stay if I'm needed."

Her mom exhaled slowly, stood, and hugged Marta. "Thank you, honey. I know all of this is overwhelming, but life's always changing. Every decision is a gamble. You'll see. Everything will work out the way it's intended."

At eight thirty that evening they drove to Lindsay's home. Lindsay greeted them with a smile, but the strain on her face didn't fool anyone.

"The dance studio is important to us and to the community," Marta's mom said. "We want to work with whomever buys the dance studio. Or, if it means we take out a home loan, we'll do our best to secure enough for a down payment to buy the building. We'll work on getting the funds for buying the business as well."

Lindsay shook her head, and bit her bottom lip. "That's wonderful, but it may be too late. The bank received an offer from an anonymous source to take over the loan and pay an additional twenty percent above the loan amount to buy the building and close the deal within a month. But he hinted he could hold off submitting the offer for a few days so someone else could bid on it. Do you know anyone who might be interested?"

Marta and her mom looked at each other. "Maybe," her mom said.

A week later on an early May evening, a gentle tapping brought Marta to her front door. Her mom stood looking across the road. "Hi, Mom."

"Great view. I see why you love this place. And your primroses are lovely."

Marta laughed. "I doubt you came to look at my primroses."

Her mom handed over a packet of paper. "No, I came to share this with you. I've got a loan in the works with Mr. Gleason at our bank. He doesn't see any problem in our plan to buy the building."

Marta hugged her mom. "This is a gigantic step. Are you certain you can handle running a studio *and* owning a building?"

"Together we can." Her mom stepped into the house and sat down. For the next two hours they discussed all the issues associated with owning a business, if Marta stayed.

As they prepared to say good night, her mom hugged her before she headed for the door. She stopped and turned back to Marta. "When I started working at the studio, Lindsay was in her late twenties. It was a part time job. Lindsay had rented two studio spaces two days a week and had four classes. Her first few recitals were in the studio. Her students wore their practice clothes with tutus and headbands to dress themselves up. Do you remember your early years in the old building?"

Marta shook her head.

"I've watched the studio grow by leaps and bounds these past ten years. When she moved to this location it felt like home. I know that if you and I work together, if you stay, we'll be fine."

"I'll think about it." Marta looked down at her hands and inhaled deeply. "Each day it looks more and more like I have no reason to consider anything else."

"Really? You've decided you won't pursue dancing? Have you told Lynne or Steve? I know they care about your plans."

Marta shrugged. "I've not spoken to either of them. There's nothing to tell, yet." She walked to the window and closed the blinds, keeping her back to her mom. "Perhaps I should tell you something else, though. I've been seeing Betty's dad."

"Sam, huh? I'd have never thought of you two together, but I guess it makes sense."

"It does. When I'm with him and Betty, I feel comfortable, but it's confusing me. I still think about Steve. I don't know what that means." Marta put on the tea kettle and took down two cups. "Stay and have a snack. I'd like your company. We can talk about the men in our lives. I could use some advice."

As May slid into its second week, the last days of classes ended. Any decision on resolving the bank loan needed to be made. Focus at the studio moved on to recital rehearsals.

Sweat slipped along Marta's body. Her snug bun escaped its thin red ribbon and hung in wisps against her damp head. She redid her hair as she prepared to tackle the rest of her list tonight then sit down with her mom, finalize the program, and call Lindsay for her input.

She exercised and tidied the upstairs, then continued downstairs to the practice room to clean up. Marta heard the door to the studio open. Expecting her mom to pop in, Marta started her normal after-hours conversation before she turned around. "Well, that was a fun bunch. They're as ready as they'll ever be. Do you think…?" Marta turned and gasped. It wasn't her mom. It was Steve.

Marta dropped the papers she held and stared. "Steve?"

"Hi Marta."

Her face heated up as she bent down to collect what she'd dropped. "What are you doing here? I mean, where did you come from? I mean...."

"I've been in the area since yesterday."

Marta stood and stared at his face, then let her eyes trail down his shoulders and arms before looking back to his face. "How did you know I'd be here?"

"Your mother. We've stayed in contact. I phone her about once a week when you're busy teaching a class or after hours. I hope that's okay."

Marta's eyes opened wide. "My mom?" She inhaled and walked to straighten records and tapes and adjust her dance skirt before turning back to face him. "How long are you staying?"

"A day or so. I missed you and I wanted to get things right between us, so I thought I'd take a chance and stop in so we could talk." He paused and looked around the room. Marta wondered what he saw when he looked at a near-barren room with *barres*, mirrors, and a long, cluttered counter. Surely nothing glamorous.

He smiled. "Marta, I'm sorry for all that's happened. I didn't mean to be so insistent about my planning a future somewhere and expecting you to follow me. But you didn't seem sure about what you wanted for yourself or from us, so I laid out my ideas. I admit I sounded pushy, but I needed a reaction from you. I just got way more than I expected."

"You said us. After New Year's, I didn't think there was an us."

"I'm still hopeful. Let's go somewhere and talk, okay?"

"I have to finish up recital details tonight. My mom's expecting me."

"No, she isn't. I spoke with her yesterday. You'll work on it tomorrow."

Marta put her hands on her hips and stared at Steve. "You talked to her *yesterday*? She didn't say anything to me."

"I asked her not to tell you." He ran his hand through his hair, then fidgeted with the keys in his pocket. "I thought I should come and see you face to face. I have a lot to tell you. And I want to hear all about everything that's happening here and about how your life is progressing."

Marta turned away from Steve once again, this time to hide her impending tears and the ache pressing against her heart. Emotions coursed through her with such force she couldn't breathe for several seconds.

"I've been just fine! That's what you want to know isn't it?" Her knees and her bottom lip trembled, but she straightened and lifted her chin. "I'm sorry. That was rude. It's just that you took me by surprise."

"I know, but I wanted to see you and I was afraid you'd refuse to talk if you knew I was coming." Steve reached out to touch her fingertips. "Can we talk? Please?"

"Let me get things cleared up with my mom first." Marta stuck her head out into the waiting area. Her mom was gone. When she turned back toward the studio, she saw a note attached to the door:

Gone home. Don't get too mad. I meant well.
I haven't mentioned anyone or anything else.
Talk with Steve, honey.
XOX
Mom

Marta wadded up the note and tossed it toward the wastebasket but missed and bent to retrieve it. She circled like a cat settling in and stared at the floor without seeing the leftover pointe shoes and the jacket tucked under one bench. She hadn't felt this nervous since her first audition. She felt his eyes follow her as she fussed over the waiting room cushions, then the small magazine table.

When she looked up, Steve stood in the doorway. "Well?"

"Okay. Let's talk, but not here. Give me a minute to change. We can go to the grill up the street." Marta walked into the bathroom and closed the door. She leaned against it letting tears stream down her face. Now what? Given how they left things, could she go through another confrontation with Steve even though she thought of him most days and nights?

She changed into her street clothes, then studied her reflection in the small mirror above the sink: pale face, clenched jaw, and messy hair. Did Steve see the tired person she saw staring back at her? The one who'd taken on a recital and maybe a dance studio? Would talking with him complicate her life or help straighten out their relationship? Deep down inside she knew she wanted to know what he was thinking.

They walked side by side to the local grill leaving space between them. The waiter seated them at a small table next to the window. For a weeknight, the grill was crowded. Marta fidgeted with her hair while the waiter took their orders.

"Just a salad, ma'am?"

"Yes, that's all, thanks," Marta said.

Steve watched her hand the menu to the waiter. "How's your recovery progressing?"

Marta clenched her jaw, thinking about what he left unsaid. "Do you really care, or is this your way of hinting yet not talking about our diet pills argument? Didn't my mom answer all your questions?"

"Ouch, Marta. That's an unexpected reaction from you. Can we just eat and get caught up? I've only spoken to your mom about you, nothing about what was going on between you and me on a personal level. Yes, I have lots of questions, but I don't think you want to hear them. Maybe I should leave now so you can go back to all your issues and your anger."

Marta let his words hang in the air. As he started to leave the table, she grabbed his hand. "Wait. I'm sorry. It's just that you arrived without warning, and now you expect me to sit here, smile, and carry on a conversation? Give me time to adjust."

"Time to adjust to what, Marta?"

She held onto Steve's hand, looking up into his eyes. "Please?"

He stared down at her, then returned to his chair, never taking his eyes from her face. She noticed his usual carefree tone had an edge. Did she see anger or hurt or impatience?

The sounds of plates, glasses, voices, and laughter filled the grill with ample background noise. Their salads arrived. Both ate in silence, watching their plates as if afraid someone might whisk them away if they didn't keep an eye on their food.

Marta set down her fork and leaned forward. "Look, Steve. I'm glad to see you. It's just so unexpected. I don't mean to sound so angry. I'm just tired and a bit taken back. You've been checking up on me with my mother. How am I supposed to react? Why didn't you stay in contact with me? Why my mom?"

Steve looked away, then back at Marta. "The ball was in your court, Marta. You never wrote. You never called."

"I *did* call, Steve. The first time your father said you weren't there. The second time no one answered."

"Two calls? You called me twice?

"I know that wasn't much of an effort, but I didn't know what to say after our blowup at New Year's, especially when you left me in charge of making the next move. Time got away from me. I got involved in working at the studio, helping two young girls prepare for their auditions, and… I was embarrassed about how we left things. I'm sorry."

Marta looked up. Steve stared at her. She felt his silence stretch out like the final chords of music when a song ends. Did he care enough about her to forgive her? As his silence continued, she realized that his next comment mattered to her more than she'd anticipated.

A faint smile caught on Steve's lips. "You matter to me, Marta." He reached across the table to touch her fingers. "I wanted to find out if there was still something between us. I think there is, but listening to you talk and watching your face, I don't think you've reached any decision yet."

"You're right. I don't know how I feel right now. Numb is probably the best word." She paused. "I'm flattered you came, and I still care about you, but I'm trying to restart my life, try new things."

Steve pulled back his hands. "Who is he?"

Marta looked around the dining room avoiding Steve's eyes. "A school counselor. He has a young daughter who comes to the dance studio."

"That didn't take long. Are you two serious?"

Marta pursed her lips and shrugged. "He's comfortable; easy to talk to. We never have the frustrating conversations I seem to have with you."

Steve's jaw tightened. "Sounds safe. Does he love you?"

She looked away before she answered. "I don't know. We're friends, Steve; that's all but,…."

The waitress arrived with Steve's main course and refilled their water glasses. Neither spoke for several moments.

Marta watched Steve focus on his meal. Seeing him triggered images of their time together: trips around Billings, bouquets of flowers, his buying her a winter coat, their conversations from the vantage point of The Rims, his coming to believe ballet was more than fluff.

Steve looked up and caught her trace of a smile. He touched Marta's fingers again. "Have you spoken to Lynne lately? Things are changing at the ballet company."

"No. She's been remote...maybe because I'm so slow at writing."

"Call her, Marta. The last time we spoke she was considering a huge change. Did she tell you the ballet school needs new instructors? I thought maybe you'd want to return to Billings and teach, be with your friends in Billings again."

Marta pulled her hands free of Steve's. "No. That portion of my life is closed. I decided when I left last year I'd not return except to visit, and we know how *that* went. Too many reminders that I'm not dancing yet. Are you saying you're going to be working in Billings?"

When Steve opened his mouth to answer, Marta held up an open palm. "Stop. Don't answer. I can't do this right now. I'm going home. Stay and eat the rest of your dinner. Call me tomorrow if you're still around. This is too much to think about right now."

Steve started to protest, then shrugged. A faint smile played in his eyes but didn't reach his lips. "Okay. I get it. I've reappeared and thrown you off kilter. May I drive you home?"

"No. Mom left her car at the studio."

Steve rose as Marta put on her jacket. She shook her head, warning him away. Picking up her purse, she turned for the door and left without a single backward glance.

She drove to Corbett without knowing how she got there. She parked the car in the driveway, walked into her little home, and looked around seeing only a blur through the tears that cascaded down her face. She heard sobs, as though from another person, not herself. It was hard to breathe. Holding herself tightly, she let the past and present flow over her like an icy stream. Seeing Steve stirred up so many emotions. Maybe he was still part of her future and not her fading first love. And why did she act so snarly? He'd kept in contact with her mom and he'd come all this way to see her. What was she afraid of?

The phone rang. She let it ring. Nothing felt important right now.

All night when she tried to close her eyes, a strange black and gray fog circled through her and a wild throbbing pulsed in her chest. Marta pushed aside her covers and paced her tiny house. Her muscles twitched as though she'd taken too many diet pills.

In the past, she'd coped with her confused feelings by taking pills and keeping herself busy. Tonight no activity distracted her. She almost wished she'd stashed a few diet pills to lean on since nothing else worked.

Hour after hour she struggled with a roiling tangle of thoughts. How did Steve figure out she was seeing someone? How did that make him feel when she confessed she was seeing Sam? How did Sam and Betty fit into her life? Was it love or concern she felt for them?

Tonight after seeing Steve, she realized she still missed him. He'd seen her through her happiest and saddest moments. When he looked into her eyes and smiled, her body melted. Maybe she still loved him.

At dawn Marta showered, put on clean clothes, opened her living room blinds, and froze in place. A man stood leaning against a blue car parked next to her mom's car. It was Steve. He'd done the same thing when they'd first met and again when she'd lost her position with the ballet company. Was he for real or just playing with her?

She put on her blue sweater and walked out to the car. "What are you doing?"

"Nothing." He moved to stand free of the car and stared at Marta.

She frowned, but inside she realized his caring touched a special place. "Where did you stay last night?"

"Here. I thought...."

"I get it. You thought if I looked out and saw you, I might want to go for a ride or talk?"

A half smile played on his lips. "Something like that."

"Steve, I don't know if I can do this. You just popped back into my life. Do you expect me to go back to the way we were and resume our relationship?"

He opened his hands and shrugged. "Marta, I have absolutely no expectations. I took a chance, that's all. I've tried to get over you, but I think about you every day. I wonder what Marta's doing? Is she happy, is she getting healthy? Does she ever think about me? I'm ready to settle down, move my life forward, but you're still in my head." He took her hands. "You're my favorite unresolved issue, so I keep coming back."

Marta nodded and pulled her hands free to button her sweater. "I know. I guess I'm still stuck with you in my head, too. Come on. I'll fix you something to eat and we can talk."

Since Marta had no classes to teach, they spent the morning talking and walking along the shore in front of her house. That afternoon when he drove away, she collapsed, drained as though she'd danced for hours. She sat in her rocking chair, absorbing the steady rhythm of the motion. The next step still belonged to her.

Their conversation had zipped from one topic to the next, including her confirming that she'd stopped taking diet pills. When he spoke of job interviews and the difficulty of finding the position he desired, she realized that his life contained issues she'd not associated with someone graduating from college. That confused her more than thinking about their tattered relationship. She wanted the best for him and realized that she wanted their lives to interconnect as they moved forward.

A knock on her door woke her. The clock showed eight-thirty in the evening. When she opened the door, Sam looked at her with concern. "Hey. I tried to call yesterday. Are you okay?"

Marta nodded. "I'm fine. I've needed time to think, so I haven't answered the phone. Come on in."

He stepped inside and reached for her hands. "I drove by yesterday, but I didn't stop because I saw you had company." Sam paused. "Marta, are you sure you're okay?"

"No." She walked to the window and fiddled with the blinds, opening and closing the slats. "My life is crazy busy. I need some alone time right now. Call me after the recital is over. I promise I'll be more focused by then."

"Sure." Sam looked puzzled as he hugged Marta and headed out the door. "Call me if you need anything."

Before the hour ended, Marta found herself parking her mom's car and walking in the back gate of her family home. She knocked on the kitchen door and called, "Mom?"

Her mom came to the door drying her hands. "Hi, honey. I…are you okay? What's happened?"

Marta let herself be hugged. After a long moment, she pulled back to look into her mother's eyes. "Why didn't you tell me you were talking with Steve?"

"He asked me not to. I didn't know if you even wanted to know he was calling, so I kept quiet. I'm sorry if you're mad."

"I'm not mad. I feel like my life is flying out of control again. First I had nothing; no one who cared about me, but you. Then I met Steve and my loneliness ended. After my career fell apart and I came home, I was alone again, except for you and my confusing conversations with Steve.

Then I met Sam. I thought I'd put my life back together and making everything jell again, but now I have two people I could love. Why is life so complicated?"

"Did you and Steve have a chance to talk?"

"We did. I apologized for being a jerk and not staying in contact. I told him about the dance studio problems, and...I told him about Sam and Betty."

"How did that go?"

"He was hurt. For now we're letting our lives settle down. After the recital and dance studio business, we'll sort things out." Marta inhaled deeply. "As much as I try to move on or forget about him, Steve holds a large portion of my heart. I owe it to him to figure out my next steps."

arta left her mom's house and walked to the dance studio. She inhaled the fragrances of May flowers as she walked the familiar route. Not much traffic this time of evening. All the homes looked snug with their curtains closed against the darkness. Tonight she'd take a step closer to making a decision about what place dancing held in her life.

She turned on the upstairs practice room lights, pulled out several classical ballet records, and cranked up the volume. She played *Swan Lake*, followed by *Sleeping Beauty*, the *Nutcracker*, and *Coppélia,* filling the entire space with memories of performances and visions of dances yet to be learned. Her soft ballet slippers slid smoothly across the floor as she danced, then walked each piece of the choreography.

When exhaustion overpowered her, she collapsed on the floor allowing her performance images to float across her mind like a motion picture. What should she do about her dancing career, the situation with the dance studio, and her feelings for two different men who said they cared about her? Why did life give her so many options when all she wanted was simple day-to-day satisfaction? That was what she wanted, wasn't it?

When the chill of the linoleum soaked into her body, she got up, went to the lost and found, and pulled out a pair of *pointe* shoes that looked her size. She rummaged through the drawer of Bandaids and wads of lamb's wool and found a pair of bunnykins. Such a comfortable change from wadded up lamb's wool. The furry insides of the rabbit fur covers protected her toes from the rough interior of the *pointe* shoes. That meant tighter fitting shoes, but delayed her getting blisters, which she appreciated.

As she tied the ribbons, the familiar crowding of her toes in the box of the shoes sent mild pain up her legs. She stood, shook out her arms and legs, and walked around to settle her feet into the shoes. How long had it been? Close to a year since she'd worn *pointe* shoes. Oh, how her feet ached just walking in them, but now was not the time to chicken out. She turned on the record player and slid the needle into the correct groove and waited for the familiar strains of *corps de ballet* dances to begin.

She ignored the electric flashes of pain and rose *en pointe* as she played one melody after another. On and on she danced, embracing every move as if she danced in a ballet company performance. She circled with tiny, pecking *bourres*, her feet fluttering up and down fast as a hummingbird's wings. She faced the mirror and inhaled, then performed *changements*, feeling the rise and drop of her center of balance as she jumped, allowing her feet to move from fifth to second to fifth position, again and again. *Pas de bourres* carried her to one corner of the room where she completed her challenge by performing *chaine* turns *en pointe* diagonally across the room until she bumped into the counter where the record player was plugged in.

Marta bent over with her hands resting on her knees, panting, drawing in deep breaths. "That didn't go well."

She walked in circles then sat on the floor and removed the pointe shoes, brushing past newly-forming blisters. Her left ankle began to swell. Pain surged through her body as her career slipped away as if she'd never danced professionally. Time to move on.

She lay on the floor until the gray of dawn yielded to morning light. In four hours her Monday exercise class began. After she returned the *pointe* shoes to the lost and found, she wrapped her ankles in ice-filled socks, curled up on the small couch in the little upstairs apartment, and slept without dreaming.

For the entire day she moved through her classes on auto-pilot, then sat down to finish recital details with her mom. Neither mentioned last night until they'd crossed off the last chore and prepared to leave for the day.

"How are you feeling, hon'?"

"Tired, lost, confused; ready for the recital to be over. I never realized how much work this entails."

"It's worth every minute when I see the happiness it brings to everyone. I hope we can keep the studio running. Have you decided what you'll do?"

Marta swiveled her head, releasing the knots that gathered in her neck. She looked down at her hands, which she grasped tightly together in her lap. She exhaled slowly before she spoke. "Last night I came here and danced en *pointe*. Even though I've practiced and danced most every day, I've lost so much strength and flexibility that my dream to dance is no longer an option. It's time to walk away and not look back or regret any part of what's happened.

"What will you do ?" her mother said.

"I love working with the students. The studio gives me the opportunity to remain creative, so my years of lessons still have value. But right now, I feel I'm unraveling."

Her mom reached over and squeezed her shoulder. "I know how hard you've worked on recovering. You gave it all you had. You're a wonderful dancer, but you're also a great teacher. I'm impressed with what you pull out of the dancers. I swear I can see them improve by the minute. That's an amazing gift, Marta. When you teach you're sharing your passion."

"Teaching and helping dancers is better than most anything I could imagine doing with my life, now that performing is out of the question." Marta stood abruptly and smiled as she pulled her mom to her feet. "Let's see if we can stop the anonymous purchaser. With Mr. Gleason's support and Lindsay wanting the studio to continue, what could possibly stop us?"

"That's what I needed to hear. I'll call tomorrow and schedule a follow-up meeting. You understand it might mean selling the house?"

"I do," Marta said. "Once you and Robert are married, you're moving to his home anyway, and I'm comfy on Corbett Drive."

"You don't mind? Because if you do, we can look for another way to gather enough money to buy the studio. Robert offered to help us, but he recently refinanced his home. He's whittling away at his payments, so adding on the studio loan is out of the question for now. He's offered to sell his car, but that won't help. Plus, starting our lives together will be a big enough challenge on its own."

Two days later, Marta's mom returned to the studio with a packet of papers in her hands and a smile on her lips. "It looks like I'm buying the studio. Mr. Gleason assured me that with a thirty-year loan, I'll be able to make payments and buy the building. We'll need to talk with Lindsay about buying the business with a separate agreement."

"Why is Mr. Gleason willing to go out on a limb for you?" Marta asked as she sank down onto the entry cushions.

"He's frustrated and ready to retire," her mom said. "He doesn't like the ethics of some of his fellow loan officers. Also, it doesn't hurt that he's heard about you from his wife's brother, who is on the community theatre committee. It appears that you have made a favorable impression and you didn't even realize it."

Knowing people in the community found value in what she'd done gave Marta renewed conviction in her decision. Maybe she'd consider dealing with her love life next. She headed upstairs but stopped to listen to her mom's side of her conversation with Mr. Gleason.

Her mom looked up when she'd finished her call. "You heard me tell him we're in the midst of a recital, but they might need to inspect it immediately so we need to get busy. Have you noticed how important things wait and then cascade down like huge waves?"

Marta chuckled. "Oh, believe me, I know." She stood and stretched side to side. "Better get out a notice about your plans with the rehearsal and recital information. Maybe this time we'll announce the news before Zandora gets wind of it and distorts it."

By the following afternoon, the studio phone rang so often that Marta's mom hired a parent to sit and answer it so she and Marta could complete details for tonight's dress rehearsal. One small blessing: the hectic pace didn't allow Marta time to dwell on either Steve or Sam.

The parents and students filled the main floor of the Coontz auditorium as Marta, with her mom beside her, stepped onto the stage to speak with everyone. "Please be seated as quickly as possible. We have a lot to cover tonight. We need to be out of the building by nine o'clock, so we'd appreciate everyone picking up after themselves.

"As in the past, we're slowing things down so you students may watch the entire program. During the real recital, you'll not be seated in the audience. You'll be in classrooms waiting for your turn to dance and then returning there to wait for your parents to pick you up. We expect you to be on your best behavior tonight and tomorrow, to be ready on time to dance, and, most of all, to have fun sharing your dances with the audience.

"Our first dance for our *Imagine* theme will be the two kinder classes dancing their "Twinkle, Twinkle" dance, followed by the beginning ballet class dance, "When You Wish Upon a Star." When we turn down the lights, that's your cue to sit quietly. We'll call your classes up in groups of three."

Everyone clapped and started talking. When the lights dimmed to half, the students and their parents stopped chattering and sat back.

Three hours later, Marta and her mom sat on the apron of the stage and looked out over the empty seats. "Not bad for our first recital rehearsal together," Marta said. "But I'm so tired I don't know if I can move off this spot."

Her mom laughed. "Me too." She looked at her watch. "It's time to head out. Let's call it a night and meet tomorrow morning to iron out the glitches."

Recital day. No classes, just time spent ironing out small problems and checking that Lindsay knew the evening's order of dances, except for the special tribute planned in her honor. The recital committee parents had gathered cards, money, and gifts from dancers and families and arranged everything in a large basket along with a huge bouquet of red and white roses. After the finale, everyone was cued into staying for a special celebration commemorating Lindsay's ten years as owner and director of the Holland Dance Studio.

Lights, costumes, makeup, and an audience of family, friends, and relatives combined to make a recital memorable for the dance students. Wrong turns, sassy show-off moves, and kinder tears set the stage for the evening. With Marta standing in the wings and Lindsay seated nearby, the young students danced with greater confidence than if left on their own.

The music followed the theme of *Imagine* with wishing, dreaming, and finding happiness. The intermediate ballet students and first year pointe dancers took every step seriously, the way Marta remembered herself. Almost perfect toes and arms and students pulling in their lips as they focused on getting everything correct resulted in encouraging applause. Relief to have completed their dances with few errors appeared in their shy smiles as they took their bows.

The advanced dancers, including Paige, gave the audience a glimpse of what years of training produced. They performed classical selections wearing costumes that matched the ballet themes. Their gracefulness and precision brought tears of joy to Marta as she remembered her performances and realized she'd be helping them further their skills over the next year. Staying on to teach was the correct decision.

As the final dance ended and the curtain closed, Marta stepped onto the stage in front of the curtain. "Thank you for coming tonight. We hope you enjoyed our theme, *Imagine*. Before you leave, we want to pay special tribute to Lindsay Holland. Her move to San Diego saddens us as dancers and friends, but we wish her our very best with her soon-to-be-born baby and her new home."

Applause filled the auditorium.

"Lindsay and Adam, please join me on the stage."

More applause and a few whistles filled the time it took Lindsay and Adam to arrive on stage. They smiled and waved as thundering applause greeted them. Marta's mom joined them on the stage carrying the basket of gifts.

Marta signaled for quiet, then stepped back to the microphone. "On behalf of ten years of grateful students and parents, we want to present you with flowers and a basket of special gifts to thank you for starting the studio. We assure you and everyone in the community that we'll keep Holland Dance Studio open for business. We hope you'll return to

Bremerton many times over the next years. May your baby be healthy and grow to be a wonderful person like both of you."

Applause filled the auditorium as Lindsay accepted the gifts and wiped away tears. She moved to the microphone. "Thanks, everyone. Leaving is one of the most difficult things I've done in my life. But, after seeing how well everyone performed, and the quality of the dancing, I know I'm leaving the Holland Dance Studio in good hands. My wish for Elle and Marta is continued good fortune with all the new classes we're providing this fall. For the rest of you, enjoy your summer and return to classes with renewed energy. Best of luck, everyone. I'll stay in touch. Thanks."

More applause followed Lindsay as she exited the stage. A cookie party in the front entry kept dancers and their families talking with Lindsay and each other until the custodian began dimming the lights. Within ten minutes the guests cleared out, leaving Marta, her mom, and the parent committee time to speak with Lindsay and Adam.

When the Hollands left, the hugs and goodbyes from dancers and parents alike continued to the doorway. They waved as they exited the building, giving Marta a feeling of sadness followed by elation to think that she and her mom planned to carry on a tradition that gave so many people such happiness.

Robert returned from checking the dressing rooms with a giant smile on his face. "All the rooms are clean and locked. The custodian only took his regular fees. Said he enjoyed the program and the lovely people who cleaned up after themselves. He's sending his granddaughter down to arrange classes for her kinder boy. See, your planning yielded another potential client."

Marta and her mom looked at each other and yawned amid their smiles. "Let's head home," her mom said. "I can sleep for at least a week, or until tomorrow afternoon."

As Marta left the school, she saw Sam sitting on the bench by the front entrance. "Hi, hope you enjoyed the recital," she said.

He stood and smiled. "It was a lot of fun, even when Betty started showing off, adding her little touches to her group dance. She's a born performer."

"She is. I'm glad she has such confidence. Will she continue with lessons next fall?"

"Of course. Will you be here?"

Marta smiled. "Maybe."

Sam fidgeted, holding Betty's dance tote. "You said we could talk after the recital, so I stayed in hopes of seeing you for a minute. Do you have any plans for summer? I thought maybe we could go to the county fair or for a swim at Kitsap Lake."

Marta looked away before she spoke. "I'm not certain. I may have plans. I'll let you know." She placed her hand on Sam's arm. "I have a lot to think about over the summer. Give Betty my best. Have a nice summer, Sam. I'll call you."

Sam's smile faded. "Okay. Well…ah…have a nice summer yourself." He backed down the steps, turned, and walked toward the parking lot.

Marta's heart ached from brushing him off. But whatever she decided about Steve or Sam, she'd need a few weeks or maybe the summer to figure out how and where and with whom she wanted to spend her life.

The light on the porch welcomed her home. So did a bouquet from Mark's Flower Shop. She opened the tiny rose-colored envelope and removed the card.

Dear, sweet Marta,

I know the recital will be a gigantic success. You are talented and caring. That's why I must tell you that I love you and that I dream of you every night.

Think of me,
S

Marta's brain did a double take. Who was "S"—Steve or Sam? The accompanying florist information contained no details. Had Steve sent them to remind her he continued to think of her, or did Sam send them, and she'd just sent him away for the summer? Maybe if she called, the florist would be able to tell her more. Suddenly Monday seemed so far away.

⁓

Sunday morning Marta slept in. Every muscle in her body ached, but the success of the recital put a smile in her heart. The flowers created a conundrum: Steve or Sam? If it was Steve, that meant he had not given up on her just yet and was waiting for her next move. Her conversation with Sam created a dark cloud she'd need to deal with after she took a brief break from classes, especially if he'd sent the flowers as a shy way of sharing his feelings. Maybe she'd get answers on Monday.

When she finished a cup of tea and a slice of cinnamon toast, she retrieved yesterday's mail and found a letter from Lynne.

Dear Marta,

Waited for your call. Fat chance, huh, what with a recital to handle.

Hope the recital went well. Call me soon as you recover. I'll be waiting to tell you about everything and maybe one special someone in my life that

*may keep me from swearing off dating altogether.
Mr. Could Be Almost Perfect may be circling. If so,
I'll exchange my grumpy thoughts for a romantic
movie, popcorn, and a few kisses in the theatre
balcony.*

*Big news. I'm done dancing in good ole' Bill-
ings. It would take me too many pages to write it
all out. I'm too lazy to do it! Just know it's all OK.
Both Madame and I are happy about this. BUT...
you need to call me before June 12th or it will be
a long time until you hear from me again 'cuz I'll
be G-O-N-E.*

If I captured your curiosity, call me!

Lynne

Something had changed with Lynne. She didn't mention her dad, so
he must be feeling better. She didn't mention her aunt moving or any of
her usual funny views on life.

In the afternoon she dialed Lynne, waiting for the ringing to give way
to her friend's perky voice. After ten rings, Marta started to hang up when
Lynne came on the phone breathing heavily.

"Hey, you called. How was your first recital from the other side of
the lights?"

"It went well. Only a few tears during the dances, then buckets of
tears when Lindsay said her goodbyes."

"I bet. Wish I'd been there, but I'm home, planning my getaway. I was
on my deck, sorting my boxes and tossing out junk when I heard the
phone. Found it buried under a pile of clothes going to Goodwill. I take
it you got my latest letter."

"Yes. Even before that, Steve mentioned you had news. Then your cryptic letter arrived. What's going on, Lynne?"

"Back up, Marta. When did you see Steve? How did that go?"

Marta sighed. "I saw him recently and it was a typical Marta-Steve reunion. We got into arguments about commitment and future plans. He left me holding the bag on where we're headed. For now I'm staying in Bremerton."

"Really? Even if he's in Timbuktu?"

"That's the current plan. I'll help the studio during the changeover. Who'd have ever thought I'd be talking about staying in Bremerton and teaching dancing? The worst thing is that I have no idea where Steve's working or if he found a job. Last time we spoke he mentioned Billings, so I guess he's planning to settle there."

"Talk to him soon, Marta. It will be interesting once you two get caught up. As for myself, I've found an almost right guy. He's a college-educated rancher. Have you ever heard of that combination?"

"Not really, but why not?" Marta debated if she should tell Lynne about Sam. "I dipped my toe into dating a local college-educated guy."

"Wait. What about Steve? Have you decided to end things?"

"No, but I'm sorta seeing a guy named Sam. So far it's just ice cream and going to his daughter's school programs." Marta paused, then dove into telling Lynne the details. "I'm getting confused. Got any advice?"

"Me? I date a hundred guys a year. What do I know?" Lynne remained silent for a long moment. "Answer me this. How do you feel when these guys are around?"

"It's like a carnival roller coaster: exciting and scary with a jittery stomach. My emotions are all over the place."

"Okay, Marta, which guy do you dream about?

"Both of them."

"Which one makes time drag when you're apart?"

"Sam, because I get to see him and Steve is who knows where."

"Which one supports your passion about dancing?"

"Steve. See what I mean? It's confusing."

Lynne laughed. "Yes. I can see how you'd be confused. Guess you're on your own in more ways than one. I'm leaving for France the end of June. I've accepted joining a summer dance troupe. I'll be part of a small group of American dancers. We'll be training in Paris and touring during the summer."

"Wow! In France? Really? But you'll be back in the fall, won't you?"

"Nope. I'm staying on for a while. Uncle Leo wants to tour Europe. It's been his dream to see the sights once he retired. We'll met up after I finish touring. He'll pay my way if I do all the driving of the car he's buying, plus, if the car survives, he's giving it to me. Can't beat that deal, huh? I can see myself now, driving around in a BMW or a Mercedes. I did tell you Uncle Leo is rich, didn't I? Anyway, maybe by the time I return you'll figure out where your heart will be happiest. Do you know what you're going to do about dancing?"

"Not yet. For a long time I thought the music had stopped in my life when I stopped performing. I realize it shifted to a different type of melody. For now I'll teach at the studio. Maybe my life will shift again. I've decided to not worry about the future and try to get through the present."

"Wow, Marta. That's a huge change. Maybe my craziness is starting to rub off on you."

"Maybe," Marta said. "I'll let you know where my heart lands. Now, back to you. What's up with your Mr. Could Almost Be Perfect guy? Do I detect a change in *your* dating frenzy?"

"Could be. Noel is an amazing guy. We met at the spring celebration. I've seen him almost every night since then. I'll send you the verdict once I know. Strange, huh? Makes me almost sorry to be leaving Billings."

Marta giggled. "I bet it does. Promise to call before you leave. I'll want to know any new details and how I can stay in touch with you while you're gone."

After she hung up from her talk with Lynne, Marta thought about the two men in her life. Steve always surprised her. He brought out her playfulness as well as her feisty side. He'd stuck by her through so many events: her first days of professional dancing, her injury, Bartley's death, and Marta's continued reluctance to become a couple. Even with his internship in San Francisco, he'd stayed in contact. He understood her moods, her stubbornness, and her passion to resume dancing. She understood his desire to find the perfect job and loved his energy. Sending flowers had become a signature trait of Steve's. Had he sent them?

What did she know about Sam? He was a loving father to Betty, a gentle man who gave off a sense of calm. He knew her as a dance instructor and was beginning to know her as a person, but that was only a recent development. Maybe it was too soon to know his personality, but she already sensed his sincerity and openness. Did he send the flowers because he was too shy to tell her how he felt?

Monday morning Marta called the florist but got no answers. "Sorry, miss. We have no further information." A dead end.

For now, she'd be busy at the studio, scheduling next fall's classes. Monday afternoon she, her mom, and Lindsay interviewed and hired Veronica Osborne to teach tap and baton. Together they planned their summer class sessions and room assignments. Having a near-complete offering of dance classes fulfilled Lindsay's dreams. They'd provide something for every dance interest.

Mr. Gleason, the loan officer, promised to contact Marta's mom during the week, but while they waited for his call, Marta and her mom began deep-cleaning to spruce up the house and yard before the bank's inspection. Mr. Gleason said he liked the fact they were expanding to offer a variety of classes and he'd work to see that they received his highest recommendation.

Later that week, after the bank inspection, the loan office scheduled a follow-up appointment, but only Marta was able to attend because her mom had an important dance association meeting in Seattle.

Click, click, click. High heels echoed off the marble foyer of the First National Bank of Washington. A woman walked toward the entrance. Her chin and slightly protruding teeth preceded the rest of her body.

Marta noted how her feather-cut red hair bounced except where a child's yellow barrette held back the front left edge that framed her face. A curious style statement from a woman wearing a tailored gray pin-stripe suit with an almost too short skirt.

Something about the woman reminded Marta of Zandora Marcus. Certainly not the hair color. Perhaps it was the way she moved with quick steps and her chin thrust forward. Maybe it was the way she looked at Marta. A shudder slid down Marta's spine.

The pinstripe-suited woman stopped short of stepping on the toes of Marta's black leather flats. She scanned a paper in her hand. "Miss Ser, Ser-berth?"

"Yes?" Marta stood and extended her hand.

The woman looked at Marta's outstretched hand. "I'm Miss Elliott. Follow me."

Marta lowered her hand and picked up her purse and folder. *Click, click, click.* Miss Elliott's heels clacked along the hallway with Marta trailing behind like a calf following the bell of the lead cow.

They entered a wood paneled office devoid of personality. The two guest chairs directly in front of the desk reminded Marta of the ones in her high school vice principal's office: the place where you sat to receive a lecture or notice of your suspension.

Miss Elliott signaled for Marta to be seated, then circled her desk, sank down into a black leather swivel chair, and folded her hands on her desk blotter. "So, tell me about your qualifications for a loan."

Marta slid the sheaf of financial papers across the desk. "My mother prepared these for Mr. Gleason. He's handling the loan."

Miss Elliott ignored the folder and continued staring at Marta, who stifled the urge to squirm around in the chair. "He's no longer with our company. I believe he retired. I'm your loan officer now." She opened the folder and scanned the top page. "Where's the primary signer, a Mrs. Ser-berth?"

"My mother is unable to come today. She'll attend future meetings."

"I see." Miss Elliott folded her hands over the papers. "Tell me your work experience, your present income, and how other financial considerations will affect our decision to grant you a loan."

Marta straightened. "I danced professionally with the Intermountain Ballet Company last season. Now I teach at the Holland Dance Studio off Callow Avenue, which is the studio we're trying to purchase."

The woman leaned back and furrowed her brow. "Why would you give up a professional career to move here and teach children?"

"I had an injury that ended my career. I'm assisting my mother and requesting a personal loan, but I have no assets to be part of the business loan. There is a note in the file in front of you, however, that gives me permission to represent my mother."

Miss Elliott raised her eyebrows at Marta. "I see. What's your mother's work experience?"

"She's been the office manager at Holland Dance Studio for ten years."

Miss Elliot rifled through the papers rapidly, then stopped. "Is this your mother's total salary? For a year?" She held three pay stubs by the corner as if touching more of them would infect her with a disease.

"Yes." Marta felt her blood pressure begin to rise, but she held herself taut.

Miss Elliott tapped a tattoo with her stubby fingers on the papers, then leaned her left elbow on her desk. As she slid her fingers through her hair, she stopped. Her eyes widened. She casually slid the yellow barrette out of her hair, looked at it, then slid it into her pocket.

The office remained library quiet as she scanned page after page in the folder. Finally she withdrew a single sheet and pushed it toward Marta. She tapped the paper, pointing to the heading: Loan Verification Form. "I can't approve this loan with such meager earnings. Plus, your mother owes two thousand dollars on the home you're requesting be used in the loan."

"You can't approve the loan?" Shock swept through Marta. The feeling reminded her of the crushing experience after her injury when she realized she'd not dance again. "Why?"

"There's not enough value for us when you default."

"What if my mother—"

The woman put up her hand to stop Marta. "No what ifs. Banks don't loan money unless they are protected *when* the owner defaults."

When. The woman said *when*, not *if*, twice in the last two sentences.

"But Mr. Gleason said that he'd—"

Miss Elliott stood abruptly and opened her office door. "Now, if you'll excuse me, I have more pressing business to attend to."

Marta felt a wave of disbelief at being dismissed so quickly. She straightened her shoulders. "My mother will be available next week with whatever you need for this loan to be completed."

"Save your time and money. I'm stamping this loan as rejected."

Marta felt her frustration rise. She fished around in her purse and withdrew a small mirror, which she placed in the center of Miss Elliott's desk. "Remember to check your hair before your important business. My young dancers know to look professional even for rehearsals."

Marta gave Miss Elliott her brightest stage smile as she exited the office. She opened and closed her fists and drew in deep breaths as she walked out to the sidewalk. That woman! No "I'm sorry"? No "come back next month"? No future meeting to discuss ways to make the loan happen? She'd not let Lindsay's hard work fade just yet. There had to be a way to buy the building.

She rushed home to call her mom, who'd be back at the studio by now. She'd be more disappointed than Marta, but what could they do? Miss Holland's time constraints forced her to leave with her husband within the month. Bremerton deserved a dance school where young dancers could grow and learn, where families could enjoy music and applaud at recitals, where future professional dancers could get a start. There *had* to be a way to make it happen.

$\mathcal{L}$indsay, Marta's mom, and Marta sat in the downstairs office with the doors locked. "Their rejecting you doesn't make any sense," Lindsay said. "If you can't find a way to buy the building, we're sunk; I'll need to go with the other buyer. Adam and I may consider moving back here after he retires, but that's a dozen years from now. I can't keep paying the building loan. Navy pay isn't that good."

Marta's mom sighed. "I'll do my best to keep the studio going. I'll call to schedule another meeting with the loan officer. Maybe she'll reconsider."

Lindsay looked around her office. "I'm going to miss this place. Not my messy shelves, but the entire studio. Lots of fond memories are hiding in this office. Once you take over and clean it up, you may uncover a few treasures. If you do, keep them as a remembrance of what we started. Of course, if you find a hundred dollars tucked away in a shoebox, I'll expect my share in the mail."

Marta stopped by her mom's house for a hamburger barbecue. Robert greeted her at the door. "I'm sorry about the loan. Wish I could help."

Her mom stepped to the door, wiping her hands on a kitchen towel. "I told him having him offer means a lot, but that we'd find a way. For now we'll get this old house ready for sale and see what happens."

"Our friend, Connie Norton, called me today." Robert hugged Marta's mom as he spoke. "She acted so sweet you'd never know Elle told her off last summer."

"I suppose she wants to sell the house for mom?"

"Yes, but I told her you ladies had an agent who's trustworthy and speeding things along and were considering several offers."

"Mom, you have offers?"

"One, maybe," her mom said. "But I didn't sign with an agency yet. Veronica Osborne lives in an apartment in Manette. She'd like to buy the house now that she has a position at the studio. Her husband loves to garden and is a Mr. Fix-it. Lindsay says they're nice people and will take care of the property."

"Good," Marta said. "Maybe more good news will float down at the goodbye luncheon tomorrow."

Lily Rose greeted everyone on the wide veranda of the Kitsap County Country Club wearing a flowing green shirtwaist dress with matching heels and gloves. "I'm so glad you're here. Trixie and Frann are modeling. They'll join us for lunch after the show. Irene saved our table for ten up front."

Bremer's department store provided an informal summer fashion show while the ladies sat at luncheon tables sipping cocktails and nibbling on tiny canapés. Club members wearing capri pants, summer shirtwaist dresses, and chiffon baby doll nighties walked among the guests, offering closer views and glimpses of the price tags. The one-piece hot pink strapless Catalina and the polka dot Jantzen swimwear caused the most stir.

Lindsay turned to Marta. "How could anyone swim without a strap to hold up the top?"

Marta laughed. "I don't think the people who wear those suits plan to get even their painted toes wet."

After Trixie and Frann finished modeling, they joined the ladies for lunch. Waiters in white shirts with black bow ties and black slacks served salmon with dill sauce and green salads with artichoke hearts, then offered dainty rolls with pats of butter.

"Trixie, you looked great in that teal green Jantzen swimsuit," Irene said. "I loved the empire detail. Of course it wouldn't look good unless we had your curvy figure."

Trixie laughed. "I tell everyone I'm keeping my curves because of Marta's exercise class. Expect a few women to call you."

"There's always room for more classes when we hire more instructors."

"Hope he's a cute guy with strong shoulders who wears tight shorts," said Irene.

"Speaking of shorts, I can't believe boy shorts are still in style," Frann said. "They camouflage my thighs, but how long are we expected to wear unflattering patterns?"

"Did you notice all the shirtwaists?" Lindsay said. "I am so sick and tired of all the flouncing material and the petticoats. I'm glad sheaths are becoming popular. Of course right now I'd be happy to wear either."

The ladies laughed.

"I saw a lovely sheath in Seattle at I. Magnin," said Sally from the exercise class. "I loved the polka dot tie. Can you believe they wanted thirty dollars for one dress?"

"Check out the Montgomery Ward catalog," suggested Miriam. "They're showing several at $4.98. Unfortunately the fabric looks like colored flour sacks."

"You know, my mom and I sew," Marta said. "We'd make you ladies dresses or capris any time you want. Just find the fabric and pattern you like."

"I doubt you'll have time to sew," Lindsay said. "The studio will take all your time and energy. Assuming you still find a way to buy it.

"Wait. What do you mean?" Lily Rose said. "We thought this was settled."

"It was," Marta's mom said. "But there's a technicality. We're going in later this week to straighten it out. But let's forget about that for now and toast Lindsay and her baby."

"Cheers," the ladies said as they raised their glasses.

While the conversation circled the table, Marta excused herself and headed to the ladies room. On the way back to the table, she heard a familiar voice and saw Zandora Marcus seated at the bar near the banquet room. Miss Elliott sat next to her. Marta stepped behind a post to try to listen to what they said.

"I knew if I shared that information with you, the loan might be rejected," Zandora said. "I'd have loved to see Elle's and Marta's faces when you turned them down. My friend is excited to know she has an even better chance to buy the building now. There's no way any agent will turn down a hefty commission and an offer higher than the asking price, unless he's a fool. Of course it will need to be repainted. You should see the colors Marta selected. So passé; certainly not appropriate colors for an Arthur Murray dance studio."

Marta leaned against the wall, catching her breath, waiting for her body to stop shaking. She backed away, returned to her luncheon table following a different route, and sat down. "I think I know who helped the loan get rejected." She explained the conversation she'd overheard.

"That woman!" Lily Rose said, then looked around and lowered her voice to a whisper. "We've got to stop Zandora and her friend."

"Let's not talk here," Frann said.

Lily Rose stood. "Meet me at my home in thirty minutes. There must be something we can do to save the studio."

The women sat in a circle of chairs in Lily Rose's living room ignoring the amazing view. Lindsay sat in a club chair and took in deep, ragged breaths. "I think you need to forget your bank and go to mine. Northwest Merchants Bank may be more willing to work with you since they've handled my business for years."

Heads nodded.

She continued. "I paid $4,500 as a down payment, and the monthly loan costs $175. With taxes, insurance, and utilities for the studio, I'm paying out $225 a month. There isn't time to apply for a small business loan, so we'll need a different solution."

"Would your bank transfer the loan to Elle?" Irene asked.

"Probably." Lindsay's face contorted and she closed her eyes. "Oh, ah, I need to go home. This baby is dancing around and telling me to rest. I trust you ladies to sort this out." Frann drove her home, promising to agree to any action they decided.

Lily Rose stood behind a chair and looked around the circle. "We can sit here all day and talk, but we need a plan as soon as possible."

Marta cleared her throat and inhaled deeply before she spoke. "Would you ladies consider becoming partners in the dance studio? If my mom and I talk with Lindsay's bank and they transfer the loan and we sell our home, we'll have a large part of the expenses handled. If we could tell them we had partners supporting the studio, they might take a chance on a loan for us."

All heads nodded.

"I like that idea," Trixie said. "My husband will draw up legal papers if we can work out how much each of us is able to contribute."

Marta's mom frowned. "I don't want anyone to feel pressured to help financially. Perhaps people will consider donating services as a way to support the studio."

Lily Rose smiled and tapped her hands on the back of the chair where she stood. "That's a great idea. Let's all go home, talk with our families, and decide what we feel comfortable contributing: money, time, whatever. Call me tomorrow and I'll compile our information. I'll keep it confidential and only share details for legal purposes."

The women stood, gathered their belongings, and started to leave. "One more thing, ladies," Lily Rose said. "Don't tell *anyone* about this. We don't want Zandora Marcus to get wind of our plans."

On the drive home, Marta sat deep in thought. "Mom, would it help if I stayed? I have no plans so I could stay on."

Her mom smiled. "It would make things easier. How long would you stay?"

Marta shrugged.

Two days later the ladies met again, without Lindsay since she had a doctor's appointment. Lily Rose's living room buzzed with energy as she shared the results of their efforts. "Lindsay transferred the loan to Elle. The bank allowed Elle to assume the loan payments, and with our merged resources we have enough for two months of loan payments. We'll send Lindsay and Adam, and the baby, to San Diego with their down payment money in their pockets, plus Lindsay will allow Elle to buy the business of the dance studio over time."

Applause and smiles circled the group.

"Tell them the rest of the news," Irene said.

Lily Rose smiled. "With our merged resources, the studio has people to provide legal help, inventory studio assets, design advertising, studio cleaning and maintenance, holiday sewing, provide hair cuts and perm services with part of their proceeds benefiting the studio. Even though we tried to keep this quiet, several dance families have called me. House cleaners and adult babysitters, holiday bakers, and even a yard cleaning service have offered to split their profits with the studio for one year. As new issues and problems arise, we'll have most everything covered.

"Each person will receive a written contract listing their contributions, the value of those contributions, and the anticipated payback schedule if money was loaned. The best part of this higher level finance scheme is that Elle will still have enough for her wedding and a brief honeymoon."

Marta watched her mom blush at the mention of a honeymoon. When her mom and Robert talked last night, they'd scaled down the already simple wedding to family and close friends in Robert's backyard. By mutual consent, their honeymoon shrank from a ten-day trip to the Oregon coast down to a day at the ocean with the money saved going to help with dance studio expenses.

Marta emptied her savings for a car into the studio fund and signed on to sew for the community theatre productions to increase her contribution. She offered reduced fees on lessons to all the contributing families to repay their generosity in saving the dance studio. Next came another hard decision. How long was she willing to put her personal life on hold?

The tide was low on the beach along Corbett Drive as Marta took off her shoes and stood in the chilly water. She watched the shore crabs circle her feet then scoot away when she wiggled her toes. She couldn't scoot away from her decision much longer. It wasn't fair to Sam or Steve if she wavered about getting serious with one of them. As she returned to her little house, she gave herself an ultimatum—two weeks.

The phone was ringing as she stepped into the house. It was her mom.

"It's happened. Lindsay had their baby boy this afternoon. Jeffrey Rahe Holland. Six pounds, seven ounces. Adam said both were doing well and we're on the list to visit this evening."

Marta laughed. "I'll bet she's happy. Did you wrap our gift to her yet?"

"No, I wanted to call you, but I'll add his name, wrap it, and pick you up at seven."

The maternity ward had two rows of beds; all were full. Marta and her mom spotted Lindsay holding a small bundle to her breast with a nervous Adam standing beside her. They clapped silently as they approached Lindsay's bed.

"Brava," Marta said. "How are you three feeling?"

"Like we waited too long to do this," Adam said. "Isn't he beautiful?"

Lindsay handed the sleeping baby boy to Adam, who handed him over to Marta's mom.

"I remember Marta as a baby," her mom said as she swayed with the baby in her arms. "Seems like yesterday. Where did this handsome boy's name come from?"

"He's named after our fathers," Lindsay said. "I'm sorry you won't get to see him grow up. I hope he loves music and wants to dance."

"Wait, Linds," Adam said. "We also want him to be an athlete, love boats, and be a good student."

Marta laughed. "This will be one busy boy." She handed the gift from her mom and herself to Lindsay. "We hope you will think of us when you use it."

When Lindsay opened the package, tears formed in her eyes. "Oh-h-h. This quilt is gorgeous. You even wrote his name on it. Thank you so much. Some of these squares look familiar. Are they...?"

Marta's mom nodded. "They're squares from various costumes we've made for the studio over the years, plus colors we knew you loved. You know us, we never throw anything away."

When they left the hospital, Marta and her mom drove to Rhododendron Drive and sat in the backyard. "It's been quite a month, hasn't it?"

Marta said. "The Hollands will soon be gone, and we'll be on our own. It's exciting and kind of scary as well."

Her mom nodded. "But since we got our feet wet taking over the recital, I think we're in good shape. We've received amazing support. I think we'll be okay."

Her mom was right. The studio business was handled. Time for handling her personal life decisions, like sending a letter for Lynne to her family home before she scooted off the Europe.

Dear Lynne,

Lindsay had her baby. It's a boy, Jeffrey Rahe Holland. The new family will drive to San Diego this next week, stopping to show off the baby to friends along the way. Please call to say good bye. I'm glad for you and sad for me.

You never made it to the northwest. I had so many places I wanted to show you. I might have found a handsome guy you'd like, but too late. It's becoming the story of your life, unless Mr. Almost is hanging in.

I'm teetering on how I feel about Sam and Steve. It's like having two doors with no windows, so I can't peek inside. No matter which one I select I'll be happy. It's just that they'll be different kinds of happiness.

Write letters or send me postcards. I'm excited for your up-coming adventure. Try to stay out of trouble. Ha, ha.

Love and hugs,

Marta

Marta stood in the dance studio office sorting the boxes delivered that morning. It felt strange opening boxes addressed to Lindsay; she'd need to change the addressee name with all the accounts as well as the post office to keep things current.

The door to the dance studio opened, but no one entered immediately. *Thump.* Something bumped against the door, then it closed. A tiny fussy sound followed.

"You're okay. I want you to say hello to some special people." Lindsay entered the office pushing a baby stroller. "I haven't gotten the hang of opening doors without waking Jeffrey."

Marta smiled. "I guess this is your final good bye?"

"It is. We're packed and ready to drive south. I wanted to thank you for everything one more time and tell you how happy I am that the studio is in such capable hands."

Marta's mom hurried into the entry carrying a box, which she set down so she could look at the baby. "You know we'll be calling you when we run into something we don't remember how to handle. But don't wait for us to call you. We'll expect you to keep us updated on Jeffrey's progress."

"I will, and I'll send photos," Lindsay said as she hugged Marta and her mom. "I'll miss this building and all the music and dancing that's gone on in here. I expect great things from you ladies." She hugged them again, then walked out for the last time.

Marta wiped away a tear. "This feels so strange."

"It does, but we can handle it. We need to keep the dancing going and the music flowing and hope not too many Zandoras walk through the doors."

೨

Back at home, Saturday's mail arrived with a postcard from Lynne. Three cows stood with their noses pressed against a fence. It said, "Looking a-head to that green pasture just beyond our reach."

> *Marta,*
>
> *Last of cows for awhile. Looking for <u>my</u> next green pasture. Stopping to see Bartley's parents. I expect to find your letter waiting for me at my parents'. Excited about visiting New York City before I sail away like someone's pop music says. Watch out world!*
>
> *Can you believe it? I'm scared but excited too.*
>
> *Lynne*
>
> *P.S. Letters to follow when I find or create anything worth reporting back to you. Ha!*

Marta laughed and shook her head. Lynne created a stir wherever she landed. She imagined Paris and the rest of Europe would be in for a big shake up. Funny, though, she didn't mention anything about anticipating a shipboard romance. Something must be happening with the Billings rancher.

On Monday afternoon as Marta cleaned up the dance studio entry, the office phone rang.

"Hi, Marta."

A jolt rushed through her. Steve. "Hi. Where are you?"

"I'm nearby. I've had a couple of interviews and wondered if I might talk with you tonight."

They agreed to meet at her house. Now, as the time of his arrival moved closer, Marta began to fidget, straightening up her already tidy living room, then walking onto the porch and back inside. When the same blue car from Steve's last visit drove up, she backed away from the open door and waited.

Steve stepped onto her porch and knocked on the door post. "Hi, Marta."

She swallowed hard. "Come in."

He moved into the room and looked around. "You've changed things."

"A little," Marta said. "Is that why you've come?"

He frowned, then laughed. "Now, now. Let's not start out with you in a huffy mood. I was nearby and thought we should talk face to face." His expression changed to a guarded smile. "I like your hair down. Looks grown-up."

Marta nodded, not certain she could speak without crying or saying something she'd regret. Seeing him standing in her little house left her feeling happy yet anxious.

"Your mom says you're buying the studio. Yes, we're still talking from time to time." He ran his hand through his hair and sat down on the couch. "Look, I'm out here interviewing and…we need to talk and stop this craziness between us one way or the other."

Marta sat in the rocker and studied his face. "I agree. So you haven't found a job yet?"

"'What do you mean? I accepted a job in May in Portland, Oregon."

"Why didn't you tell me?"

Steve shrugged. "I didn't know if that mattered to you."

"But you just said you were nearby for interviews."

"I was. I had interviews at Fort Lawton, Sandpoint Naval Base, Fort Lewis, McChord Air Force Base, and here in the shipyard. I'm writing about the effects of the northwest military bases on the region's economy."

Marta dipped her head, feeling Steve's intended put down. "Oh. Guess I deserved that. I'm sorry I've acted so self-centered. I'm trying to change, really. The fact that I'm staying on as a dance instructor shows I'm changing, doesn't it?"

"Yes, it does." Steve stood and walked to the front window and looked out. "I've held onto my hopes for us for a long time. Lately I've had dreams about you teaching my children to appreciate music."

Marta reeled from his comment "my children." Her brain took in the information, sending shock waves through her body. "Congratulations. When are you getting married?"

Steve turned and smiled. "I'm not until you say you'll marry me." He moved to stand behind her with his hands resting gently on her shoulders as she rocked. "Marta, I've tried to erase you from my mind, but I love you; I have since the first time we met." He moved to kneel in front of where she sat. "Will you marry me or not?"

Marta twisted a strand of hair around finger and looked away. "Now that the dance studio business is settled, I've found a new focus for my life, teaching dancing."

"That's good, right?"

"It is, but I've promised my mom I'd stay awhile. We're expecting dozens of new students and we'll need to hire another ballet instructor before next year ends."

"I understand, but you haven't answered my question. Will you marry me or not?"

Marta stood up and smiled. "It depends." She pulled his hand and walked toward the front door. "Come with me. I want to show you something at the dance studio."

As they exited his car and entered the dance studio, Marta felt a gnawing in her stomach. What if Steve didn't see the potential she and her mom saw? What if he thought her decision to stay here and teach was an ill-conceived idea?

Marta dragged him into the large practice room. "I want to show you what's happening in my life over the next little while." She reached out her arm in a sweeping circle. "This is my mom's new dance studio. We have three studio rooms, a waiting area and office, a messy director's office, plus a small apartment upstairs."

Steve nodded. "And the fact that your mom will own the building is a smart business move. I'd like to see the rest of the space."

She smiled and dragged him from room to room, pointing out all the details that made the building a special place. "I want to stay and be part of what we're building. Does that fit into your plans?"

"It could," Steve said. "I have to say, when you talk about this, your face lights up like it did when you danced in Billings. Do you still dance for yourself?"

Marta nodded.

"Will you dance for me?"

"Yes. Of course. Let me change." She hurriedly to the bathroom, changed, returned, then selected a favorite record. "This is the last ballet company choreography I learned from Damien. I modified it for my ladies' ballet class." She lowered the needle onto the first ring, closed her eyes, and waited for the opening clarinet slide of *Rhapsody in Blue*.

As she moved from one step to the next, she felt Steve's eyes follow her. She pretended to ignore him, but inside her spirit soared as she shared her passion to dance with him. When she ended, he stared at her but didn't speak for several moments. She couldn't read his face. Had she disappointed him?

"That was beautiful. You are still the most graceful person I've ever met. Thank you for dancing for me."

Marta curtsied. "My pleasure. But before you say anything more, I have questions for you."

"Okay. Fire away, Miss Fluff." Steve stood directly in front of Marta and saluted.

First, Mr. Mason, do you continue to steal flowers from your aunt's flower shop?"

"No, I only did that when you were in Billings. But more recently I was forced to call her and have flowers delivered to you. I hope you liked the ones I sent for the recital. Someday I'm hoping to have a home where I can grow my own."

"Good answer," Marta said. "Second, do you still think ballet is fluff?"

He shook his head and laughed. "That comment will haunt me until I'm too old to remember it. Ballet is not fluff. You may quote me on that." He leaned over and kissed Marta's cheek.

Steve reached out for Marta's hands. "Now I have questions for you. First, are you still seeing that counselor guy?"

"No, but I need to talk with him before too much longer."

"Second, do you ever wear the bracelet and necklace I gave you, and if so why don't I see you wearing them now?"

Marta reached into a tiny pocket sewn into her dance wrap. She handed them to him. "I carry them in my pocket when I'm at the studio. I don't want them to get damaged or sweaty. I'll admit that for a brief while, I didn't wear them. And, in the hurry flurry of the recital, I left them here. Usually I wear them or carry them in my purse."

"Fair enough," he said as he placed them back in Marta's hands. "Third, will you marry me or not?"

Marta closed her hand over the jewelry and looked at Steve. "I've spent lots of hours thinking about us. I dream about you, and if we can stay in this area, I'll marry you."

"But Marta—"

"Hold on; I'm not finished. But, if we'd need to move away from my home and the dance studio, I could manage as long as two things get resolved. First, I need to help find instructors for this studio. That might take as long as a year. Second, I also want to continue teaching ballet. It fills my need to dance."

"Really? You'd move to be with me?"

"Yep. I'd move. I've discussed this with my mom, and she's okay with my moving away once we find qualified instructors. Portland is close enough I could still get home to see her and help her when she's overextended." Marta smiled. "As a bonus, I might even share *my* ocean with you."

"*Your* ocean? I like the sound of that, Miss Fluff." Steve hugged Marta, then held her at arm's length. "So, should I get this in writing in case you change your mind?"

Marta absorbed his smile like a sweet fragrance that erased any of her doubts. She laughed. "Nope. I've made up my mind. You'll be stuck with me if you can be patient while the studio gets its dancing feet settled."

Steve drew her close, then relaxed his grip to cover her face and neck with kisses. Marta felt his heart beat in unison to hers as she returned his kisses. She closed her eyes and listened to the music of her life crescendo.

Elle Selbryth and Robert Marsden
announce their private family wedding ceremony
Sunday, July 12, 1959
at the Marsden home
Bremerton, Washington

You are cordially invited to attend their
Reception Celebration
Sunday, July 12, 1959

Drop-in between
4:00 - 7:00 PM
Holland Dance Studio
Burwell at Montgomery
Bremerton, Washington

Dear Lynne,

Here's an article you may want to save. I expect you to be home to be my maid of honor.

Love,

Marta

(*Seattle Times* reprinted from *Portland News Tribune* article)

Mrs. Robert Marsden of Bremerton, Washington announces the engagement of her daughter, Marta Selbryth to Steven Mason, son of Diane and Neal Mason of Billings, Montana.

The future bride is a former dancer with the Intermountain Ballet Company and is the current co-owner of the Holland Dance Studio in Bremerton, Washington.

The future groom is a recent graduate of Rocky Mountain College in Billings, Montana, and a reporter for the Portland News Tribune.

A June 1960 wedding is planned in Bremerton, Washington. The couple will make their home in Portland, Oregon.

Chat, Comment, and
Connect with the Author

Book clubs and schools are invited to participate in FREE virtual discussions with Paddy Eger.

Chat:

Invite Paddy to chat with your group via the web or phone.

Comment:

Ask thought-provoking questions or give Paddy feedback.

Connect:

Find Paddy at a local book talk or meet and greet. Visit her blog and website for dates, times, and locations or to set up your group's virtual discussion. For excerpts, author interviews, news and future releases, visit PaddyEger.com

Acknowledgements

Novel characters, like the rest of us, look for solutions. While some rush to a speedy conclusion, many unravel slowly. In Marta's case, the story dances out across three books. I hope you'll 'stick around' for the conclusion in *Letters to Follow*.

Getting a book on it's feet requires early readers like Gretchen Houser and web and social media support from Julie Mattern and Emily S. Hill. My young writing friend, Lucile Marshall, created the energetic character Lily Rose Costello. Together they provided direction and encouragement.

Technical details add to a book's authenticity. My thanks to Russell Warren for Bremerton, WA history, Judge Goodwin and attorney at law David Murdach for legal language and issues, Mark Allen for military details, and my husband for owning and remembering how eight-track tapes work. Also, I thank Camille Saint-Saëns for creating *The Carnival of the Animals* in 1886, furthering the notion that good music lasts.

Once the words are written, a good editor helps shape the story. Thanks to Sarah Overstreet's amazing patience and scrutiny *When the Music Stops* found its way from the first page to the final curtain. She made it possible for my publisher and creative designer, Karin Hoffman, to envision artistic details that embellish the pages of the book.

Marta's story began two decades ago with a writing class I took from my friend and author, Lauraine Snelling. I had no vision that writing about a young girl, dreaming to become a professional dancer would become three novels and begin my career as an author. Thanks to Lauraine as well as my critique groups. Your valued suggestions changed my life.

Special thanks to Margie Speck for being my principal dance instructor from the time I was seven until I left for college. Your studio and your commitment to all forms of dance were my inspiration for the fictional Holland Dance Studio.

About the Author

Paddy Eger is an award-winning author in Washington state. Her love of story, coupled with her years as an educator, encourages her to write for teen and older readers, to share glimpses of reality through one young dancer's struggle to face new challenges as she steps into adulthood.

Paddy's multiple award-winning debut YA novel, *84 Ribbons*, springs from her years of dance lessons. Between age three and twenty she performed ballet, character and tap routines for local recitals, hospitals, area musicals and for a World's Fair. *When the Music Stops: Dance On,* the second book in the trilogy, continues Marta Selbryth's story as she returns home and begins to face new challenges.

Although she never became a professional dancer, Paddy is an avid supporter of dance and the arts. She says, "The world of ballet is a wonderful, graceful place peopled by extraordinary dancers, musicians, directors and choreographers. I hope my ballet stories help readers understand more about the sacrifices each make to bring the world of dance into all our lives."

General Reader's Guide

All of us lead complex and multi-faceted lives.
    What are Marta's strengths? Her deficits?
    What factors contribute to Marta's reluctance to begin her
    personal life?
    What advice would you have given her during her recovery?

Marta is eighteen when the story begins and nineteen when its end.
    What growth do you see in her over the year she's at home and
    helping at the Holland Dance Studio?
    What do you imagine happens over the next year?

The world of ballet and American society have made major changes since the late 1950s.
    What changes have you noticed or heard mentioned?
    How do you view those changes?

Check paddyeger.com for more information, articles and news as the ballet trilogy continues.

School Reader's Guide

For an extensive guide that follows the Common Core State Standards for ELA 6-12, download the guide file from paddyeger.com The guide covers:
    Key Discussion Questions
    Post Reading
    Creative Writing Prompt
    Internet Resources
    Related Readings
    Select Interdisciplinary Activities

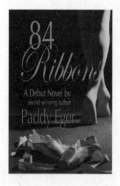

84 Ribbons

"A pure coming-of-age tale with moments of quiet drama *84 Ribbons* is about thriving despite the imperfections of life." YA Foresight, *Foreword Reviews,* Spring 2014. *DanceSpirit* Magazine's Pick of the Month, April 2014. "Any young dancer will find herself in Marta's story", Newbery Honor Author, Kirby Larson, *Hattie Big Sky.*

Coming Soon from Paddy Eger

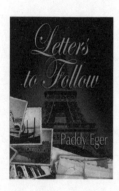

Letters to Follow

Marta's best friend Lynne begins a grand adventure when she travels to Paris to join a dance troupe. Her move to a wacky boarding house is not a good fit for an outspoken American dancer but it creates humorous encounters with the tenants. At the end of the exchange, Lynne becomes the travel companion for her harebrained Uncle Leo. She sends postcards and letters to Marta to retell her madcap adventures.

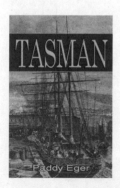

Tasman

In 1850, sixteen year-old Irish lad, Ean McCloud, steps off the boat, his legs in iron shackles, and steps into serving a three-year sentence at the Port Arthur Penal Colony in Tasmania. Falsely convicted, he must now survive the brutal conditions, the backbreaking labor, and time in the silent prison—a place that breaks men's souls. Follow Ean's adventures as he seeks not only to survive but to escape!